RICH KILL
POOR KILL

NEIL HUMPHREYS

Marshall Cavendish
Editions

With the Support of

NATIONAL ARTS COUNCIL
SINGAPORE

Published by Marshall Cavendish Editions
An imprint of Marshall Cavendish International
1 New Industrial Road, Singapore 536196

Other Marshall Cavendish Offices:
Marshall Cavendish Corporation. 99 White Plains Road, Tarrytown NY 10591-9001, USA • Marshall Cavendish International (Thailand) Co Ltd. 253 Asoke, 12th Flr, Sukhumvit 21 Road, Klongtoey Nua, Wattana, Bangkok 10110, Thailand • Marshall Cavendish (Malaysia) Sdn Bhd, Times Subang, Lot 46, Subang Hi-Tech Industrial Park, Batu Tiga, 40000 Shah Alam, Selangor Darul Ehsan, Malaysia.

Marshall Cavendish is a trademark of Times Publishing Limited

National Library Board, Singapore Cataloguing-in-Publication Data
Name(s): Neil Humphreys, author.
Title(s): Rich kill poor kill / Neil Humphreys.
Description: Singapore: Marshall Cavendish Editions, [2016]
Identifier(s): OCN951640941 | ISBN 978-981-47-5197-1
Subject(s): LCSH: Murder--Investigation--Singapore--Fiction. | Foreign workers--
Singapore.
Classification: DDC 823.92--dc23

Printed in Singapore by JCS Digital Solutions Pte Ltd

Glossary of popular Singapore terms and Singlish phrases (in order of appearance)

Lah: Common Singlish expression. Often used for emphasis at the end of words and sentences.

Talk cock: To speak nonsense.

Prata: A fried pancake usually served with a fish- or meat-based curry.

Aiyoh: To express frustration, impatience or disgust.

Cheem: A Hokkien expression used when someone or something is deep, profound or particularly clever.

Ang moh: A Caucasian (literal Chinese translation is "red hair").

Wah lau: A mostly benign expression that can mean "damn" or "dear me" in Hokkien. (See *wah lan eh* for a more vulgar variation.)

Kakis: Buddies or mates.

Catch no ball: From the Hokkien "*liak boh kiew*", the expression means to not understand at all.

Sarong Party Girl: A derogatory term used to describe Asian women who go out with Caucasians and adopt western affectations.

FT: Foreign talent.

Tekan: A Malay term to hit or whack someone, but not always in the literal sense. *Tekan* means to abuse or bully. An abusive workplace might be accused of having a "*tekan* culture".

Kelong: A colloquialism for cheating, corruption or fixed, often used in a sporting context. (In Malay, kelong is a wooden sea structure used for fishing.)

Xiao mei mei: In Mandarin, it means little sister. On seedier websites and blogs, it can also refer to attractive women and prostitutes.

Longkang: The Malay word for "drain". But *longkang* is commonly used to describe man-made water passages.

Basket: A local, more benign euphemism for "bastard", often used to express one's frustration.

Owe money, pay money: A popular expression scrawled on the walls and doors of debtors' homes by loan sharks.

Ikan bilis: The Malay term for anchovies, but often used to describe something small or a skinny person.

Kan ni na: Perhaps the most abusive phrase in Singlish. It can mean "fuck you" or "fucking" (e.g. *Kan ni na ang moh*).

Jia lat: A Hokkien adjective meaning to sap energy and used to describe something that is exhausting, troublesome or time-consuming (also written as *jialat* and *chia lat*).

Chao chee bye: In Hokkien, *chao* means smelly and *chee bye* is the rudest term for vagina.

Gahmen: A colloquial term for the Singapore Government.

CPF: It stands for Central Provident Fund, a social security savings plan for Singaporean citizens and permanent residents.

Tahan: Malay expression to take or endure. (e.g. cannot *tahan* roughly means cannot take it.)

Hao lian: Arrogant.

Siu mai: Pork dumplings.

Ah beng: A popular stereotype, an *ah beng* is often depicted as a scruffy, skinny Chinese guy who favours Singlish and Hokkien vulgarities.

Teh tarik: A popular tea in Singapore, particularly at *roti prata* stalls. Literally translated as "pulled tea", the hot, milky drink is poured into a cup from a considerable height, giving it a frothy, bubbly appearance.

Lelong: In Malay, *lelong* means "auction", but it is also a common Singaporean term for selling something cheaply.

Teh-c: Tea with evaporated milk and sugar.

Sotong: A popular seafood dish. *Sotong* is Malay for squid. But it is commonly used to describe an idiot, often by saying, "Blur like *sotong*".

Ah long: Loan shark (in Hokkien).

Kiasi: In Hokkien, *kiasi* means "scared of death", a criticism directed towards someone for being cowardly.

Kiasu: Singaporean adjective that means "scared to fail" in Hokkien.

Wah lan eh: A naughty relative of *wah lau*. In Hokkien, it means "oh penis" or even "my penis".

Mat salleh: In Malay, a pejorative term for a Caucasian.

Shiok: A fantastic, wonderfully pleasurable feeling.

Towkay: The big boss or leader (in Hokkien, *towkay* means head of the family).

Laksa: A rice noodles dish served in a curry sauce or hot soup.

Ice kachang: A dessert of shaved ice covered in colourful fruit cocktails, toppings and dressings.

Chapter 1

TALEK Maxwell closed his laptop. The reflection in the screen was annoying him. He knew he had aged, but at 3am he looked dreadful. The dark puffs beneath his blood-streaked eyes hardened his already coarse complexion. Some of the old handsomeness remained, but he had stopped posting Facebook photos. The broad-shouldered, muscular swagger of Chatham Boys' rugby captain had gone, replaced by a fat, balding, angry stockbroker. The English private schoolgirls once called his name from the touchline. In Asia, they shouted "white man" over their loud mini-skirts. He once had the prefects. Now he had prostitutes. He paid them to take him back. For a night, he was the captain of the team again. In the morning, he at least had the memories.

Aini wandered past the dining table. Pencil-thin with small breasts, her nakedness usually aroused Maxwell. But it was late. And he had seen himself in the reflection. She leaned over the breakfast bar, her chest brushing against the kettle, and grabbed the percolator.

"You want coffee?" she asked.

"No." Maxwell didn't bother looking at her.

"I want coffee," she said.

"I gathered that. Any chance of you putting some clothes on? I do have neighbours."

"You say you like it."

"I like it on Saturday night, not when I've got to be up for work in three hours."

Aini turned on the tap and filled the percolator.

"I've got to be at work in three hours too."

Maxwell snarled a little. "You're already at work."

Aini hit the percolator against the marble breakfast bar.

"I am not a hooker OK."

"So what are you doing now? An impression?"

"I am a cleaner. I clean apartments. That's how you meet me, OK."

Maxwell peered down at his stomach and flicked the waistband on his boxer shorts.

"Met me. It's 'how you *met* me.' Past tense. You can't even speak properly."

Aini muttered something under her breath.

"Don't start your Bahasa shit. I know you're criticising me when you start waffling on in your own language."

Aini was suddenly embarrassed by her nakedness.

"Why you treat me like this? Why you so mean to me?"

Maxwell stood up and violently pushed his chair under the dining table. The timber chair legs screeched along the tiled floor.

"Mean to you? What is this, primary school? Grow up."

"Me grow up? You are the child. You are the one who so nasty."

"*Is*. For god's sake, it's '*is* so nasty.' I live in a first-world country where no one can string a proper sentence together."

Aini felt the shame. She hated this man, *hated* him. But she needed him and so did her family. She pointed towards the bedroom.

"You never make fun of me in there. In there, you don't complain what I say."

"Maybe in there I'm too distracted thinking about the meter."

"What meter?"

Maxwell was lunging forward fast enough to alarm Aini, joining her behind the breakfast bar. He jabbed a chunky finger towards her groin.

"That meter there, the one between your legs, charging me by the hour."

"I am not a prostitute OK."

"No, of course you're not. I just buy your clothes, and your shoes, and give you extra for remittance, and give you money to buy your boy something for his birthday, or for his first day at school, or for another birthday. He has more birthdays than the bloody Queen and he's probably not even your son."

Aini suppressed the anger, considering her response. She appeared to rise slightly. She looked at Maxwell. Sweat pulled clumps of his chest hair together. He disgusted her.

"He is my son," she whispered.

She pushed the percolator plug into the socket and flicked the switch. The unexpected bang made her scream. She ducked as sparks danced in the air.

"It's only a blown fuse, you silly cow." Maxwell brushed past her and pulled the plug out. He yelped as he dropped the plug.

"Ah, you bastard, it's hot," he shouted. "You see? Are you happy now? You can't even make a cup of coffee without blowing up my apartment."

"It was an accident."

"You're an accident."

Maxwell pulled open a drawer near the sink and rummaged around. He took out a long, slender Phillips screwdriver with a yellow handle and bent over the blackened plug socket. He tapped it with the screwdriver handle.

"Look at this. I'm gonna have to replace this now. That's more money, isn't it? Plus the coffee pot might be blown. Put all that in with the remittance money I gave you, and it would've been cheaper to pick one up at Orchard Towers."

Aini moved the percolator away from Maxwell's hefty frame as he leaned on the breakfast bar. He began to unscrew the plug socket plate.

"But no, I've got to pay for one with the world's smallest tits who can't even make the coffee." He sighed. "In some ways, it's not even your fault. It's my fault. Asia has done this. Too much money, too much cheap food and too many cheap women like you. You should've seen me before I came out here, at university. I was unstoppable. I had them all, on their knees, rugby firsts, cricket firsts and Kelly Stewart. Best-looking woman in the college, daughter of an old Tory boy and I had her first. And now look at me."

He stopped to face Aini.

"I'm in a sweaty apartment at 3am with you. It's like swapping champagne for a pint of warm piss."

"You want me to leave?"

"No, please stay. I paid for the full night, didn't I?"

Maxwell leered at her. The tears in the Indonesian girl's eyes pleased him. He returned to the plug socket.

"Does your son know what you do? Surely he doesn't think you make all your money from cleaning expats' condos. When he opens his birthday presents, does he know they were paid for by a fat white man you fuck at weekends?"

Maxwell heard breaking glass behind him. He reached around to feel the water already trickling down his back. The percolator hit him again, smashing against his fingers. Glass splinters pinched all over his back. He turned towards Aini and smiled. She swung again. He threw up his left arm and watched as the flesh opened up beside his elbow. Aini was screaming. He couldn't really hear her. But he was sure she was screaming. His neighbours wouldn't like that.

Using his good right hand, he picked up the screwdriver and stopped her screaming.

Chapter 2

SLUMPED in his office chair, Detective Inspector Stanley Low picked up his obituary. It was written on his new name cards. There they were. The words on his death warrant: *Technology Crime Division*. The Singapore Government had a sense of humour after all. He couldn't be fired. He had too many notches on his truncheon. The Tiger Syndicate and the Marina Bay Sands murders made him a recurring character on true crime TV dramas. But cybercrimes was worse than a sacking. It was a living death. The desk job came with rigor mortis. Low had lived his investigative career outside of an office. Now he was dying in one.

His stained T-shirt was not as messy as his desk. In open defiance of his anal, geeky, computer-obsessed director, Low ran a loose ship. His workspace collected pizza boxes. His spreadsheets were dotted with coffee stains and he could never find his files because he never kept files. He was tasked with finding online hackers, invisible seditionists and confused, loud-mouthed teenagers. He had effectively been spayed like a whiny stray. His tool was always his tongue, but it had been ripped out.

Low opened the boxes and tipped out the name cards across his desk. Using them as Frisbees, he flicked them one at a time at the heads of colleagues peeking above their cubicles.

"Come on *lah*, Stanley," a voice shouted.

"Trying to work over here," cried another.

He childishly sniggered. "It's 3am, go home already."

"You go home. Learn how to use a computer."

Low craned his head to locate the heckler.

"Eh, balls to you. No need. I got you to wipe my arse for me."

Low found the silence crushing. No one really bantered with him at Technology Crime Division. They were boring and he pulled rank. Singaporeans didn't make fun of their superiors, even in a jocular environment, even if their superior happened to be a government pariah and an alcoholic mess. Just in case.

Low swigged from a plastic water bottle on his desk and shuddered. He smelled the vodka. His own breath left him nauseous. The phone made him jump, but he was eager for the distraction.

"Hello . . . Ah, yeah, working on it now. You know it's 3am, right? No, I appreciate that, but do we have to shit ourselves every time there's a negative story? I know the Minister shouldn't have commented on low-paid workers, but she's always talking cock. Election coming is it? I'll check the websites again. Couldn't get interns for that? No, I'll do it. It's 3am on a Monday morning, what else would I be doing, right? But can I ask one thing, *ah*. Wouldn't it be easier if you just fired me?"

The sudden dial tone made Low smile. His cheeks burned as he savoured his childish victory. They hated him, but they couldn't quite get rid of him, not yet. He tapped his keyboard and the blog reappeared on his screen. Low refreshed the page for updates. The homepage had the Singapore flag as a background with an index on the right listing the latest salubrious stories involving beer sellers from Mainland China sleeping with their coffee shop customers, Filipino nurses criticising Singaporean "dogs" and teenage anarchists mocking religious leaders; same shit, different names. Even the website's name irritated Low. *The*

Singapore Truth. True news for true Singaporeans.

He picked up the phone and waited for the answering machine.

"Hello, I know you're not there, I know it's 3am and I know this isn't an emergency," Low muttered. "But if I have to read one more racist blog, I will kill everyone in this office. Let me know when I can see you."

Low returned to his screen. *Fuck you, The Singapore Truth and fuck your racist followers.*

Low manically scooped up as many name cards as he could. He stood up and starting throwing handfuls around the room, flicking them towards office cubicles.

"Hey, got a new name card, must take *ah*. Singapore style, everyone must take my shiny new name card."

He spotted a colleague with oily hair peeping at him from above his terminal.

"Hey, computer genius, you want my new name card? There you go."

Low was hurling bundles of name cards at the nameless guy.

"Got enough or not? Hey, Alan Turing, you want more or not? You know who Alan Turing is? No, of course not, you're a first-year computer grad. You are sitting here at 3am because you can't get laid out there. All networking? Eh, you want to network, take my new name card."

The guy ducked as the name cards sailed over his head.

"No, don't duck, Alan. Take my name card, will be very good for your career. Everybody knows me. The Minister is my good friend."

Low swigged from his bottle again. He flinched before picking up the last of his name cards.

"Come on, no one wants my name cards? They will get you out of here. You don't want to get out of Technology? You don't want to get a girlfriend, is it?"

As the last of the name cards fell, everyone else at the Technology Crime Division returned to work. No one criticised or comforted the inspector. They left him alone. They all hated him that much.

Chapter 3

MAXWELL held Aini in his arms. He pressed her head against his bare chest. Her eyes had saddened him. They were confused, pathetic even. She lifted her hands to his chest and gently pushed away. Her blood covered them both. It had stuck to Maxwell's chest hair, which peeled away from Aini's neck. She made to scream, but couldn't find the sound.

"No, it's OK, it'll be fine," Maxwell said.

He tried to pull her towards him again, but she recoiled this time. She stood still in the minimalist apartment as blood seeped from her wound and trickled down her legs. A red streak snaked its way across the kitchen's marble tiles towards Maxwell.

"No, no, no, we can't have that," he whispered.

MAXWELL walked quickly along Spottiswoode Park Road. He adjusted the suit jacket he had thrown around Aini's shoulders and buttoned across the front, covering her dark T-shirt and the stain beneath. Her tight, dark blue jeans absorbed most of the blood around the waist. Any patches were hard to see in the darkness. The drizzle helped. Chinatown was mostly deserted. But there were 24-hour coffee shops filled with dozing taxi drivers and a handful of bookies even at 3.30am. They were nearby, but not near enough. Maxwell paid $8,000-a-month rent for a reason. As he passed the deserted, silent restored houses of the private Blair Plain district, he cherished the exclusivity. Questions were rarely asked of anyone living in such neighbourhoods, not in Singapore.

Aini's head rolled towards her chest.

"No, no, no, stay awake, Aini, it's going to be fine."

Aini's eyes were closing.

"I'm tired Talek."

"No, you're not tired. You're fine. Everything is fine. We've just got to get you somewhere, somewhere nice."

Aini tumbled towards Maxwell. Her legs buckled like a newborn foal. Maxwell propped her up, ignoring the searing pain in his back. He knew his black T-shirt was sticking to his bloodied skin. He hoped the jean jacket offered enough cover.

The distant streetlights of Kampong Bahru Road danced before Aini's eyes.

"I can't see anything," she whispered.

"It's dark, just dark."

Maxwell realised the scraping sound was from her stilettos. He was dragging her. Taxi drivers might assume she was drunk. The gallant white man had offered his suit jacket and was chaperoning her home.

"I'm so tired."

Aini's eyes closed.

"No, it's OK. Wake up, Aini. You must wake up now, it's OK. You can't go yet, not yet."

Maxwell heard the sound of a TV coming from the prata shop on the corner. Plates were being stacked. He also picked out voices. The lights were too bright. He dragged her towards an alley behind the *prata* shop.

"This will be OK. This will be a good place to rest."

The odour of the dank alley stunned Maxwell. Cockroaches scattered as he pulled Aini's failing body past fruit boxes filled with food scraps. He propped her against the wall of the *prata* shop and lowered her across an open drain. A rat scurried away through the foul, stagnant water.

"Just wait here for a minute, just for a minute."

Maxwell stepped back, utterly exhausted. His breathing was laboured. He ran his fingers along the spine of his T-shirt. They were damp with sweat and blood. He examined his hands. Most of the blood wasn't his. He bent down beside Aini and washed his hands and arms in the drain.

She stirred.

"My boy," she whispered.

Her voice unnerved Maxwell. He grabbed a nearby plastic barrel and hoisted himself up. His hand slipped into the barrel and he recoiled in disgust. The barrel was filled with the *prata* shop's dirty crockery. Its cold water was curry red. Chicken bones and used tissues floated on the oily surface.

"My beautiful boy," Aini muttered.

Maxwell watched her closely. Her head had rolled towards her left shoulder. She couldn't move. She was almost certainly dying now.

"He is a beautiful boy," Maxwell agreed, examining her broken body.

"So beautiful."

"He takes after his mother."

As Maxwell moved towards the plastic barrel, he thought he saw Aini smile.

"Talek, can you?"

"Of course. I have the address."

Maxwell crouched beside Aini and pulled her towards him. He took back his jacket and hung it on a crate. He dragged the plastic barrel away from Aini. The slop spilled over the sides and splashed onto his trainers. He jumped back to spare them.

"Photo."

"What's that?"

"My boy, pocket."

Aini tried to lift her arm, but her strength had deserted her.

"Yes, the photo in your pocket, of your boy, yes, I like that one." Maxwell flicked a cockroach off the rim of the plastic barrel. "You want me to get that photo for you?"

Aini said nothing. Maxwell grabbed the sides of the plastic barrel.

"That's the one with him holding his new football right, with his friends in the village. Lovely photo. Make sure you look after that one."

Maxwell pushed the plastic barrel over.

The oily, curried water washed over the dying woman. The grubby plastic plates and cutlery clattered against her body. She slid along the wall until her right arm and shoulder wedged in the narrow drain. Maxwell picked up the plastic barrel and shook it over Aini's body until the last half-eaten chicken wing had tumbled out.

Satisfied, he rinsed his hands in the drain a second time, picked up his jacket and returned home to clean his apartment.

Chapter 4

"WHY do they always leave them in alleyways," Professor Chong said theatrically to the investigators squeezed around him in the confined space. "And why does the Major Crime Division always send too many men down an alleyway? Can I have some room please gentlemen?"

Asia's leading pathologist used his gloved hands to usher the crowding officers away. The white-shirted men moved back. In crime and punishment circles, Chong commanded reverence. From his earliest days as a cadet dealing with Toa Payoh's cult killings, his professionalism demanded respect. His portly frame and avuncular personality made him every officer's favourite uncle.

"Thank you, boys. Let the old dog see the poor rabbit."

Chong was a happier man these days. Nearing retirement, he had found a cottage with his English partner in the East Sussex countryside, not too far from Brighton, where they had married a year earlier. After that wretched business at Marina Bay Sands, Chong was insistent that he scrubbed the stains away with a long vacation. His partner suggested a cottage in Kent and surprised him with a marriage proposal. They still couldn't get married in Singapore of course. Technically, they still couldn't have sex in Singapore. But the public mood was softening beyond the increasingly marginalised fundamentalists. Chong knew that. So did the fundamentalists who tried to shame him by regurgitating old stories on vulgar blogs using uncouth language. But Chong's civil partnership ceremony was covered, to his surprise, by all the major newspapers, including the Chinese and Malay press. The overwhelmingly positive response had privately reduced him to tears. And the archaic jokes had mostly dried up at crime scenes, at least to his face.

With considerable effort, Chong kneeled beside Aini's crumpled body and sighed. It never got any easier; more detached, yes, but never any easier. He gestured towards an assistant to take notes and photographs as he spoke into an iPhone.

"A young Malay woman, presumably in her late 20s, maybe early 30s, slim, with no obvious wounds except the solitary wound in her chest. It's a round puncture, rather than a slash, suggesting a sharp-tipped instrument, such as an ice pick or a screwdriver, rather than a knife, and was pushed in far enough to catch her lung, resulting in heavy blood loss, more internal than external due to the size of the entry wound. She probably didn't die immediately; she might have had some time while the pleural cavity filled up. There's blood in the mouth and on the teeth. She probably spat out quite a bit before she died. Judging by the wound, she probably wasn't attacked here. Even allowing for the waste-water washing away a lot of the blood, there's still not enough either in the alley or out in the street. No. She wasn't killed here."

Chong followed a voice in the background and found a familiar face. He rose slowly.

"Detective Sergeant Chan, I heard you were with the Major Crime Division now, the murder squad no less. How are you, young man?"

Charles Chan was aware of the audience in the alley. He was

also aware of his recent promotion. He had earned his stripes quicker than those around him.

"It's Inspector now, actually, Professor."

Chong smiled and patted his hand warmly.

"For Marina Bay Sands?"

"That and one or two smaller cases."

"You're being modest. I read the papers. Working with that old scoundrel James Tan obviously helped in the end."

"It did, sir. Working with him and, you know, Stanley Low, I got, how to say *ah*?"

"Both ends of the spectrum?"

"Exactly. So you don't think the girl died here either then?"

"No, there's not enough blood here."

"We found some spots out in the street. The killer washed down most of it around here, but missed a bit in the darkness. How long you think she's been dead?"

"Around four, maybe five hours now."

Detective Inspector Chan stepped back as Chong's assistant took photographs. He folded his arms.

"Yeah, table cleaner from the *prata* shop found her. From China. At first, scared to tell his boss, then scared to tell us, usual *lah*, over here on social visit pass, no work permit, no declared income. The *prata* shop staff said the victim never came into the shop, never seen her before."

"You believe them?"

"Not really."

Only now did Chong notice the puffiness around Chan's face. He was still attractive, but heavier, darker. The boyishness was fading.

"So what do you think?"

"Ah, same as everyone else here. There's no CCTV in the *prata* shop or around here and we got no ID on her yet, just some photos in her pocket, but this is a very *ulu* side. Once you get away from the houses, it's quiet streets and open fields until you reach Tiong Bahru, not many cars or witnesses, got privacy, empty streets, places to park cars. Why else would you come here? Go coffee shop first maybe. Argue over price. Fight. Dump her in the alley. Finish."

"I'm impressed, inspector. You don't sound like the old Charlie Chan anymore."

He didn't. Even being called Charlie Chan didn't bother him anymore. The job had desensitised him. He was becoming immune to criticism and crime scenes. He had a second child on the way and his wife wanted their Punggol apartment renovated. She had told him to get his priorities sorted out. He needed to spend more time discussing nursery colour schemes than dead prostitutes. Something had to give.

"In this job, no choice right. How long for the lab report?"

"Ah, not too long, you need it in a hurry?"

"Not really. If she's a foreign prostitute, they won't make her a priority."

Chan gently patted the pathologist's shoulder. He stepped over the corpse and wandered out of the alley. He needed some air.

Chapter 5

DR Tracy Lai nodded and thought about her next appointment, the pervert in denial. He still protested his innocence, even with her, despite two convictions for taking up-skirt photos on shopping mall escalators. He insisted the photos were accidental and his dutiful wife had stood by him. They had three children and had recently moved into a condo with a partial view of the Bedok Reservoir.

But the up-skirter would offer a welcome reprieve after Detective Inspector Stanley Low.

She took the longest showers before and after his sessions. She could never be clean enough. She had no qualms about wearing skirts for the up-skirter, but rarely on days when Low was scribbled in her diary. He undressed her psychologically and left her feeling unworthy and cheap. More than that, he made her feel unprofessional. Her doctorate that she hung so proudly in her office withered away whenever he flopped into one of her leather armchairs. He penetrated her. He weakened her. Her affluent, sheltered background reeked of bullshit. She couldn't wash it away. She was always left with a residue of phoniness. He was the real deal, a raw, natural intellect capable of understanding his own case file, blessed and cursed with the ability to harness his bipolar condition for his own ends. And it made him such a prick.

"Have you slept yet?" Lai asked.

Low rubbed his bloodshot eyes and slid further down the armchair.

"What for?"

"Have you been working all night?"

"You know I have."

"Sleep deprivation can be a contributing factor in a manic episode."

"So can having a shit job, but you never ask me to quit."

"It's not getting any better?"

Low turned away slightly and smiled. "I work for the Technology Crime Division. *The Technology Crime Division.* Even the name is boring."

"A desk job may be less stressful for you right now. It's a change of pace."

"It'd be a change of pace if I stuck a fucking chopstick in my eye."

"We talked about the language before, didn't we?"

"The what?"

"You said the f-word again."

Low laughed loudly and clapped his hands. "*Aiyoh,* the great Asian hypocrisy strikes again. I know we're all full of shit outside, but now we got to bring it in here? We keep half the country in poverty and the other half in denial, but we can't say the word 'fuck'. Because that will be our downfall, right? That will be the moment when the sunny island sinks, when we all start saying 'fuck' to each other. How's your up-skirter doing?"

"I don't talk about my other patients in here."

"He's your patient. But he's my case, remember? I caught him last time, thanks to my hard drive-cracking geeks in the office."

"He's not your case any more."

"No, he's yours. You try to keep it clean in here, right? You don't want to sully yourself with sick people saying sick words. You think you can spray nice words through the air like disinfectant and keep it clean, is it? My job is shit because it stops me from catching up-skirt, photo-taking bastards like your patient. Your job is to make them better, find their redemption, find their good side like Darth fucking Vader. I catch them. You make them feel good. And you want to give me shit for saying 'fuck'?"

Lai considered her response carefully. "Feel better?"

"No." Low bit the inside of his cheek. "Do you really think there's a point to all this? You think we can be cured?"

"Not cured."

"*Yah lah, yah lah*, not cured, treated. I know the drill already."

"To a certain extent."

"Anyone? Like Adolf Hitler or the North Korean with the funny haircut?"

"Those are extreme examples often cited when someone seeks to disparage the treatment of mental health, but that's exactly what they are, extreme cases. You don't think you are getting any better?"

"It depends on the circumstances."

"Nurture over nature?"

"Not so *cheem*, just a fucked-up life over a good life." Low raised his hands in apology. "Sorry, a messed-up life over a good life. See? I feel better already."

Lai smiled. And then felt terrible for smiling.

"What do you think?"

"Please *lah*, the same as you when you put away the textbooks," Low said, sitting up. "I've got this website now to monitor, *The Singapore Truth*, you heard of it?"

"I'm familiar with it, can't say I read it regularly."

"But you do. We all do. We say we don't, but we do. My guys

have the stats to prove it. The site gets more unique visitors than all other mainstream news sites combined. And it's shit, right or not? Racist, sensationalised shit. Every day it's the same. Send back the Indians, the Filipinos, the Indonesians buying our condos, the Bangladeshis scaring our women in the shopping centres, it's all bullshit. But we read it. We check with the tech guys overseas and it's the same everywhere—blacks and whites in the US, asylum seekers in Australia, Eastern Europeans invading England and France, the Mainland Chinese taking over Hong Kong, the Islamic State taking over the world—same stories everywhere, right? Globalisation makes us all fear being swamped by the invader, right or not?"

"Perhaps."

"Please *lah*, we monitor. It's the same all over. Almost overnight, we are all racist again, even in Singapore. You think that's true?"

"No."

"No. But *The Singapore Truth* website says we are. That blog says we must make Singapore for Singaporeans and take the country back before it collapses. And do you know why? Do you really know why one country is supposedly being overrun with racists?"

"Go on."

"Because one Chinaman's wife got shagged by a white man."

Chapter 6

HAROLD Zhang sat on the side of his bed and watched his wife get dressed. Li Jing was still so beautiful. That's what hurt the most. If she had gone to seed, he could channel his infuriating sense of impotence and fling it back in her fat, saggy face. He could make her understand how she had scooped out his insides in Australia and left him empty. She had disemboweled him. He didn't think it was possible to loathe another person quite as much as he loathed his wife. But she was still so beautiful.

The early-morning sun streaked through the grilles of their bedroom window and her face glowed. Zhang continued watching as his wife brushed her tousled hair, still damp from the shower. He wanted her, right now, with her damp hair and her clingy underwear and her tight thighs and her pink cheeks and her early-morning bloom.

And he despised himself for it. He controlled Singapore from his laptop, but she still controlled his loins. He'd do anything to lose the puppy-dog adoration that emasculated him. Out there, he was the blog master. In here, he wasn't even the master of his own bedroom.

"Very nice," he said.

"Hmm?" Li Jing muttered, still brushing her hair in the mirror, not bothering with eye contact, reasserting the balance of power.

"That underwear, very nice."

"Yah."

"Where you get it?"

"Don't know. Had it long time already."

They had been married for 15 years and always struggled with small talk. After Australia, it was agonising.

"It's nice."

"Yah," Li Jing uttered as she grabbed a couple of clips from the dresser and pulled her hair back tightly.

"Got yoga today?"

"Yah."

"Same instructor?"

"Yah."

"From China?"

"Don't start, OK."

"I won't, I won't. Just don't know why we cannot find a local yoga instructor to give lessons at our local community centre."

"Maybe because we think a yoga job not good enough for our children."

"Maybe. Maybe got no choice."

"Look, I'm not doing this again, OK. Save it for your blog."

"OK. I'm sorry."

"Yah."

Zhang tried to look away as his wife bent over to pull up her Lycra leggings. But her tautness teased him. His old friends—the ones he had left—their wives had lost their figures. Childbirth, reunion dinners and hawker centres all stuck to their hips in the end. But his wife had always taken pride in her appearance. Good genes gave her the complexion and the slim build. Bad genes gave him the potbelly, the receding hairline and the myopia. He knew strangers played the numbers game with them. He watched their cogs turn. He heard their voices in his head: *What was she doing with him? She was at least a seven. He was barely a three. It must be the money. He's got that famous blog. It must be the money. Can't be anything else. Just look at them.*

He always anticipated the scrunched faces as they registered their disgust, unable to hide their contempt for the middle-aged, balding, fat xenophobe dragging around the beautiful, reluctant wife. Zhang didn't mind. He agreed with them. He had to shave in the mirror. He saw what they saw.

But they were only half-right. It wasn't his weight gain or the hair loss. She wasn't superficial in that way. Her beauty made it easier for her to be less vain. She radiated natural confidence, not artificial arrogance. It was the ugly ducklings that chained themselves to mirrors in a desperate search for swans. Li Jing didn't care about her appearance, because she didn't have to.

And then she went to Australia and found herself; found the mirror image of herself in another man.

He was a surfing instructor, taking out coach parties of Japanese and Chinese tourists who could barely swim. He was shabby, bearded and wore faded T-shirts and shorts all year round. None of his clothes were branded. Some of them came from second-hand shops. He didn't own a computer and his phone was an old, cracked Nokia. His battered Ford was more than 10 years old and rarely washed. He had built his seafront shack himself. He ran his surfing business by placing ads in the local newspaper. He didn't even have name cards.

Zhang didn't understand him at all and thought the surfing lesson was pointless. Li Jing fell in love with him almost immediately.

She started private surfing lessons. Zhang started his blog soon after, from a suburban home in Australia. He called it *The Singapore Truth*. It was the right time for true Singaporeans to take back Singapore. The website was worthy and necessary, and Zhang couldn't find a job in Australia.

He squeezed the side of the duvet as his wife pulled the leggings towards her hips.

"*Wah*, you still look good, *ah*."

"Hmm." Li Jing focused on her sweat top.

"Still got a bit of time before work."

"Not really."

"It won't take long. Definitely will not take long."

"No time really."

"Made time for him though, right?"

Zhang spat out the words. Li Jing stopped.

"Maybe I'm the wrong skin colour," he went on. "White is right?"

Finally, Li Jing gave her husband the attention he craved. She looked at him. She had once loved this man.

"I'm going to work."

She didn't look back.

"Yah, and who owns your company again? Who's your boss again?"

Zhang heard the door slam and got up. He shuffled into the office and opened his laptop. Anti-government activists monitored and updated *The Singapore Truth* for him overnight. Bigots and fundamentalists were always his favourite volunteers. Their contributions usually garnered the most hits. He didn't even correct the dreadful syntax, knowing it further irritated the English-educated, bleeding-heart liberals. True believers were the best. They answered to a higher ideology. It would only undermine their purity to pay them.

He clicked on the latest news and there was the headline.

Young Woman Killed in Chinatown

He read the story and learned only in the second paragraph that she was a cleaner from Indonesia, so she was probably working illegally in the country. And she was a foreigner. That should've been in the headline. He'd speak to the fool who uploaded the story later.

But an illegal worker had been murdered. And she was a foreigner. Zhang smiled and settled down for a productive morning's work.

He had needed cheering up.

Chapter 7

DEAD bodies no longer bothered Chan, but the smell still lingered. He applied some Vicks VapoRub beneath his nostrils. Professor Chong rolled his eyes.

"What? This is good for the sinuses," Chan said. "They do this in the US, you know."

"Only in the movies, my dear boy."

Chan didn't want to admit the truth. He hadn't picked up the idea from the movies. The stench of a rotting corpse had driven him to distraction for months until he watched a Liverpool match and saw that a couple of the players had rubbed Vicks VapoRub on their jerseys, just below the neck, to help their breathing. He tried it once at a police morgue and immediately blocked out the dead. Now he never left home without it.

"Eh, it works OK. Don't smell them anymore."

"Nor do I," Chong replied.

"Really? What's your secret?"

"Almost 40 years of experience. Are you ready?"

Chan nodded as the pathologist pulled back the sheet. The morgue's freezing air-conditioning had slowed the deterioration of Aini's body, but the effects of almost five hours in a drain beneath a slop bucket hadn't helped. Her right arm and shoulder were greying after being exposed to the drain's wastewater. But she was in reasonable condition. Chan had seen worse. The growing rich-poor divide, and those damn casinos, had turned up more floaters in the reservoirs. Some still jumped from apartments, which pulped body parts. But those who opted for a romantic way out at the nearest reservoir had no idea just how decidedly unromantic their suicide location really was. The fish turned them into zombies. The water leeched the soul.

Chong pointed to the puncture wound beneath her breasts. There was still the faint outline of a tan and flecks of glitter polish on her toenails. Aini had worked hard to keep up appearances in her new country.

"Pretty *ah*," Chan said, adjusting his gloves.

"They often are, these poor girls."

"Why *ah*?"

"Why would you kill an ugly one? Why would you be with her in the first place? They work in the coffee shops selling beer, or themselves, and they have to look their best. There is so much competition now. It's a global market. And the unlucky ones end up here."

"So she was definitely a prostitute?"

Chong pointed towards her vagina. "Maybe not, actually. She had intercourse reasonably regularly, but only in the way a regular couple might. There was no swelling or bruising and no medical work. But there had been intercourse that night, nothing unusual. A condom was probably used. So that won't really help us, which brings us to this."

Both men pored over the puncture wound.

"Only one circular wound," Chong continued. "A thin instrument, certainly not a knife, but at least 12 to 18 cm long, long enough to penetrate the bottom of her lung, which caused internal bleeding into her pleural cavity. She slowly choked to death on her own blood. It's a wretched, terrifying way to die."

"Why?"

"There is no room for misinterpretation, inspector. The mind knows that the body is dying."

"Do you still think she was moved?"

"Without a doubt. There wasn't enough blood in that alley on the whole."

"So, what? An angry partner lashes out? An argument over money with a customer?"

"That's for you to decide, but I might lean towards the former at this stage." Chong lifted a hand. "Her hands were butter soft, with heavy traces of detergent."

"A moonlighting cleaner."

"*Voilà.*"

"So no fixed job or regular income. That's gonna make it tougher."

"No ID then?"

"Not yet, nothing on her."

"Is she not Indonesian? I thought I read that online."

Chan fiddled with his latex gloves. "Got a lot of angry people these days posting rubbish, even in the police force. Work long hours, understaffed, not paid enough. And that website pays good money. It can be more than a month's salary, you know."

"So she might be Singaporean?"

"How many local Malays end up in a drain with no IC and no one declaring them missing?"

"You've got a tough one then."

"That's why. And no one will come forward. Her friends will also be foreigners with no work permits. And locals won't really know her, because she was a cleaner. It's just more paperwork for me."

"Welcome to the Major Crime Division," Chong boomed. "Come. Let me help you."

The pathologist gathered his notes from a stainless steel trolley beside Aini's body. "We found hair under here and here."

His clipboard hovered over the victim's armpits.

"And?"

"Being an Asian, she had exceptionally coarse hair, very long and straight, as you can see, and her hairs were particularly wide, even for an Asian, a fine head of hair. But under her armpits we found different hairs. The *prata* shop waste that was thrown over her was rather devious, washing away most fingerprints and covering her with the saliva, hair and fibre of the dozens of people who went for *prata*. But there were stray hairs kept snug and dry under her armpits. The long hairs you pull from a hairbrush or a jacket. The hair strands were very fine and consistently the same, somewhere between brown and blonde."

"*Ang moh* hair?"

"Based on those hairs and some preliminary tests taken on a couple of stray pubic hairs we found in her panties, I'd say the last person she was with that night, certainly the last person she had sex with, was a Caucasian."

"Oh shit."

Chong winced as he pulled the sheet back over Aini's head. He abhorred bad language in the workplace.

Chapter 8

USING her arm like a crane in a video arcade game, Sue Parry swept Billy's toys off the dining room table and into a plastic container. One of his cars scratched the Burmese teakwood.

"Billy, will you stop watching TV and clear up your own bloody toys," she shouted.

"You said the b-word again, Mummy," Billy's voice drifted back.

"Never mind that, I haven't got time to clear up your toys."

Parry licked her thumb and tried to rub away the minor scratch, but it stubbornly clung to the table's polished surface. She had bought the table at Dempsey Hill. Her new friends from Thursday coffee mornings had recommended an antique house that specialised in Mongolian, Tibetan and Burmese furniture. She had sighed appreciatively at the time, sipping her skinny flat white and desperately hoping no one picked up on her indifference. She had no interest in stick furniture from Mongolia or Burma. She just couldn't picture a Tibetan statue either side of her Laura Ashley sideboard. But she went along while Billy was at kindergarten and fell in love with the Burmese dining table.

And now it was in need of repair because the place hadn't been tidied properly for days.

Where was that bloody woman?

Parry dumped the plastic toy box in Billy's bedroom and pulled a phone from her shorts pocket.

If I get her answering machine again . . .

"Oh, hello, Aini. It's me Sue Parry again, the British lady with the condo at Joo Chiat. Look, I know you've only been here a few times, but you didn't turn up and you didn't let me know beforehand and I can't get hold of you now. I really need you to come around. Call me as soon as possible."

She put the phone on the Burmese dining table, covering the scratch.

"Lazy cow."

"Who's a lazy cow, Mummy?"

Billy appeared at his mother's hip. He was a handsome five-year-old boy, with his mother's blue eyes. His face was smothered in chocolate.

"You've been in the fridge again, haven't you? Just because I'm on the phone doesn't mean you can sneak into the fridge and eat chocolate, OK."

"Who's a lazy cow, Mummy?"

Parry had hoped the minor telling off would throw him off the lazy cow thing.

"No one is, all right. I don't want to hear any more about it."

"Is Auntie Aini a lazy . . ."

"No one is lazy," Parry interrupted. "Except you when you don't put your toys away. Go on. Go in the living room. You can watch TV for 10 minutes before I put the dinner on. Give me 10 minutes rest. I haven't stopped all day."

Billy cheered and ran off to grab the remote control. His mother picked up her phone and played Farm Heroes.

Parry waited.

"Mummy."

There it was, less than 10 seconds of silence.

"Auntie Aini is on TV."

Parry focused on Farm Heroes. "No, she isn't. Switch over to Tom and Jerry."

"The TV says Auntie Aini is dead."

"What?"

Parry followed her son into the living room. Half of their LED screen was filled with their cleaner's image, and the other half with contact numbers and email addresses for anyone with further information.

"See, Mummy. Auntie Aini is dead."

As Parry froze in horror, Billy ran to the kitchen to steal more chocolate.

CHAN smoothened his tie before he spoke. He always wore a tie for house visits. The old guard at Major Crime Division made fun of him for his stuffy dress code. Even the Prime Minister didn't bother with a tie in Parliament, but Charles Chan tied a Windsor knot to tell *Ah Beng* of Bishan that his bike had been stolen from the town park. Initially, Chan saw the tie as a shield. His attire exuded the authority he didn't have as a rookie on the murder squad. He didn't need the tie now, but felt strangely naked without it. He smiled as Sue Parry gently placed his cup of tea, with an English saucer, on one of those weird, wooden Asian tables that *ang mohs* liked more than Asians.

Parry joined her husband, Ben Parry, on the other side of the table. Chan took the time to stir his tea, buying time for superficial observations. The wife was younger and more attractive than the husband, but he earned good money for a shipping company at Keppel Harbour, so the relationship made sense. Her nails were flawless, buffed and polished, and she had swimming costume tan lines from daily trips to their condo pool. The living room was scruffy, with the kid's toys, remote controls and interior design magazines featuring black and white bungalows, but not dirty. There was no live-in helper. Homes with live-in helpers rarely looked like homes, but sanitised show flats. They were not real. This apartment was lived in, scruffy, but mostly clean. So they had a part-time cleaner.

Chan knew most of this before he visited, but it was useful to sharpen the senses before beginning.

"It's a lovely apartment," he said, honestly.

"Oh, thank you," Mrs Parry replied quickly, nervously. "It's hard when you have children, you know?"

"I do. I've got one and another on the way."

"Congratulations."

"Thank you."

Mrs Parry moved a couple of colouring books and piled them at the end of the long dining table. She was trying too hard, eager to alleviate the guilt of the stay-home parent. Mr Parry hadn't said a word. Chan focused on the wife. That's what Stanley Low would do. She was the weak spot.

"So how did you hire Aini?"

"She had left a handwritten ad on the clubhouse noticeboard."

"And you hired her?"

"I tried her first, and I liked her, and Billy liked her so I gave her the job."

"How often did she come round?"

"Twice a week."

"Twice a week?"

"Yes."

"But you don't work?"

"No."

Chan didn't feel particularly guilty for enjoying her discomfort. His pregnant wife worked full-time and put up with his mother in a much smaller HDB flat in Punggol.

"I'm sorry. Is this about my wife or about Aini?"

Chan turned towards the husband.

So you do have a voice.

The inspector could see the deep rings under Mr Parry's eyes. His regional accent was also harder to understand than his wife's. He was rougher. His wife had married down, but into more money.

"It's about Aini, sir. I'm trying to work out her daily patterns, how often she came here, you know."

"My wife has told you already twice a week."

"And you were never around when she cleaned?"

"No."

Mr Parry expected his wife to react, but she did nothing except lick her thumb and try and wipe away a scratch on the dining table. He hadn't noticed the scratch before.

"I haven't seen her since her last visit more than a week ago," said Mrs Parry. "I've been leaving messages on her phone."

"And you were both at home on Sunday night?"

Mr Parry adjusted his body shape to face Chan. "The night she died? Where did that come from?"

"I'm just asking . . ."

"Just asking what?"

"I'm just establishing Aini's daily patterns and trying to work out where she might have been at different times of the day."

"Fine. What's that got to do with us?"

"Nothing, I'm sure, but so far you're the only people we've interviewed with a direct connection to Aini. Were you both at home on Sunday night?"

The silence was interrupted by the faint, rhythmic sound of Billy rummaging through the toy box in his bedroom.

"I was," Mrs Parry said finally.

"And I was out," her husband said, raising his voice. "So I

suppose that makes me her killer then."

Chapter 9

LOW was at his table, grinning as he listened on the telephone. He kicked a pizza box aside to make more room for his legs on the desk. He waved at Chan as his former protégé made his way past the clinical cubicles of the Technology Crime Division. Low noted the younger man's posture. He didn't stoop as much. He walked purposefully. His dress sense had also improved. Little Charlie Chan had the makings of a fine department director, as long as he lost that silly idealism first.

Low held up a finger, gesturing for Chan to wait as he returned to the phone.

"*Yah lah*, I know that already, but your estimated reading is wrong. I spend most of my time in the office, you understand or not? You think someone is holding air-con parties when I'm outside, is it? . . . That's not my problem. I'm not paying this bill."

Low waved a final demand utilities bill at Chan. The younger inspector shook his head.

"Excuse me, what are your qualifications for this job? Did you quit school to pursue your dream of working in customer service? Hello? I'm talking too fast for you? My England too powder-ful is it? Hello? Hello? . . . She hung up. Can you believe that? She hung up."

Low threw the office phone across his desk and watched it fall between chicken rice boxes. Chan offered his hand. "Still an asshole then?"

"Of course."

"So, using the company phone to whack utility companies now, is it?"

"Hey, I finished night shift hours ago, man."

"So go home."

"What for?"

Both men left the question hanging in the air. Both men already knew the answer. Chan changed the subject. "Still a messy bugger then?"

"Hey, I work in Technology, man, big time now *ah*. Got no time for that."

"They're still screwing you?"

"Of course."

"I'm sorry, man."

"What for?"

"Last time."

"*Wah lau*, enough already. Everyone has moved on. And look at you, got a promotion. You kept going."

"I kept my mouth shut."

"Ah."

"And so did you. About me."

"Nothing to say."

"Please *lah*, Marina Bay Sands, The Indonesian. That was my fault."

"Look, I was finished either way. One mistake, two mistakes, ten mistakes, it didn't matter, might as well take one more, right or not?"

"I want to help you."

Low glanced up. Chan had more lines on his forehead. Tiny

crows feet were tiptoeing away from his eyes.

"I did tell you before," Low muttered.

"What?"

"Major Crime, murder squad, no different to CPIB, it's where we go to burst bubbles. You go in, you never come out the same. I told you that, right?"

"Shall I get a couch and lay down?"

"*Wah*, smart arse now, *ah*? Don't be too smart. You end up here chasing bloggers."

Chan wheeled over an executive chair from the next cubicle and sat down. "I've got a lead."

"No."

"What?"

"I'm not helping. It's not my case. I got no influence anymore, no jurisdiction."

"Just one chat *lah*. You won't get into trouble."

"You think I give a shit about me? Look at me." Low pointed at his stained shirt and rubbed his scruffy stubble. "You want this to be a cautionary tale or a bloody mirror? I'm finished, blacklisted, career over. You want to be toxic, too? Look around you. You're sitting in an empty chair. No one wants to be near me. I'm contaminated, man."

"You finished?"

"Yeah, that'll do."

Chan edged his chair closer. Low peered down at his old partner's shuffling feet. "You going to kiss me or what?"

"One interview, just observe. Watch the guy with his wife, see what he says."

"Why?"

"They employed the dead girl, this Aini from Indonesia. She was their cleaner. We don't know who else she worked for yet."

"So?"

"The husband was out the night she was killed. His alibi checks out. He was with friends at a bar, got witnesses."

"Then he didn't kill her."

"But he's lying. They're both lying."

"About what?"

"I don't know. But you will."

Low drank from his water bottle. "If anyone finds out, they'll whack you, not me."

"Come on, you've finished your shift. One hour. Just sit and watch them. See if I'm right, just like last time."

"Don't do the nostalgia shit. You don't want me there. I don't want to be there. I can't bring Ah Lian back anymore."

Chan smiled at the filthy desk. "He's a white guy."

"Who?"

"The husband. He's an *ang moh*."

Low's eyes widened. "Really *ah*? Fuck it. Let's go."

He emptied the water bottle and shook his head clear. He wiped his forearm across his mouth and pretended the bottle really was filled with water.

And Chan pretended he couldn't smell the vodka.

Chapter 10

SUE Parry made a point of easing the tray onto the Burmese teakwood dining table. She handed out a cup and saucer to her husband and the two Chinese policemen. She smiled at both visitors, even the older, grubby one who kept staring at her. She didn't smile at her husband. Instead she pushed the small plate of biscuits towards the inspectors.

"Help yourself," she said.

Low watched her manicured fingers grip the plate. Her kindness was genuine. So was her fear. He grabbed a biscuit and held it in the air. "Eh, custard cream, right?"

Mrs Parry smiled at the recognition. "Yes. You like them?"

"Reminds me of my university days."

"You studied in England?"

"I did, LSE, London School of Economics."

Ben Parry examined the unkempt guest for the first time. "Really?"

"Yeah, more than 20 years ago now, but great time to be in London. It was all happening then, the music, Britpop right? Great time."

Mr Parry nodded at the memory. "Yeah, it was."

Low turned his attention back to the nervous housewife. "So where do you get these biscuits in Singapore?"

"Oh, er, Marks and Spencer. They're expensive really, more than double the price, but it's a taste of home, I suppose."

"Definitely," Low mumbled through a mouthful of custard cream. "My mother used to send me a big box, every two months, to my hall of residence. Big box, you know, with SingPost down the side. All the *ang mohs*, sorry, white guys used to make fun of me you know, but soon stopped making fun of me when I made them Maggi noodles for the first time, much better than the one in England. What was it called? The one in that plastic pot?"

"Oh, a Pot Noodle," Mrs Parry interjected.

"That's it. *Wah*, that one *ah*. Lousy. Like eating plastic. So my mother always sent me Maggi noodles and Maggi chilli sauce, couldn't survive without it."

Chan tapped Low's leg beneath the table.

"Anyway, sorry, it's easy to get nostalgic. I enjoyed my time in England. And now I know where to get custard creams in Singapore."

Low reached over for another. That was Chan's cue.

"So, Mr Parry, we've made some checks and you were at the German bar you mentioned in Joo Chiat for a number of hours on the night of your cleaner's murder."

Mrs Parry shuddered as she sipped her tea. Her husband looked straight at Chan.

"We've spoken to the bar manager and everything is fine," Chan went on.

Mr Parry pointed a finger at the munching inspector. "So why is he here then? Why have you come back?"

"Just a follow up. I hope you understand. And I hope you're willing to help. We were very grateful that you called us, Mrs Parry. I can understand why you might have been reluctant, initially. But you did the right thing to call us in the end. Right now, you guys are the only connection with the victim."

"Aini. Her name was Aini."

Everyone looked at Mr Parry. His wife used the cup to cover as much of her face as possible.

"Sorry, Mr Parry, of course you're right. Her name was Aini," Chan acknowledged.

"Were you having sex with her, Mr Parry?"

Now everyone looked at Low. No one appeared more horrified than Chan. He squeezed Low's leg much harder this time.

Mr Parry's eyes focused entirely on his accuser. "What? Where did you? Who are you?"

"I told you who I was when we came in, showed you my credentials. I'm Detective Inspector Stanley Low. Now, did you sleep with . . . Aini?"

"No. I didn't."

"Something else then. Hand job? Blow job?"

Mrs Parry almost dropped her cup. "What?"

"What my colleague means," Chan interrupted, cutting off Low by discreetly grabbing his wrist and pressing it against the antique table, "is maybe you knew the victim, Aini, a little more?"

"You're asking my husband, who I've been married to for almost eight years, if he slept with a foreign cleaner, someone he had known for less than a month and had only met once or twice?"

Chan let go of Low's wrist. "Once or twice?"

"What?"

"Once or twice?"

"Once or twice what?"

"You said 'once or twice'. Your husband had only met Aini once or twice, but the last time we met, you seemed to suggest he hadn't met her before. You hired her from an ad she'd left on the clubhouse noticeboard. You were here with your son, when she cleaned twice a week, while your husband was at work. Just you and Billy, that's how he recognised her on TV. That's why you called us. So did you meet her or not, Mr Parry?"

Mrs Parry looked away. Low leaned forward to take another biscuit to see her eyes. She blinked away a couple of stray tears. He bit hard into the biscuit and chewed loudly.

"I love custard creams. One thing about England, they know how to make cakes and biscuits. *Ang mohs* can't cook like Asians, but they do bake better than us. Cakes, biscuits, pies. We got BreadTalk, but it's not the same, just like Singapore noodles in the UK are not like noodles here. So Mr Parry, when you met her once or twice did you sleep with her?"

"If you say that again . . ."

"What? You going to punch me, is it? We're not in university now, man. This is Singapore and I'm a Singaporean police officer, most of the time. Here, we rule, OK? So, did you buy this table?"

"What?"

"This table here? You bought this table here, very nice, no?"

"My wife did."

"How much was it?"

"Almost $10,000."

"*Wah*, steady *lah*. That's a lot of money, man. You know what that is? That's more than an *ang moh* showing off at dinner parties; that's roots, man. That's you planting roots in Singapore. You've been here a while already and just moved to a nice, big apartment. So you applied for PR right?"

"Why?"

"It's important, permanent residency. It means you want to stay here, raise little Billy in a nice country, good international school, stable economy, low crime, not like London last time, right? So when did you apply for PR?"

"About nine months ago," Mr Parry said.

"Yah, just nice. Takes about a year, a year plus, so you get your furniture together, start to build the nest and then get that PR, no need to pay foreigner stamp duty any more and then buy a nice condo like this one, correct?"

"Something like that."

"Well, you're fucked."

"Excuse me?"

"I know everyone at Ministry of Manpower, everyone. Last time, I worked for CPIB. You know who they are? They are the Corrupt Practices Investigation Bureau. And I know everyone there, too. So I can screw your job and your PR application."

"You can't do that."

"Of course we can. We're the Singapore Government."

"The PR application . . ."

". . . Is already gone. That's it. Finished. You're going back to England. A month from now, you'll be scraping ice off your windscreen with your credit card, moaning about your high taxes and free-loading foreigners, pretending to be all liberal and tolerant of foreigners because you lived with so many in Asia, but you'll soon be putting your house on the market, joining that white flight, heading for the village or the countryside and dreaming of Singapore, where you could go anywhere safely, at any time and buy anything, and then you'll realise, finally, that there really is more to life than custard fucking creams," Low said as he shoved another into his mouth. "Still, they will be cheap though. Why were you home alone with Aini?"

Mrs Parry faced her husband. "Tell him."

"No."

"Tell him."

"What's the point?"

"Because we're going back to England if you don't."

Low raised his teacup to the teary-eyed woman. "I like you, Mrs Parry. I really do. So, Mr Parry. Do as your wife says. You were home alone with a woman who was found dead in an alley and covered in leftover curry because . . ."

Mr Parry sneered at his wife. "*She* had insisted on joining some expat women's charity group and didn't want to miss the first meeting, but she had also forgotten to leave money for Aini on the table. And she didn't want to make a bad impression, didn't want to seem like one of those expats who treat the hired help like shit. So I agreed to drop the money off in my lunch hour."

"You paid cash? No receipts? That doesn't look good with the Ministry of Manpower."

"Yes all right, don't labour the point. I came home and she had gone out with Billy to her bloody mother's meeting. I introduced myself to the woman, we shook hands, I gave her the money and left her polishing the bedrooms."

Mr Parry glared at his partner. "As I didn't have time to go out for lunch, I made myself a sandwich when she called out to me from the bedroom."

Mrs Parry snorted. "Called out to you, did she?"

"She did, all right? She called out saying she needed help with something and . . . when I went in there . . ."

"She was lying naked on the bed," Low said.

Mr Parry looked surprised. "Yes. That's right."

"What, you think you're the first one, is it? You people make me laugh. You pay these poor women shit and then you do the aw-shucks routine when you find out they moonlight to top up their income. Pay these women a living wage and they wouldn't have to make up the difference on their backs. But no, you pay them the bare minimum so your wife can go out and do her charity work while another woman scrubs your toilets for 10 bucks an hour. And then you find her, lying there on your king-sized bed, and she's stunning, right? She's so tanned and slim. No *ang moh* can ever be that slim, especially after they have a baby.

Everything changes once you had a baby right? Everything.

"It used to be all the time, after a few wines and a DVD, now it's between feeds and diaper changes and nightmares about monsters. Now all you can do is talk about it, because you're not doing it, so you're talking about it all the time at work with your shipping pals because you no longer do it. You find yourself looking at the Asian secretaries in your office. How can they be so slim? And that olive skin, makes their teeth look like a toothpaste commercial, right or not? And then you come home from work, pissed off with your wife for dragging you away from lunch, and there it is, right there, on the bed, no one would ever know. And you work so hard for the family you hardly ever see, for the wife who rarely sleeps with you, that you deserve this, you have earned this. It's right there. It's yours. She is yours. So you shagged her in your own bed."

"NO I FUCKING DIDN'T."

Mr Parry swept his cup and saucer off the table. The flying crockery narrowly missed Chan before it smashed against the wall, leaving a dramatic splatter of tea dregs, slowly dripping down the egg-white paintwork.

Chan wiped a couple of tea spots off his cheek. "Mr Parry, please don't do that again."

"I didn't sleep with her, all right? For god's sake, you're a social leper in this country if you don't shag anything that moves at Orchard Towers. Yes, they all do it at work, OK? Yes, they cheat on their wives. But I met the woman of my life 12 years ago in a pub in Camden. And that's it. And if you suggest that I slept with that poor woman one more time, I'll take my work visa and shove it up your arse."

Low grinned at his partner. "Not bad *ah*, this guy."

"So what happened, Mr Parry," Chan said softly, brushing biscuit crumbs off the table.

Mr Parry rubbed his hands across his face. "She opened her legs and told me to get undressed. She told me that I could be hers, every week if I came home at lunchtime, or if my wife was ever out. I started to walk away and told her to get off our bed and put her clothes back on or I'd fire her. She jumped up and grabbed my arm and told me she really needed the money for her son back home in Indonesia. She said I should understand because I have a son. I didn't look at her, but she sounded like she was crying. I shrugged her off and said she should've come to me with her clothes on first, and walked out of the room.

"And then?" Chan asked.

"And then, she strolled into the kitchen, still naked, and said she was discreet. She said she already cleaned another white guy's home, some banker."

"A banker?"

"Yeah, a banker or a stockbroker, and maybe one or two others and they all trusted her and I should trust her too. Then I said I'd had enough and told her to leave the house. So she said she was going to call my wife and tell her I'd had sex with her in our bed unless I gave her $500."

"What did you do?"

"What did I do? I threw the rest of my sandwich down the chute and left her standing naked in my kitchen. I didn't touch her. I didn't talk to her. I came home that night and told my wife here exactly what happened, and she hasn't spoken to me properly ever since. My wife threw away all the sheets. Now she wants a new bed. Our marriage is a mess because I was honest with my wife."

"That woman was naked in my house," Mrs Parry whispered, "in my bed. We shipped that bed from England. Our son was conceived in that bed."

Low put down his teacup. "So why didn't you do anything

about it?"

"I did. I kept calling. She never came back after she stripped naked in my bed. That was more than a week ago. I left messages on her phone. I kept leaving messages right up until my poor son saw her on TV."

"She was already dead by then."

"Yes, I know," Mrs Parry said, dragging the biscuit plate away from the policeman, "but she still managed to wreck my marriage first."

Chapter 11

DEPUTY Director Anthony Chua liked to think he ran a tight ship. He peered through the glass of his partitioned office and watched his investigators, chained to their terminals. They never went home. They were loyal, committed employees, but lousy policemen. The government's scholarship programme gave him industrious civil servants. Collectively, they had the balls of a female eunuch. They filled every form and met every key performance indicator, but they couldn't crack an egg between them. He had more of an animal farm than a murder squad, filled with battery hens and bleating sheep. The street-smart detectives died out with the kampongs.

Well, most of them had.

What the hell is he doing here?

Chua tapped the glass with his wedding ring and beckoned Detective Inspector Charles Chan and the unwanted associate into his office.

Chua realised he was adjusting his crisp white shirt and flicking his hair back. He admonished himself. He was the deputy director of the Criminal Investigation Department. He was smart, qualified and appointed more than six months ago. He didn't need to prove anything to anyone, least of all to a fallen star drinking his way to an early retrenchment.

He closed the door behind Chan and Low.

"Sit," he said, quickly asserting control.

Chan, a fellow government scholar, immediately complied. The so-called genius from the poor housing estate, Singapore's legendary undercover cop, slumped into a chair, smirking the whole time.

Chua felt a sudden urge to punch Low in the face. Low did that to people.

"What's up boss?" Chan tried to be breezy, but misjudged the mood.

"Yeah, fine, so the Parrys how?"

"Err, yeah, not bad. It's definitely not the husband, but I knew that already. The victim tried to sleep with the *ang moh*, but he turned her down. So somewhere along the line, one of them said yes, it got awkward, and he killed her. Oh, and he might be an *ang moh* banker or a stockbroker."

"Well, that narrows it down to around 10,000 then. OK, send some guys to their condos, speak to other cleaners and the Indonesian helpers. They all talk to each other, see if she told them about this *ang moh*."

Low turned away from the deputy director and watched the hive of inactivity beyond the glass cocoon. He chuckled.

"Sorry, I'm funny is it?"

Low faced his friend's boss again. "What?"

"I see you smiling there."

"No *lah*, never mind. Carry on."

"Oh, I can carry on in my own office is it? *Wah*, thanks *ah*. I don't need your permission in my office."

"How many times are you going to say it's your office? I guessed that already. Your name and title are on the door already in a really big font."

"Stanley," Chan interrupted. "It's OK, sir, he just helped me out."

Chua raised a hand to silence the probationary inspector.

"Wait, you took him with you to interview the *ang mohs*, is it?"

"He was only an observer."

"Observe what? He's not in Major Crime, he's not even in CPIB anymore, he's in . . . where are you again?"

Low grinned. He was enjoying this.

"It's one of your divisions. The Technology Crime Division, deputy director, with capital letters and everything."

"Is that where they post you? *Wah*, you must have really pissed them off upstairs. And what do you do at Tech?"

"I track bloggers, sir. I chase hackers. I keep an eye on the political opposition and, on Fridays, if I'm a really good boy, they let me press control-alt-delete."

Low stood up.

"What are you doing?" Chua asked.

"I'm leaving."

"Did I say you could leave?"

"You didn't say I could come in."

"Hey, Stanley, come on," Chan interjected, his eyes darting between the two men. He was aware that he was sweating.

"It's true what they say about you *ah*," Chua said, pulling his shoulders back and putting his hands on his hips to emphasise his muscular frame in front of the skinny inspector.

"What they say *ah*?"

"You're an asshole."

"No, really? They say much worse than that. And what do they say about you? Do they say anything about you?"

Chan reached out for Low's arm and thought of his family and his pregnant wife, and his cramped apartment and his mortgage repayments. He didn't need this, not now. His friend brushed him off.

"You know what they say about you?" Low continued. "Nothing, because they've never heard of you. You've done nothing. Got all these big letters after your name, but you stink of antiseptic. You'll never smell of the street like me. Look at your office, everyone in a tidy little box. But crimes aren't like that. They're messy and dirty and improvised and all the things that a civil servant is not. You got nothing in common with the people you're trying to catch. You know nothing about the victims. You say go and see the victim's friends. What do you think they're going to say *ah*? They all moonlight, all take extra cleaning jobs or work a few nights at Geylang, all illegal. Most don't have correct work visas, got social visit passes. You think they're going to risk getting kicked out of Singapore to help a dead *kaki*? No chance. But you don't care. You just tick boxes."

"Get out of my office."

Low opened the door and stopped. "I just realise why I've never heard of you. You're clean. No gambling, no women, no tenders, nothing, right? *Yah lah*, that's why. Must have a clean one now after the last one. No corruption, no casinos, no debts. So they picked you, a shiny new scholar in a white shirt. No scandal, no problem, no brains, just nice."

Chua undid the top button on his shirt.

I smartened up for this? This is the man who brought down the Tiger syndicate? This is the best we had last time?

The deputy director spoke slowly. "I'm going to have you fired."

"Really? Best news I've had all day."

Low slammed the door and didn't look back.

Chapter 12

CARRYING a coffee and a plate of kaya toast, Zhang made his way into the office. The toast slid from the plate and onto his laptop, such was his excitement. He methodically placed his toast on the left of his laptop and the coffee on his right, just as he did when he was once employed as a sales manager for a computer software company. Even at home, he maintained the same, fastidious work habits and always dressed smartly. When he caught his reflection in the laptop screen, it made him feel like he still had a proper job.

He carefully laid out everything he needed. The latest newspapers were behind the laptop, the relevant articles and paragraphs circled when he was still in bed. Attacking the mainstream media was almost too easy these days. Every time he opened his laptop, he shot fish in a barrel. They were snacks for the masses at suppertime, the junk food for the thoughtless. He already had his main course.

He pulled out the iPhone from the holder on the left side of his desk, away from hot beverages of course, and read the message from his police source again. He was a reliable source, the best kind, a shiny badge with a chip on the shoulder. He was a disgruntled, middle-aged officer who'd been passed over for promotion for kids half his age with twice as many qualifications and a better grasp of Standard English. He'd been tipping off Zhang for more than a year. Sometimes he wanted money. But often he'd pass information to *The Singapore Truth* website just to watch the alien world around him burn. In Harold Zhang, the alienated officer thought he'd found a kindred spirit. They always did.

Zhang checked the post-it notes on the white board above his desk. He had a busy day ahead of him. There was the rival female blogger to deal with first. He despised female bloggers, with their forthright opinions on gender equality, abortion and workers' rights. He found the hypocrisy nauseating. She posted about equality for women beside a photo of her pushed-up breasts. She was destroying healthy, traditional Asian values and Zhang couldn't tolerate that. And the more he stared at her photo with her cleavage, the more he thought of his wife's flat chest. And he couldn't tolerate that either.

Then there was a short video of a ranting taxi passenger to upload. Zhang knew who the passenger was already. He was a typical, put-upon office minion feeling oppressed by his foreign bosses so he'd lashed out at the benign driver, the dog kicking the cat. He was also Singaporean, but only Zhang was aware of that. One of his angry, young hackers had tracked down the bully's personal details. But Zhang knew he could hint that the passenger was Malaysian, as there were some similarities in accent. He couldn't push the xenophobia any further on that one. Even his more rabid readers wouldn't fall for any other nationality.

Right now, China was the cash cow. Any videos or contributions depicting the Ugly Chinese tourist or the Crazy Rich Chinese always rated well. Clips of South Asian workers were less popular, unless they came across as threatening towards women. At a blogging convention in the US, Zhang had once met a white American from North Carolina who'd said that nothing generated more page views than a minority male intimidating a majority female. A white man attacking a black woman doesn't cut it. But a black man attacking a white woman is a conservative blogger's wet dream.

And Zhang had never forgotten the blogger's parting shot.

Find your BNBG, man, and you're golden.

Nothing sold fear better than "big Negro, big gun" in the United States. Singapore had neither African-Americans nor guns, but it had globalisation. Every foreign worker was a big Negro. Every retrenched local was a smoking gun. Zhang didn't need a phantom figure waving a weapon in a dark alley. The economy was raping everyone. The invader was the violator. Every upstanding citizen was being bent over and pummelled by globalisation. It was so easy. Each blog picked low-lying fruit on behalf of the knuckle-scrapers. Once repressed by political correctness and a vigilant government, racists and xenophobes suddenly poured through cyberspace like an army of invisible ants, all blindly following the same line, all hiding behind their anonymity. All they needed was a little direction and Zhang proved to be the perfect navigator. He had found his BNBG. And the goose of globalisation had just laid another gloriously golden egg.

The killer was white. The killer was *white*.

Singapore had rich foreigners killing poor foreigners. The island really had gone to the dogs.

Zhang was angry now. That pleased him. The bile would come more easily. He chewed the last of his kaya toast and began to type quickly.

Chapter 13

ON some level, Low begrudgingly admired Harold Zhang. They both knew how to push buttons. And Zhang had the patter down, the tone, the language, the fine line between indignation and outright xenophobia; the blogger had undoubtedly mastered his craft. The proof was in the hit counter at the bottom of the stained screen of Low's office computer. Thousands of shares, tens of thousands of likes and the piece had only been up for an hour. Low gripped his water bottle and read Zhang's blog again:

FOREIGN 'TALENT' KILLS FOREIGN PROSTITUTE

Dear True Singaporeans,
   So now got foreigner killing another foreigner. We already got Pinoy being rude to Singaporeans at Changi Airport, got Indian workers causing problem at Little India, got PRC women spitting in our faces because they think they high class and now got this: an ang moh killing an Indonesian prostitute in Chinatown.
   Singapore was safe last time. Last time, can take our family anywhere, can do anything. But now, cannot be safe in own home. Our whiter than white Minister keep saying Singapore cannot survive without FT, no FT Singapore sure die one. Like broken record already. Need Pinoy in service, need Indian workers to build

apartments, need ang mohs in Marina Bay. Otherwise, catch no ball, cannot make it. Our Gahmen all act like Sarong Party Girl.

But we don't get best FT, we get FT who cannot make it in their home country. We get no-class FT come and take our jobs. We get FT dogs fighting and killing each other. Now got our police waste time looking for an ang moh for killing an Indonesian whore. For what? If they never come, we never have this problem. How they make Singapore better?

The Minister keep saying we are now a dirty city. Why? Last time we were clean city. The Minister say our customer service drop. Why? Last time we manage OK. Now got CCTV in all our apartments, in our lift lobby and still crime keep rising. Why? What change in last 10 years? You know the answer already. And the Minister know the answer. But cannot say. I cannot say. They tekan me with the same stick. If I say, then sure say I xenophobic one. Nonsense. We are an island of immigrants for 100 years plus. We are all immigrants last time. But this too much. When foreigners are murdering foreigners, cannot tahan already.

Singapore must be for Singaporeans first, for National Servicemen first, but now got our NS boys looking for ang moh killer. What are we now? We are no longer a whiter than white city. We are a dirty city with too much trash, cannot recognise anymore. This is true Singapore today. Our Singapore die already.

Low nodded at the screen. Zhang was rather good. The simple, poor man's broken English, the lack of plurals and the deliberately mangled syntax and Chinese sentence structure, a hint of Singlish without entirely collapsing into caricature, Zhang's blogs deserved to be studied in psychology classes. The blogger was a better undercover operative than Low ever was. Low once played the scrawny Ah Lian, the mouthy, anarchic loan shark and gang member, which was easier because it was theatrical, a pantomime performance. Zhang had to be more subtle. He had to pander without ever patronising.

Low dug his hands into the desk mess and pulled out Zhang's file. The blogger could write. He was a graduate from the National University of Singapore, with a business management degree and a decent salary at an international IT firm before his wife convinced him to throw caution to the wind and head for the bigger, greener pastures of Australia. She wanted to step back from the Asian rat race. He wanted to keep his wife happy. She found the clichéd suburban dream in the arms of a surfer. He found Hell.

Zhang also found his muse. His hatred and self-loathing fuelled his creativity and gave him a sense of purpose. He would stand up for men like him, those twisted souls always looking for someone else to blame. In a nanny state, there was always someone else to blame.

The phone rang. Its sudden trilling surprised Low. It was his other phone, the one from his previous incarnation as an undercover investigator for the CPIB. The phone was from a past life. It was Ah Lian's phone. Low had kept it and charged it daily, just in case.

He hesitated before answering. "Yah . . ."

"Eh, *kelong* bastard, it's me *lah*," said a familiar voice.

Low suddenly brightened. He checked around the office, but the place was almost empty. The vindictive bastards had given him the graveyard shift. They wanted him out of the way during the day.

"Eh, man, you OK? What's up?"

"You know that *ang moh* bastard, right?"

"Who?"

"That one *lah*. The one who kill the *xiao mei mei* in the *longkang* before."

"Oh, that one *ah*. Why?"

"I know who he is."

"Eh, come on *lah*."

"Bastard, I'm serious OK. The killer. He's *ang moh*, right? I definitely know him."

Chapter 14

LOW made his way through the bustling Marine Parade hawker centre. An elderly Chinese worker clipped his thigh with his crockery trolley. The inspector winced as he passed a younger Chinese man carrying four bowls of fish-ball noodles on a brown plastic tray. His sweat dripped into the noodle soup. With its high ceilings and insufficient lighting, the cavernous hawker centre was a humid, dark place even during the day. The only colour came from the garish stall signs. Low was pleased with the location. Asians didn't like to be disturbed when they were eating. They kept their heads down.

He spotted Dragon Boy sitting at a round table with a cracked stool seat beside the closed wet market. Most of the stalls around him had pulled the shutters for the day. Dragon Boy waved a tattooed arm, but the skin beneath flapped slightly. He had gained weight. His potbelly poked at his oversized NBA singlet. He put down two phones and a packet of Marlboro Lights to hug his old friend.

"Eh, you put on weight *ah*," Low said.

"Make money, eat money, right?"

They both sat down.

"So how?" Low asked. He realised he was grinning. Dragon Boy was the first warm, friendly face he'd seen since babysitting

Chan at the Parrys' apartment. He was genuinely pleased to see the violent, remorseless recidivist. They shared a past.

When he was undercover as Ah Lian, Low was once with Dragon Boy at a steamboat restaurant when a rival gang member made fun of his tattoos. Dragon Boy picked up the steamboat and poured its boiling contents over the joker's arms and shoulders. Now they both had something on their arms to laugh about. Dragon Boy returned to his table and finished his fish head soup.

"Like that *lor*," the gangster shrugged.

"Still busy?"

Dragon Boy flicked his cigarette box around the table.

"Eh, you called me, so you know I don't care, right," Low said. "You knew what I was already before you called me."

"*Yah lah*, I know what you are, basket."

"So why you call me?"

"Owe money, pay money, right."

"You know we don't pay money."

"I pay you."

"What?"

"Last time, after Tiger, you never tell me who you were, never arrest me some more."

"No need. Tiger enough, got all the big fish."

"So? I'm *ikan bilis* is it?"

"No."

"You don't think I'm big time is it? Insult me *ah, kan ni na*."

"No. I figured no need."

"You saw things last time. I did some fucked-up stuff."

"Yeah."

"But you never arrest me. Why?"

"No need. We both saw things, right or not?"

"That's why."

Dragon Boy spun his phone around and smiled. "You

remember that fat one *ah*, Queenstown, damn *jia lat*, never pay so long already. Tiger tell us throw red paint against door. Remember?"

"Of course."

"And then what happen?"

"He opened the door."

"Fucker opened the door as I throw red paint. He looked like a fucking traffic light, *chao chee bye*."

Both men laughed. Low pointed at both phones. "Busy time *ah*?"

"Always, man. EPL season finishing already and La Liga some more. Plus casinos. Casinos the best, boss. Every fucker lose money one. Can make more than last time. Need three phones already."

"Eh, come on *lah*. You know I cannot hear this. Close one eye. Cannot close two."

"Please *lah*, you know how many policemen come to me. I got three on east side."

"Is it?"

"Of course, cannot make it at casino. Lose so much money. Idiots. And *Gahmen* the best, you know why?"

"Why?"

"CPF."

"CPF?"

"That's why. They hold back the savings right, cannot release, so I got all the aunties and uncles coming to me for money."

"Serious?"

"I'm serious, boss. Should pay the *Gahmen* commission I tell you. Each time they push back CPF, old people cannot retire, come straight to me, borrow money. It's the best I tell you. You should see me at coffee shop man, old people everywhere. It's like reunion dinner."

Low laughed loudly. He felt alive again with Dragon Boy. He felt a pulse. "Bugger, I should come back."

Low heard the beats of silence and cringed. The joke was poor and obviously hurt his friend. In a sudden rush of euphoria, the bastard bipolar had gone too far and pulled down the façade. They were no longer old friends reminiscing. They were cop and criminal, the betrayer and betrayed. The stupid joke cut through the pretense and the genuine warmth, and re-established the boundaries of their current, colder relationship.

"Yeah, well, cannot anymore."

Low sighed. There was nothing to hide anymore.

"No, not after Marina Bay Sands. Too high profile. After Tiger, it was still OK, can hide a bit, but Marina Bay Sands was a different story, much bigger, too many people involved, no more Ah Lian after that."

"You miss him *ah*?"

"Tiger?"

"Ah Lian."

"Why?"

"Don't know . . . I liked him."

Low didn't know what to say. He felt empty, exposed. "So did I," he said finally.

Dragon Boy sat up, as if suddenly asserting himself.

"So, bastard, you want this *ang moh* or what?"

"Why?"

"What you mean, 'why'?"

"Why you care?"

"I'm here, right? I should be in Changi, talking cock with Tiger."

"So?"

"Please *lah*. You help me last time."

"You help me with Marina Bay Sands."

"But this *ang moh* bastard cannot *tahan* already. He's a banker right, stays around Chinatown?"

Low shrugged.

"*Yah lah*, you know he is. And I know who he is, typical FT, so *hao lian* one, works in Marina Bay, so much money, buy our women, fucker *lah*."

"You know his name?"

"No."

"Then how you know him?"

"One time I see him with the *xiao mei mei* with the *siu mai*."

"*Siu mai?*"

"Small tits *lah*, like pork dumplings."

"You saw them together?"

"The *siu mai?*"

"No *lah*, basket. The *ang moh* and the girl."

"Of course."

"Where?"

"Cannot."

"Why?"

"This one cannot."

"Why? You show me where and finish already."

"No *lah*, this one cannot save me one, no bargain."

"What are you talking about? It's murder."

"Still cannot."

Like a guilty schoolboy, Dragon Boy couldn't sustain eye contact. He flicked at his cigarette box again. Low leaned back and rubbed his face.

"You dealing shit *ah?*"

Dragon Boy refused to look up.

"Eh, come on *lah*, that's the only way you meet *ang moh* bankers. They don't need you for money or women. Please tell me I'm wrong."

Dragon Boy couldn't speak.

"Ah, shit, that one I cannot protect you. Class A, you're finished. Even if you catch him, people will ask the connection, or the *ang moh* will tell everyone. That one I cannot save you, man."

"No, it's OK," Dragon Boy said suddenly. "I get you his name, finish. I get his name and everything settled already."

"But you don't even know it's him. This girl was probably seeing more than one *ang moh*."

"It's him I tell you."

"OK, so what you going to do?"

"I get his name and pass you *lah*."

"And how you do that?"

"How you think? Next time, when I . . ."

"No, cannot," Low interrupted. "Don't tell me. Dealing cannot. They'll screw you and then they'll screw me for not screwing you."

"OK, OK, understand."

Dragon Boy opened his cigarette box. "I'll still get his name."

"How?"

"Please *lah*."

"Without . . ."

"No problem."

"Yeah, right."

Dragon Boy grinned and waved his arm at a drinks seller. "Come on, Ah Lian. You want a beer or not?"

Chapter 15

THE Minister of Home Improvement's office was deliberately sparse. A tidy office gave the appearance of a tiny mind, but clutter also contained sensitive information for the prying eyes of visitors. They didn't need to know about his work or his family life, beyond the necessary ministerial prerequisites. He needed to be married with kids. He had to support the traditional family model, promote filial piety and publicly endorse Asian values. An occasional lapse behind closed doors was once tolerated, accepted even, as a perk for all that selfless national service. The Minister had been a successful Asian businessman with an expense account to entertain the region's economic whales. Entertaining and servicing prospective clients were in the job description, but extra curricular activities were frowned upon now. Social media and an upcoming cleansing of the Cabinet's old guard meant a clean slate was imperative. Singapore's stringent political regeneration policy supposedly stopped ministers from turning stale. It also stopped them from playing. Besides, some of his colleagues actually believed all that stuff about the traditional, nuclear family. It was a bit too Old Testament for the Minister's tastes, but he championed calm exteriors.

So he kept the framed photo of his wife and daughter on the desk, half facing outwards for the benefit of any audience. Visitors got his wife's profile. He got to see his daughter beaming back at him. His fundamental, unshakable faith in positive eugenics had served his little girl well. He had married a barrister, the daughter of a property tycoon, and they had reproduced a similarly smart offspring to serve the nation.

The Minister smiled at the photo. He loved his little Gabriella. After Raffles Girls' School and the National University of Singapore, she had become a leading pediatrician at Raffles Hospital. When others in the Cabinet questioned his decision to only have one child, he always had his little girl's profession as backup. His child served the children of the nation. She was engaged to a wealthy venture capitalist with three successful apps to his name, so the Minister's grandchildren might further improve on their genes, adding a greater entrepreneurial zeal. Positive eugenics was a simple cocktail really, just a matter of throwing in the right ingredients.

Of course, the shake-up occasionally went awry and poured out men like Deputy Director Anthony Chua into the country's petri dish.

The Minister pushed his intercom. "Send him in please."

Chua tried too hard from the moment he opened the door.

"How are you, Minister, thanks for your time," he said, practically bowing. "This won't take long."

"It's OK. Have a seat."

The Minister watched a bead of perspiration make its way through the deputy director's oily hair. They were always insecure in his presence. Their nervous disposition validated his belief. Most men would always be inferior to the genetically superior few. It wasn't politically correct, but a government that built a country on political correctness built on sand. Singapore's system made the most of its limited gene pool. A man like Anthony Chua couldn't be a great man, but he could be a good one. He could punch above his weight. The trouble was he lacked the natural intellect and confidence to shake off the inferiority complex to question, challenge and improvise. He ticked boxes. And after the Marina Bay Sands debacle, the Singapore Police Force needed fewer investigators and more box tickers.

Chua rubbed his sweaty palms against his trousers. "Nice office."

"Thank you."

"That's your daughter there?"

"Yes."

"She's very pretty *ah*."

"Thank you."

"Studying?"

"No, working already, Raffles Hospital. She's a doctor."

"*Wah*, fantastic, *ah*. I got two boys, primary school. Boys are such a handful."

"Great. How can I help you, Director?"

"Ah, it's Deputy Director actually sir."

"I know, but Deputy Director is such a mouthful and I know you're doing very well."

Chua felt the blood sting his cheeks. "Ah, well, I do my best."

The Minister nodded towards the clock on the wall, beside the framed photographs of the President of Singapore and his wife. "It's a very busy day for me, so, er . . ."

"Yes, of course. Well, it's a bit delicate actually."

"Go on."

"Do you know Stanley Low, Detective Inspector Stanley Low, now working in Technology?"

"Our paths have crossed."

Chua thought he heard sarcasm in the Minister's voice, but he couldn't be sure. He struggled with ironic humour. He was a very literal man.

"Ah, OK. He can be, well, how to say *ah*, he can, maybe he's not such a good team player."

"Isn't he in Technology now, as you mentioned?"

"Yes, but he's been getting involved with this murder case."

"What murder case?"

"Oh, we got a foreign worker killed in Chinatown."

"A construction worker? It's not Indian, is it?"

"No, no, this one's Indonesian, probably killed by her boyfriend."

"Oh, that one, yes. The bloggers are getting very excited about that one. So how?"

"So, Low has been helping and . . ."

"Wait, why is he helping? He was put in Technology for a reason, right?"

Chua was certain he heard a hint of apprehension that time.

"Yah, but my officers, well some of my officers and not really my officers actually, the ones I got leftover from Inspector James Tan's team, seem to listen to him, some even look up to him."

"He did settle some big cases in the past."

"But he's undermining my authority, sir. I don't think he should be involved with this case."

"Then get rid of him. Send him back to Technology."

"He doesn't really do what he's told."

The Minister stared at the personification of negative eugenics, struggling to conceal his contempt.

"You are the Deputy Director of CID. You oversee eight divisions, including Major Crime and Technology. And, frankly speaking, you're making him sound like a five-year-old boy peeing on your classroom carpet."

"Could you fire him, sir?"

"Could I? . . . I think it's probably better if we both pretended that just never happened. Right now, all we need to focus on is calm exteriors. We have an election around the corner and rather than have the Singapore Police Force washing its dirty linen in public, I think it's better if we keep it in a spin cycle. We've got hate speech and slander all over the place. We've got teenage anarchists thinking they're Guy Fawkes. We need calm. Low has his flaws, but he's keeping an eye on Harold Zhang. You heard of him?"

"Yes, sir."

"He's got more followers on Facebook than the Prime Minister."

"Yes, sir."

The Minister stood up. The meeting was over.

"Anyway, you just focus on your Malaysian victim for now."

"She was Indonesian, sir."

"Right. Thanks for coming in, keep up the good work."

Chua thought about saying something else, but the Minister had already returned to his laptop.

Chapter 16

LOW sat on the very edge of his seat. He was jittery and talking too fast, but retained the remarkable lucidity that came with his manic episodes. Lai straightened her trousers and struggled with the guilt. Her patient was experiencing a high in her office. He would relapse later. But for now, he was a fidgeting guinea pig for her bipolar research. The psychiatrist couldn't take her eyes off him.

"So you felt no guilt after each outburst?"

"Guilt? What for? I got something from all of them. The *ang mohs* told me about this guy being a banker and then Dragon Boy confirmed he was an *ang moh* banker. And now he's going to get the name of a potential suspect. Not bad, right?"

"But what did you gain from the meeting with your boss, this deputy director?"

"He's not my boss. He's an idiot. I exposed him. I showed them what he really is."

"What is he?"

"You know what he is. He's the guy running every department in the country. He's your boss and my boss. He's a scholar boy, an arse kisser, a number cruncher, he's everything we think we need and nothing we ever want. He's a robot. He'll go any direction you want as long as you tell him where to go first."

"But why is it your job?"

"My job what?"

"To expose, as you say, these people."

"Because no one else has got the balls."

"You use that word a lot. Do you define all men by their masculinity?"

"Not just men. You got balls, because you ask questions. You think differently, you probe people. You got balls."

"Thank you." Lai adjusted her trousers again. "But why must we probe anyone?"

"Coming from you, that's like a bear asking why we shit in the woods."

Lai's eyes sparkled. He could be entertaining when he was manic.

"Fair enough. But does it not make you judge and jury? You size someone up, you dissect him and then you destroy him. Why?"

"To see through them, to get to the truth, I don't know. It's what Ah Lian does. And let me tell you OK, nobody else in the police force does it better."

"What does it feel like in those moments?"

"When I'm really firing? There's nothing like it; sex, drugs, alcohol, nothing comes close. I can take down anyone. When the old Ah Lian instincts kick in, I speak faster, think quicker and get the job done."

"Do you think it's ironic that these manic episodes . . . "

"They are not manic episodes, they are my life skills. When a carpenter bangs away with his hammer, do you call that a manic episode?"

"It depends if he's abusing the people he works with."

"He does when he whacks his thumb with a hammer."

"You know what I mean."

"And so do you. I'm not putting up a kitchen cabinet. I'm

catching bad people. If I'm not in the right frame of mind, I'm finished."

"Which brings me back to my original question. Do you not think it's ironic that these manic episodes usually occur when you are with . . ."

"Sick bastards? No. That's the point. They've all got balls the size of durians."

"Can we stop talking about balls?"

"Look, the deputy director cannot make it. So I crush him. I smell weakness, like Dragon Boy and Tiger last time. I need to pick up the scent or I'm dead."

"OK, stay with that. Let's assume that's true. You need to behave a certain way in your job. I understand that. But you seem to enjoy behaving that way."

"Of course. It's the best. I never feel more alive when I'm Ah Lian."

"But you're essentially being someone else."

"That depends on your point of view. The paper shuffler sitting in front of a desk and reading shitty blogs, he feels like someone else. He's a stranger."

Lai decided to change tack.

"The loan shark gave you that nickname, right?"

Low appeared confused by the question. "Yeah, why?"

"Do you still see him?"

"No, he's in Changi waiting to be hanged. You know that. What's your point?"

"You said you feel alive being Ah Lian."

"No one needs to feel *that* alive."

"How did you get the nickname, Ah Lian?"

"How? Err, I was the skinny, loud one, just like Dragon Boy, but I was even skinnier than him at the time. I practically stopped eating to look right. Tiger said I was too skinny to be an *ah beng*,

that I looked like a girl. So he called me Ah Lian. I told you
before."

"I know, but we're getting somewhere here."

"Are we?"

"Yes. You say it didn't bother you. He was essentially mocking
you."

"He was a gangster. I was undercover. I'm going to cry to
Mummy, is it?"

"Some people might have been hurt by such a nickname."

"Ah, for fuck's sake," Low said, rubbing his forehead
repeatedly. "This is exactly what I'm talking about. People like
you give a shit about that stuff. In my world, it was nothing,
a chance to get closer to my target. And that's what Ah Lian is
for. I don't need Tiger anymore so I don't see him. But I need
Dragon Boy so I still see him. I *use* him. I close one eye to the
drug dealing because he can help me. And this kid never screwed
me. Never. A bookie once made fun of my name so Dragon Boy
whacked him with a chilli sauce bottle. I dragged him off the
bookie's face and made up some bullshit story about not wanting
to kill the guy. The truth is I didn't want him arrested in case it
blew my cover. And I know he must have found out who I really
was. At some point after Tiger went away, he had to find out. But
he said nothing. Even when I went back to him for the Marina
Bay Sands case, he still said nothing. And now he's praising *me*.
He's thanking *me* for not arresting him and for protecting our
relationship. But the truth is I don't really give a shit. I thought
then what I think now. I could use him. He might be able to do
something for me. Not Ah Lian, but me. That's the real me. And
you say I enjoy being the undercover gangster guy. I *loved* being
Ah Lian. He was honest. I could live with him. Look at me. Look
what's left behind. Why the fuck would I want to live with me?"

Lai said nothing. The inspector had a point.

Chapter 17

TALEK Maxwell used a razor blade to chop up the lines across Aini's face. He was careful not to scratch the glass photo frame. It was his favourite photo, taken at Tanjong Beach as the sun went down. She was wearing her jean shorts. He had loved her legs. When he saw the photo, he thought of her; when he thought of her, he thought of being younger and slimmer and attractive. At Chatham Boys and university, women had always wanted him. He had the tie, the crest, the rugby trophies and the family connections. He was going places. He was going to rule the world. He never felt so self-assured again, until Aini came along. She had wanted him, even if only for his money.

Maxwell picked up the McDonald's straw. He always stocked up on McDonald's straws. He wasn't like the Friday night cokeheads from the council estates, snorting their wages through a five-pound note on a cracked toilet seat. He had standards. He had his hygiene to consider. Besides, his standards had already slipped in Singapore. When he was younger, back in England, McDonald's straws came sealed in paper wrapping. Now he took his chances with straws shoved into the dispenser by a hunchbacked uncle who used the same hands to clean the foul toilets.

Everything was a compromise in Asia.

In his boxer shorts, Maxwell shuffled his trunk-like thighs closer to the coffee table and leaned over his flabby stomach. He snorted violently and thought of Aini. He dropped the straw and allowed the music to take him away. Oasis took him back to the 90s—the captain, the head boy, the clever one, the muscly one, the coveted one. He wiped his running nose and flopped back on the Italian leather sofa. Outside, he was a fat, balding, second-rate trader, over the hill and far behind the hungrier Chinese and Indians. Inside, it was 1994. He turned up the Bang & Olufsen sound system with his iPhone and waited for the dreams to return, when he was one of the boys, when he mattered.

Tonight, I'm a rock 'n' roll star.

"Hey, I know this one."

Maxwell opened his eyes. He watched the rambling fool wander around his kitchen, pogoing up and down to the throbbing bass lines.

"It's U2 right?"

"No."

Maxwell started to drift. He was fading away with the guitar solo. Lost in the soundtrack of a past, better life, he leaned to one side. By the end of the song, he'd be there again, alert and alive. The music washed him away.

The distant fumbling sharpened his senses. His nose started running. He touched it, but it wasn't bleeding this time. The idiot had a decent product at least, but what was he touching in the kitchen?

"Are you going through my mail?" Maxwell was still, but his mind was racing. He saw the guy's restless fingers. "Are you touching my letters up there?"

He swept up the last of the powder with his forefinger, removing the white foundation from Aini's face. He rubbed the finger around his gums and wiped his nose across his arm.

He stood up, allowing his gut to fall over the waistband of his grubby Calvin Klein's. He hadn't changed them for days. Aini had bought them, with his money of course, but that wasn't the point. He made his way towards the breakfast bar.

"That's my mail."

"OK, man," said Dragon Boy. "I was looking for a lighter."

"I don't smoke. And nor can you in here."

Dragon Boy pointed at a phone bill beside the empty fruit bowl. "That you *ah*, Talek Maxwell?"

"No, it's the last tenant. Why?"

"No *lah*, funny, that name."

"Why?"

"Talek, sound like *tarik*, like *teh tarik*, you know."

"No."

Maxwell picked up the mail. He stepped past the tattooed runt and shoved the letters in the drawer. The rims of his eyes were crimson. His nose dripped onto his chin and chest.

"Eh, how *ah*? Not bad *ah*. You want one more? Come, *lelong, lelong.*"

Dragon Boy slipped a small, silver packet onto the breakfast bar.

"Speak fucking English," Maxwell hissed.

"*Lelong*, man, means cheap, cheap, a sale, you know. Special price for my *ang moh towkay.*"

Maxwell opened the silver packet. He pushed the powder around with his finger. "That it?"

"Eh, man, I give you a lot already no?"

"I want more."

"Must call first."

"Then call."

Maxwell shuffled back to the sofa. He sprinkled the powder across the dead woman's face, cut it into three lines and snorted

Maxwell blinked away the tears and pulled out the cutlery drawer with one hand and threw it against the wall. Forks and spoons clattered onto the marble kitchen top. He picked up a fork and drove it into the top of Dragon Boy's head. Dragon Boy yelled as the fork scraped against his skull. He reached up, but Maxwell reacted quicker. His knee connected with Dragon Boy's jaw.

And then Maxwell found what he had been looking for. He reached for his keepsake.

Dragon Boy tried to crawl across the tiled floor, but Maxwell pulled him back by his oily hair and flipped him over. The Phillips screwdriver went in easily this time, just below the heart. Maxwell pinned Dragon Boy to the ground. The fight fell away from the exhausted gangster.

"Ah Lian," Dragon Boy mumbled.

Maxwell straddled the dying man and cocked an ear to his bleeding mouth. "Sorry, what was that, Dragon Boy?"

"Ah Lian. He will catch you one. Definitely."

"Who's Ah Lian?"

Dragon Boy choked on the blood and grinned. Maxwell squeezed the yellow handle and twisted the screwdriver. Dragon Boy heard his own rib crack.

"Who the fuck's Ah Lian?"

Dragon Boy used the last of his strength to lift his head slightly. "Come closer."

"What?"

"You can keep secret or not?"

"Yeah."

"Me also. Fuck you, *ang moh*."

Chapter 18

THE policemen admired Maxwell's car. They always did. The Porsche was a Kevlar vest. He checked his speed as he passed the crash scene. Two crumpled taxis were parked on the hard shoulder of the Bukit Timah Expressway. Their drivers sat on the crash barrier, heads bowed, as the officers scribbled in notepads. They watched the sleek, red Porsche and nodded their appreciation. Maxwell waved and then accelerated to let them hear the engine roar. The young policemen giggled.

The Porsche raced away with Dragon Boy's body in its boot.

MAXWELL turned off the engine and checked the car park. The remote, neglected spot was deserted. It often was during the day, let alone at 4am. The Upper Seletar Reservoir Park enjoyed a brief heyday in the early seventies, its quirky rocket-shaped viewing tower drawing visitors at the height of the space race. But the isolated green haven was almost inaccessible without a car, which made it the perfect spot for rich people to have sex. Maxwell often brought Aini here. They used to sit on benches overlooking the reservoir. Occasionally, they saw a star or two in the murky sky above the forest canopy. She waffled on about her son and her dream of one day moving to Jakarta and buying a provision shop to pay for his college education. Maxwell listened impatiently as he waited for his blow job. He loved sex in public places, particularly in Singapore.

Illegal sex made him the old school captain again. He once screwed a girl over a park bench at a village green in England, on the edge of a cricket pitch, imagining someone running up to bowl. She was the daughter of the local MP, a Tory safe seat, so she naturally craved something unsafe, something slightly septic. Maxwell happily obliged. The next time he saw her, she was with her father on the touchline of the school rugby pitch. They both cheered when Maxwell went over for a try.

Years later, Maxwell found her on Facebook. She had established an international PR agency and married an American. She divided her time between a Manhattan apartment and a Richmond home on the Thames. Maxwell changed his name on Facebook shortly after, took down his old photos and focused only on his new friends in Asia.

Maxwell grabbed Dragon Boy by his feet and pulled his body from the boot. He heard the Singaporean's skull crack as it hit the concrete. He couldn't see anything on the floor. He crouched behind his car and wrapped the blood-soaked bed sheet tighter around the body. Satisfied that he was alone, he lifted the skinny kid and made for the reservoir. He knew there were no CCTV cameras at the park. The first time they had visited together, he made a point of looking for any cameras while Aini's head bobbed up and down in his lap. There were none. Apart from the odd fisherman, only wealthy car owners found their way to the Upper Seletar Reservoir Park. They were the country's elite. They were trusted.

Maxwell breathed heavily as he made his way to the water's edge. He had stopped exercising not long after arriving in Asia. He didn't need to. His wallet carried enough weight. He bent down beside the reservoir. A cloudy sky softened the moonlight.

Maxwell welcomed the darkness as he unwrapped the body.

And then he stopped. He listened as the water gently lapped against the artificial rock bund on his right.

Fuck it. The water will clean him up.

Maxwell pulled the sheet back across Dragon Boy's bloody chest. He tied the corners into knots, as tightly as he could. He stood up and looked around one more time. Nocturnal anglers often appeared on the wall that separated the reservoir and the golf course, or midnight perverts hoping to catch a glimpse of something their wives refused to do at home.

But Maxwell was alone.

In the eerie shadow of the rocket tower, Maxwell kicked Dragon Boy's covered body into Singapore's fresh water supply. It didn't sink. He didn't care.

BACK on the Bukit Timah Expressway, Maxwell turned up the volume. He was speeding, his mind racing. Dragon Boy's final gift fuelled him. He hadn't felt like this for years, not since the village green, the deflowered girls, the winning tries and the bulletproof blazer. He reached for his iPhone. The volume could go no higher. He was singing, shouting, screaming. The music owned him.

Tonight, I'm a rock 'n' roll star.

Maxwell passed the crash scene for a second time. He waved at the officers. They waved back. His boot was littered with bits of Dragon Boy's body, but he knew he was fine.

No one stopped a Porsche in Singapore.

Chapter 19

LYNDA Bennett gathered her children around the orangutan. The life-size bronze sculpture usually held their attention until the post-lunch sugar rush kicked in. Then they became wilder than the mild attractions of the Singapore Zoo. She dabbed her forehead with a hand towel. The equatorial humidity was particularly insufferable at the Singapore Zoo, where the Mandai forest squeezed out every drop of sweat. As she rubbed the back of her neck, she watched the parent volunteers fanning themselves inside the shelter behind the orangutan statue. They came only for the free admission. As always, the kindergarten teacher was on her own and out in the sun.

Bennett gestured towards the orangutan. "Does anyone know who this is?"

Twenty sweaty, red faces offered open mouths and blank looks. At least they were relatively still. The Ribena hadn't kicked in yet.

"OK, this is the Singapore Zoo's most famous animal," Bennett said. "She was an orangutan called Ah Meng. She lived in the zoo for many, many years and people came from all over the world to see her. Families from different countries, famous people, presidents and prime ministers, kings and queens, they all came to the Singapore Zoo to visit Ah Meng."

The kids were drifting. Their restlessness was spreading.

"And then, Ah Meng got old and died."

Death always got their attention. Inevitably, their slender arms punched the air. She was bombarded with questions.

"How did the monkey die, Miss Bennett?"

"Did the white tiger eat the Ah Meng, Miss Bennett?"

"Miss Bennett, is the orangutan inside the statue?"

"Are there other dead animals in the zoo, Miss Bennett?"

"Miss Bennett, is that a dead animal over there?"

She found the voice sitting cross-legged at the back of the group and pointing at the reservoir behind the shelter. It was Lara, a quiet, sweet girl, not usually one for making up stories.

"What did you say, Lara?"

"Over there, Miss Bennett. Can you see? I can see the top of its body, at the front of the river."

Miss Bennett picked out the object brushing up against the rocks. Her mouth suddenly dried out, as if a dentist had gone in with a suction tube. She raked her tongue along her soft palate in search of a voice.

"Could you come here, please," she croaked.

Her scratchy voice failed to reach the gossiping mothers.

"Sorry, would you mind watching the children for a moment."

Lara was busily pointing out the dead animal to her friends, who were on their knees and craning their heads, eager for a peek.

As a small wave made its way towards the rocks, Lara's discovery rolled onto its back.

The children's screams pierced their mothers' hearts. The women were on their feet and running towards their children. Bennett and the parent volunteers turned the children away from the reservoir, out of sight, but not out of mind. The adults ushered the children towards the road in a futile attempt to spare future nightmares. But the damage was done. The image would haunt their dreams for years to come.

"Right, everyone stay here please and look for a tram, everyone look for a tram, can you do that for me," Bennett shouted, her voice cracking. "Can you do that for me please K2 class? Keep your eyes on the road and look for a tram. Can we do that, K2?"

A couple of children answered, the ones who hadn't seen anything. The rest cried. The luckier ones, the ones whose parents had volunteered for the school excursion, hid their weeping faces inside their mothers' warm hugs. The women bit their lips, unsure of what to say, unsure of what they'd just seen. They didn't expect to see such things, not in Singapore.

Finally, a tram trundled towards them. When the day started, the carriage represented a jaunty, jolly day out. Now it offered an escape from the horror. The women hoisted the children onto the tram as quickly as possible, persuading other visitors to shuffle along the seats to make room. When every child was safely settled, Bennett whispered to the tram driver and told him to wait. The startled driver prepared to explain the zoo's safety regulations, but her eyes silenced him.

Bennett ran back to the shelter to collect her belongings. She couldn't help herself. She looked down at the water's edge.

Dragon Boy's battered and swollen face stared back at her. A fish wriggled through his mouth. His skin and gums had been attacked overnight, giving his protruding teeth a deceptive appearance.

The reservoir's marine life had left Dragon Boy with a smile on his face.

Chapter 20

LOW heard the giggling. It had woken him up. He wiped the dribble off his chin. Exhaustion stung his eyes. His left temple throbbed. His back ached and his neck was stiff. He squinted at the clock on the computer screen. His body craved sleep, but the bastards on morning shift had meandered in with their clanking coffee mugs and squeaking chairs. He'd been asleep for less than an hour. They all knew that. The revulsion ran deep.

Low didn't bother to get up. He rested his head on the desk. He heard voices arguing over the previous night's Manchester United game.

"Eh, trying to sleep, basket," he shouted.

"Go home then," one of the voices spat back.

"Balls to you."

Using his forearm as a pillow, Low turned his head towards his desk partition, just inches from his nose. He faced the other way and got the same view. Every morning, the walls inched closer. They hadn't sacked him. They had imprisoned him. It was a much smarter move, keeping him on the payroll but chopping his balls off. He was alive but impotent. He was better off in Changi Prison. Tiger was less a prisoner than he was.

A cup of hot *teh-c* suddenly appeared on his desk, the steam tickling the pores of his nose.

"What the hell?"

Low sat up to find a young, neat Chinese guy fidgeting beside him.

"Oh sorry, didn't mean to wake you."

"Never mind wake up, I almost lost my bloody face."

"Sorry."

The nervous stranger focused on his polished black shoes. Low shifted some of the mess on his cluttered desk to make room for the tea.

"Who are you anyway?"

The young man straightened his white shirt. His posture stiffened. "Oh, I thought I would make you a tea, sir."

Low pointed at the cup. "Did you poison it?"

"No, sir."

"Did you piss in it?"

"No, sir."

"Then you must be new then."

"Why, sir?"

"Because I'm universally despised at the Technology Crime Division. That's why."

"No, sir, cannot be, I'm sure."

"Oh, it definitely is."

"Really?"

"Definitely."

"Why?"

"Because I'm an asshole."

Low smiled and sipped his tea. He nodded appreciatively as he raised the cup. "Eh, your tea not bad, *ah?*"

"Thank you, sir."

"*Wah lau*, enough with the 'sir' already. You doing National Service, is it?"

"Just finished."

"And they put you here? So how? Which one?"

"Which one what, sir? I mean, Detective Inspector . . ."

"*Yah lah, yah lah*, which one?"

"I'm sorry. I don't understand."

"You either blur like *sotong* or *hao lian* one. This one here, got no middle ground. If you want middle ground, you go for uniform or Major Crime. They don't mess around down here in Technology. They know the next election will be settled in cyberspace. So, which one are you?"

The young officer shifted his weight to the other foot. "I'm a government scholar, sir, fast-tracked."

"Wah, not bad *ah*, very *cheem*. Got big balls *ah*. You got a name, big balls?"

"Harry."

"Wah, you really were named after the big boss. Your parents fans of LKY, is it?"

"No, my Dad liked Clint Eastwood movies."

Low clapped his hands.

"Ah, that's hilarious."

"Yeah, people always make fun of me."

"I bet you never said that at the interviews, *ah*, dirty Harry? I bet you always say, you were named after the old man, right or not?"

"Actually, I usually just say my Chinese name."

"Hey, just like the great man himself. Ah, that's funny. That's made my day, Harry, your Dad loved Clint Eastwood, fantastic."

Harry Lim hovered at the desk. Low's dishevelled appearance had shocked him, even though he had heard all the rumours, but the emotional reaction surprised him more. He was in awe.

"Anyway, if you don't mind, it's just that, well, you know, I wanted to meet . . ."

"You wanted to meet the great Stanley Low."

"Well, sort of."

"And now you've met him," said Low, stretching out his arms. "Isn't he a disappointment?"

"No, no, sir, not at all."

"Don't start with the 'sir' shit again, please. It's like being back in NS."

"Sorry. I just wanted to ask, if it's OK, did you really catch Tiger last time?"

"You know I did, otherwise you wouldn't be here. They study the case in your classes. Last time, they asked me to go down and give a talk."

"That must have been amazing."

"I didn't go."

"Why?"

"They expect to meet a myth."

Lim watched his hero pour the rest of the contents from a plastic water bottle into the tea and then wished he hadn't.

"But you were undercover for like two years or something. It was a record."

"Yeah, Guinness never called me though."

"I, er, actually wrote a paper on you, how you revolutionised undercover work in Singapore by infiltrating a match-fixing syndicate and pulling it all down from the inside out."

"Or, talking cock for two years and waiting for someone to fuck up."

"No *lah*, it wasn't like that. I read everything on the case."

Low swivelled his chair away. "Come on *ah*, Harry. It's always like that. Someone always fucks up, or they hand themselves in, or they escape. That's it. They are the only three outcomes. You just got to be nearby when it happens."

"But you always catch them."

Low flinched as he swigged the tea mixed with vodka. "Marina

Bay Sands," he muttered.

"But that was Tiger, right? You caught him."

"I caught one of them."

"Oh, yah, we heard some rumours in class. Is that why you moved here?"

"Hmm, something like that."

Lim left the ambiguous answer alone. He was smart. He noticed the latest blog from *The Singapore Truth* on Low's screen.

"Ah, you've got to watch these sites too. You know how many hits that site gets?"

"Yep."

"He's clever though. He really knows how to control the masses."

"So does a sheepdog."

The office phone rang. For once, Low welcomed the distraction. The kid was sharp, but the adulation was getting boring. "Yah," he drawled.

"Hey, it's me, Chan."

Low was so weary he missed the anxiety in Chan's voice.

"Hey, Charlie Chan, what's up man?"

"I got to be quick. I'm not telling you this, OK, but we just found another one, maybe same kind of stab wound, at the Singapore Zoo."

"The Singapore Zoo? Serious?"

"Yeah, skinny Chinese, full of tattoos. He still had his IC in his pocket. I think it's your old *kaki* from last time. It's Dragon Boy."

By the time Low had finished smashing the phone, he had cut most of his fingers.

Chapter 21

CHAN struggled with the greyness. The water had leeched the body of its colour. Death came in all shapes and sizes, but it only came in one colour underwater. Aini's arm and shoulder had shriveled and greyed in the drain, but Dragon Boy's appearance genuinely unsettled. The fish and turtles had made a start on the gangster's flesh. Being skinny to begin with, it didn't take long to strip him back to the bone in some places. When Professor Chong pulled back the sheet to reveal Dragon Boy's bloodied stomach covered in bite marks, Chan grimaced.

"It's actually got worse you know," Chong said, addressing the inspector's discomfort.

"What's that?" Chan asked.

"The state of bodies in our waters. The cleaner they got, the uglier the corpses got."

"How?"

"We cleaned up our rivers and reservoirs, Inspector Chan. We harvested our own water supply. We built canals, waterways and dams and improved our drainage systems and channelled everything towards those great manufactured bodies of water like Upper Seletar Reservoir."

"So?"

Chong lifted one of Dragon Boy's arms. Some of the flesh

above the elbow had already been gnawed away. "We brought back the scavengers. We brought back the fish, Inspector Chan. And every nibble and chunk taken out of our friend here makes my job that little bit harder."

"I just can't believe the state of the body. He was only in there one night, right?"

"Judging by the decomposition and the charts from the Public Utilities Board, probably less than that, maybe five or six hours."

"And the fish did all that?"

"A couple of months ago, a group of school kayakers went out at MacRitchie Reservoir. A teenage boy rolled his kayak, felt a sharp pain and ended up with a bloody foot. His foot had been in the water for less than 30 seconds. That's the trouble with our mentality. We think we can control everything. But we cannot subjugate nature."

"Subjugate?"

"Bring under control," said Chua, suddenly appearing at Chan's side. The deputy director was out of breath. "Sorry about that, professor, urgent call."

Chua admired the lab's grey, sterile appearance. "*Wah*, you still keep the cleanest lab in Asia, professor."

"Tidy work, tidy mind. Now, you came to see this?"

Chong pointed towards the puncture wound beneath Dragon Boy's left nipple. He pushed his gloved fingertip into the hole.

"As you can see, the fatal wound is narrow, but deep, very deep. And the direction and force of the injury suggests the weapon was held in that position for quite some time."

"But not a knife?" Chua asked.

"No, there's no ripping or cutting, no slashing at all. This is a thin weapon, around 10 to 15 cm, at least that's the depth of the wound. I can't be sure of the handle length of course. But it was a weapon with a sharp tip, requiring a strong individual to really push through to break the skin and bone. One of the victim's ribs was cracked. This is a strong man, a powerful man."

"So the same weapon as before?"

"I can't say for sure, but certainly similar and probably the same man. Strong, right-handed judging by the direction of the impact and presumably not planned either."

"Why?"

"There are four minor puncture wounds on the top of the scalp, probably from a fork and heavy bruising around the jaw, suggesting a fight in a domestic environment. Of course, any fingerprints, blood or DNA have all been scrubbed away by the water and the fish."

"But it's the same killer?"

Chong nodded.

"Now he's killed a local, it's gonna be a problem," Chua said.

The deputy director tapped a note into his iPhone. Dead foreigners inconvenienced the statisticians at the Ministry of Home Improvement, but dead locals antagonised voters. Politics had no respect for the dead. But then, the dead had no respect for politics.

"He's definitely a Singaporean?" Chua asked.

"Yeah, his skinny jeans so tight, his IC still inside," Chan replied.

"Not an Indonesian like last time or anything?"

"No, sir."

Chong busied himself with Dragon Boy's body. Across three decades, he had come across many policemen like Anthony Chua. They cared more about KPIs than killers. That's why they rarely caught the killers, not that it particularly mattered. Victims are soon forgotten. KPI figures can always be massaged.

"OK, OK, so what do we know about this guy?"

Chan read from his notepad. "OK, Lee Kok Wah, but

everybody called him Dragon Boy, 28 years old, no real fixed address, moved all over Singapore, Malaysia, Indonesia, Macau and Thailand, no declared income, but got a BMW in his name. Convicted of loan sharking last time, twice, and assault before, started as a bookies' runner, fixing S-League and Malaysia Cup matches, and in Indonesia, worked for Tiger's syndicate, then disappeared for a while, turned up again a couple of years ago, pimping in Geylang and running illegal bookies in the East Coast, maybe selling cocaine, probably trying to make enough to set up as an *ah long*, because he's still got all Tiger's contacts from last time."

"*Wah lau*, he's only been dead for a few hours. How you find out so much?" Chua watched the young inspector exchange wary glances with the pathologist. "Well?"

"Er, Low, sir," Chan mumbled.

"What?"

"Detective Inspector Low, sir. They worked together last time, him and Dragon Boy, when he was undercover with Tiger."

"So, what? They were friends, is it?"

"Kind of, sir, yeah."

"Ah, fuck."

The deputy director took considerable pride in maintaining a sense of dignity and decorum around his subordinates. He usually avoided foul language in front of the other officers.

But Stanley Low did that to people.

Chapter 22

THE car screeched to a halt. Low took his hands off the bonnet and stepped back. His banging had caused a minor dent in the paintwork, but he had otherwise retained control. He had tried counting backwards and forwards. He had tried counting sheep, past cases and former girlfriends, but he always returned to the target at hand. A target recalibrated his focus and controlled the fizzing in his brain. A target sharpened the senses and exercised the intellect. A target gave him a chase and a chase gave him a purpose. Without a purpose, he didn't, well he didn't want to think about that. Low always found a purpose.

Chua lowered the driver's window. Cautiously, he poked his head out. "What the hell are you doing?"

"You want to do this here, deputy dog? Fine."

Low moved towards the driver's side of the car. Chua quickly pulled his head back in and put up the window. He was a scholar, not a fighter. They had only just left the pathologist's office. There were doctors and fellow officers in the crowded car park. He didn't want to cause a scene. He had also heard the rumours. Low attacked like a feral dog.

On the passenger's side, Chan was already out of the car and making his way around the purring engine. "Come on, Stanley."

"Eh, not now *ah*, Charlie."

Low tapped the window.

"We'll discuss this at the office," Chua mouthed through the window.

"No, we'll discuss it now." Low banged the window harder with his fist. The fury threatened to consume him. He had to stay with the target.

"Open this fucking window, or I'll kick it in."

Low took a step backwards as if preparing a run up. Chan grabbed his arm.

"Stanley, come on, man, this is crazy."

Low shrugged off the arm and kicked the driver's door. "No, he's the crazy bastard. I told you to put me on this case, right or not? I told you to let me follow this guy. I gave you the scent. I told you I had a lead with Dragon Boy and you dropped it, worrying about your 13th-month bonus, you *kiasi* prick."

Low kicked the car a second time. Chan dragged him away, but the provocation was enough. Chua got out and slammed the door behind him.

"OK, let him go, inspector, let him go now."

Chan released his grip on his former mentor and Low lunged forward. The men stood nose to nose.

"Right, Ah Lian. Here we are. Shall we discuss the case like men or fight like little boys in the sandpit?"

"My man is dead because of you."

"No, he's dead because of you. We had nothing because you gave us nothing, so don't try and make this about us. You went off on your own without telling us. You thought you can win the case all by yourself like last time, but those days are finished. You're finished."

"I almost had him."

"You had nothing. You had a lead. But you didn't share it. We could've watched your Dragon Boy, followed him to the guy and made an arrest. But, no, you went in on your own, playing Napoleon again."

Low visibly reeled from the comparison. The fight dissipated. Weakness spread. His body was suddenly riddled with self-doubt.

"What you mean, Napoleon?"

"You think I can't read a psychological profile? Everybody's got one. You, me, him, everybody. This is Singapore. Everybody's got a file. I've read Dr Lai's assessment. I know all about your condition."

Low looked towards Chan for reassurance, but his friend couldn't look him in the eye.

"Look, Dragon Boy is dead because you . . ."

"No, you. It's always about you. You wouldn't share him with us."

"Bullshit. He was a drug dealer. Since when does a deputy director do deals with a drug dealer. I knew I couldn't come to you. You worry about your promotion, you don't work with drug dealers."

"We would have interrogated him."

"Please *lah*. Dragon Boy sold so much cocaine it snowed in Shenton Way. He had nothing to bargain with. No way you could work with him, not now, not with all our corruption shit. The bloggers are already killing us."

"You think CPIB is the only one who can interrogate?"

"Oh *yah*, definitely, sure get Dragon Boy to talk one. No problem. Just give him the air-con treatment, right? Definitely shit his pants. Listen. I once saw Tiger hold a *parang* to his neck right here," Low said, moving his finger across his neck. "Someone had been talking to CPIB and Tiger got pissed off. He started moving the *parang* across Dragon Boy's neck, breaking the skin, the blood dripping down the blade and all down Dragon Boy's singlet. Dragon Boy never blinked. He stared at Tiger the whole time, never moved, never talked. Tiger got halfway across his neck, right next to the jugular and stopped. He knew Dragon Boy never talked. It was *me*. The only person who talked was me."

"We could've tried. If you had told us about his connection to the suspect, we could've tried."

"Dragon Boy only talked to me. That's why I never came to you. There was no point. He'd never talk to you."

The deputy director turned his back on the inspector and opened the car door.

"Maybe. But he'd still be alive."

Chapter 23

THE Chinese stone lions roared either side of the oak-panelled door. Wealth and subtlety were uneasy bedfellows in Asia. Even ministers were not immune to tacky indulgences. Standing on the gravel driveway, Low rang the doorbell again. The chimes echoed through the three-storey home in the isolated Bukit Timah street. The property backed onto primary rainforest. Singapore and Rio were the only cities to boast primary rainforest within their borders. For most it was a tourism tidbit. For the elite, it was a view from the window. As he hit the doorbell for a third time, Low heard the cicadas. The forest orchestra played only for the rich. Their performances, like everything else in the street, were exclusive.

The door finally opened. The Minister of Home Improvement filled the gap. He sighed at his unwelcome visitor. Low had aged. His hollowed cheeks accentuated his ghostly pallor. Somehow, the Government's gadfly had lost more weight. He wasn't eating properly. The Minister knew what was filling the void.

"Hello, inspector."

The Minister examined his door. "You haven't kicked it this time."

"There's still time. Put me back on the case."

"What case?"

"Come on, don't do this now. The *ang moh* with a screwdriver."

"The *ang moh* with a screwdriver? It sounds like a tourist sipping cocktails at Raffles Hotel."

The Minister chuckled at his lame joke. Low loathed everything about the man—his conceit, his innate sense of superiority and irrefutable belief in the educated few controlling the lumpen masses; the automated charm, the ingratiating smarm and the overwhelming certainty of always being right. Men like the Minister never patronised. They genuinely believed in what they were saying. Privately, in weaker moments, Low envied the absolute faith in one's abilities. The Minister had it. Ah Lian had it. But Low never would. He couldn't overcome his inferiority; he could only obscure it with aggression, shout it down and bury it.

"You want to make jokes is it?"

"It was more of a pithy observation."

"Fuck off."

The Minister laughed in spite of himself. "You haven't cleaned up your language."

"You haven't cleaned up your country. How's my Indonesian money launderer?"

"What do you want, inspector?"

"I told you already. Put me on the case. You know you need me. You can't have a double murder."

"What double murder? Is this a new case?"

"No, same one, he's killed another one, a Singaporean this time."

The Minister absorbed the information. "A Singaporean? This was carried out by the same Caucasian guy?"

"That's why."

"Who's the Singaporean?"

"Was my *kaki* last time, helped me when I was undercover, the Tiger case."

"He was a policeman?"

"No *lah*, he was an illegal bookie, *ah long*, small-time."

"Chinese or Malay?"

"Chinese."

"Ah, OK."

"Why OK?"

"No, no, it's just that the neighbours . . . never mind."

"Balls to you, never mind. He was my boy, OK."

"You told me he was a loan shark?"

"Yah."

"Money-lending is a major concern for us now. I've just launched a poster campaign across all the housing estates. Vandalism is an issue, right now, too. Loan sharks are getting bolder."

"You built the bloody casinos."

"The point is, inspector, loan sharks are not sympathetic figures."

"He was stabbed and thrown in the reservoir for a group of school kids to find at Singapore Zoo."

"Terrible for the children."

"Terrible for Dragon Boy."

"Dragon Boy? That was his name?"

"Nickname."

"Imagine the newspapers. Imagine the blogs. You're in Technology now. A murdered gangster called Dragon Boy. We're not Malaysia or Macau. This kind of thing, the timing, it gives the wrong impression."

"But he's killed twice, the woman before, dumped her in Chinatown."

"Yes, I read the reports. An Indonesian prostitute in a drain and now you say a Chinese loan shark in a reservoir."

"A Singaporean."

"A Singaporean gangster. Resources must be carefully allocated."

"To bloggers?"

"Bloggers are read every day."

"And they'll read this."

"I'm sure. The Chinese press will have a field day for a few days, but then it will return to what really matters—retirement savings, new bus routes and better healthcare for the elderly."

"You still talk cock."

The Minister gestured towards the empty street beyond his gated property. "Where's the media? Where's the national interest?"

"What about last year? You all shit your pants with Marina Bay Sands."

"That one was tricky."

"Some victims will always be more dead than others, right?"

The Minister checked his watch. "As I said, I appreciate all the work you are doing in the Technology division."

"You didn't say that."

"Well, I do."

"So I'm not going to be assigned to this then?"

"Our focus must be online sedition and obscenities. They affect national security. Anyway, thanks for coming, inspector, but I'm having dinner with my daughter later."

The Minister edged back from the door. Low took half a step forward.

"How is your daughter these days? She's the doctor, right? So you're the family man now, *ah*?"

The Minister stopped. "I kept you in the job," he muttered.

"You sentenced me to a slow death."

"Bad publicity helps no one. It's all about calm exteriors."

"Save your shit for the sheep." Low turned on his heel and

crunched his way along the gravel path. "You'll be coming to me to save your *cheem* calm exteriors."

"I think you're better suited in Technology, inspector. Thanks again."

Low reached the ornate gates and faced the Minister. "What, you think I'll come to you is it? No, no, no. You will come to me."

"Why?"

"He's already killed two. Might as well enjoy himself now."

Chapter 24

ZHANG poked a hole through the instructions with his silver Allen key. He felt better. His living room was filled with flat-packed tokens of love for his cheating wife. He sat among bags of screws, cardboard boxes and incomplete bookcases. His wife had mocked his masculinity in Australia. She had called him a bookish, *kiasu* nerd typical of the homeland she was desperate to leave behind. He made money, but he never made her laugh.

That surfer had made her laugh. He could also put up bookcases.

Before Australia, Zhang had never questioned his manliness. He wore a white collar to work. He commuted in a second-hand car and ordered underlings around in the office. He belonged to not one but two private golf clubs, the membership stickers proudly emblazoned on his windscreen. He owned an annual pass at both casinos and always took a cabin with a balcony on Star Cruises. He was a man of means, a modern Asian success story. He didn't put up bloody bookcases. Bangladeshis put up his bookcases. Indonesians mopped his floors and Chinese contractors cleaned his air-conditioning units.

But the world was back to front Down Under. The labourer was king. Air-con handymen were called engineers and owned mansions with swimming pools. Bankers built their own decking on weekends. Corporate CEOs built their own bookcases after putting up their holiday homes. Everything was alien. Zhang's experience and qualifications were suddenly more foreign than his accent.

In Singapore, he was respected. In Australia, he was irrelevant.

Zhang picked up one of the shelves and craned his head to re-examine the instructions. Satisfied, he clamped a screwdriver between his teeth and balanced the shelf on his right hand. With his left hand, he adjusted the metal stops, pulling them from one pre-drilled hole and pushing them into another. He lowered the shelf onto the metal stops, fitting it snugly across the middle of a half-finished bookcase.

"That's too high," said Li Jing, as she swept across the living room.

"Why is it too high?" Zhang shouted after his wife, who was already in the kitchen.

"Must have space for my classic novels. I've got a lot already. All that space above is wasted. That's why we got extra shelves to squeeze in more books."

"All right, I'll move it down."

Since Australia, she had started reading. It was one of her many overnight obsessions. The initial suburban coffee mornings to welcome that quaint Chinese couple from Singapore had soon turned into interrogations. A tilt of the head, a hand on the arm, a sympathetic smile and those patronising questions: *You've never read Jane Austen? Oh, you must. What about Hardy and Dickens? Do you not read the classics in Singapore? It's surprising because your English is really good.*

Zhang wasn't bothered. He understood his Asian education and championed its underlying purpose. Books that stimulated both the mind and the economy were valued. Books that provoked the mind and soul were western indulgences, an outdated liberal pandering to some warped, artistic ideal.

But his weaker wife fell for the façade and tried to win him over with pet phrases.

There's more to life than money, Harold.

That was always her favourite.

We're not in Singapore anymore. There's more to life than money, Harold.

Yeah, like blond surfers, you cheating bitch.

But he said nothing. He assumed common sense would prevail in the end.

It didn't.

Not even when they returned to Singapore. He was certain that she would see sense when she came home and learn to recognise what was really important, what truly mattered. Instead she withdrew further into her make-believe shell, losing herself in nonsensical novels and romantic, whimsical worlds filled with chivalrous, selfless men hiking across rugged terrain to put up her damn bookcases.

Zhang lowered the four metal stops and slipped the shelf on top. "How's this?"

Li Jing popped her head around the living room door. "Er, still lower I think. My books not very tall, need the shelves, not the head space."

She returned to the kitchen.

"Right, no problem, will make it lower."

Zhang angrily tugged at the two metal stops on the right side of the bookcase. His left hand wasn't holding the shelf properly underneath and it slipped downwards, its edge scrapping the skin between Zhang's thumb and forefinger.

"Bastard."

Zhang jumped up, shaking his right hand. In a fit of petulance, he kicked at the unfinished bookcase. As the other shelves came away from their metal stops, the bookcase fell in on itself.

Li Jing ran into the living room. "What are you doing?"

"Can see what? Putting up your bookcase."

"Why are you banging?"

"Well, someone's got to around here."

"What's that supposed to mean?"

"Nothing."

"Yes it is."

"Why am I putting up bookcases?"

"I like reading."

"Nonsense. Ten years we never had a bookshelf. Last time, we got our books from the library. Now you want a big shelf."

"I like books now."

"No, *he* liked books."

"Who?"

Zhang glared at his wife, but only briefly. Her beauty could diffuse his anger. And he wanted to be angry. Li Jing didn't look away.

"*Aiyoh*, this is about him, is it?"

"I don't know. I didn't screw him, did I? You did."

"Look, I'm here. I came back."

"You came back because we couldn't make it in Australia."

"Not again, OK. I'm here. I'm trying my best."

"Of course. For you, it's just nice. Over there, can sleep with him. Over here, I make money and put up your bookcases."

"You see, money again."

"What? It's what you want right? Last time, I cannot make it, but he can make it right, real big shot, teaching tourists how to sit on a surfboard."

"I'm going."

Li Jing left her husband alone in their living room, surrounded by bits of bookcases.

"Ah, you going, is it? Don't go. Come. I'll write another blog, about foreigners with no talent. Come. You can help me."

Zhang marched over to his laptop on the coffee table. "Come *lah*, Li Jing, this one is about how foreigners keep screwing Asians. Come, you're an expert."

Zhang heard the apartment door slam shut. He thought about the mess he had made on her rug, a broken bookcase for his broken marriage. She could always ring her handyman. She still had his number. She still called him. Zhang knew that.

He rolled the loose screws around his foot, flicking one against the assembly instructions. The step-by-step guide and the stupid diagrams suddenly caught his attention. He was drawn to them, to the patronising pictures listing the contents, the screws, the metal stops, the shelves, the panels, the brackets and the damn Allen key, the one-size-fits-all tool, just like that surfer. But it was the *logo*—the logo on the instructions—that had him flipping open his laptop.

Through the fog of his cuckolded fury, Zhang saw the name of the killer.

Chapter 25

SHUFFLING along the seats, Maxwell made space for Super Mario to put down a tray of beers. The Teenage Mutant Ninja Turtles sat on the next table and The Beatles leaned against the lounge's glass balcony. Charity days began back in the office at Marina Bay Financial Centre, but they usually ended at LeVeL33. The world's highest craft brewery allowed traders and bankers to soak in the Marina Bay view and wallow in their self-importance.

Thomas the Tank Engine and his pal Percy waddled towards Maxwell, sipping beers through their boxy train-face costumes. They were part of Maxwell's trading team. They sat at the same desk and shared the commission. They were younger, prettier and more successful than Maxwell. He used to *be* them. Now they carried him. They made the most commission for charity. They chose the costumes for the fancy dress competition. They *owned* him.

"Cheer up, Fat Controller," said Thomas, removing his mask and shoving it under the table. "We won. 40 grand in commission by lunchtime, fucking 'ave it."

Thomas and Percy pulled stools from another crowded table. They didn't ask permission. The stools were there. So they took them. They dragged them towards Maxwell, the metallic legs scraping along the tiled surface. The noise caught the attention of a young, Malay waiter.

"Sorry, mate," said Thomas, dropping his muscular frame onto the stool. "We're celebrating. Made 40 grand for charity this morning. How much did you make?"

"Leave him alone," Maxwell muttered.

"Sorry, Fat Controller, didn't mean to upset the natives . . . Let's have the same again over here, mate."

"Here, you know what you look like in that costume," said Percy, taking off his mask and ruffling his blond hair.

"What?" Maxwell replied.

"A cunt."

Everyone at the table laughed. They laughed in Maxwell's face. Teenage turtles and train engines pointed fingers at his painted rosy red cheeks and the ill-fitting yellow waistcoat squeezed beneath an outsized black suit. The three-piece costume made the sweat stick to his rounded face like a bonnet strap. The blusher on his cheeks ran. He took off the top hat and wiped his dripping forehead.

"Nah, don't take the hat off," said Percy.

"Yeah, you look less of a twat with the hat off."

"Fuck off," Maxwell snarled.

Percy picked up one of the beers that filled ice buckets across the lounge. "I'd like to make a toast," he shouted. "It's early days yet, boys and girls, but I reckon by the time the day's trades are settled we should be somewhere close to a million for charity."

The cheers filled the exclusive lounge and drifted across Marina Bay's sparklingly artificial vista. Wealthy foreigners chinked champagne flutes and beer bottles and toasted their philanthropic contribution to Singapore as the Malay barman wiped away the beer stains.

"So I think it's only right and proper that we do at least spend one per cent of that million tonight to celebrate our generosity."

The primal roars of greedy men and women filled LeVeL33, drowning out the conversations of bar staff. Maxwell stared at the beer bottle.

Fuck your million. You're all frauds.

Percy slammed his bottle on the table and snarled at Maxwell. The fat, old man was at least 40, almost twice his age. He was out of condition. He no longer had the stomach for the fight. He just had the stomach. He ate into the other boys' commission and hampered their hunting. Women didn't want him so he slowed them down. He was obsolete. Percy could only remind Maxwell of his worthlessness. The younger man leaned across the table.

"Here, see that girl behind the bar, the skinny Chinese bird, I'm gonna smash the life out of it tonight."

Thomas giggled. Maxwell focused on his beer.

"You reckon?" Thomas asked.

"I know."

"How?"

"Told her we had a reserved table at Pangaea. Richest nightclub in the world."

"Is she bringing a mate?"

"If she does, I'm having them both."

"Sod off."

"Who made the most commission this morning, or this week, or this year? It's a winner's privilege. I'm putting down 20 grand for this table tonight. I want it paid back here." Percy pointed at his groin.

"Is that the table with the painting of that woman hanging off the wall?" Thomas asked.

"I don't know. I just wanna be hanging out of that woman tonight," said Percy, looking straight at Maxwell. "What about you, Fat Controller?"

Maxwell smiled. "What about me?"

"Who you having a go at tonight?"

"Don't know."

"I've heard the cleaners are pretty cheap. Here, the American sailors are not around. They might give you a half-price special at Orchard Towers. You up for that?"

Percy and Thomas tapped their bottles together. Maxwell thought about the two cardboard cutouts sharing his table and the empty shells floating across the lounge on the Marina Bay breeze. And then he thought about Aini and Dragon Boy. The imagery pleased him.

You have no idea what I'd be up for.

"You boys make me laugh," Maxwell said. "You make some commission and you think you're King Kong. When we had these charity days in England, when you were still in school, I'd make a million on my own, in one day. We had so much good PR we could bring in prime ministers and Oscar winners for the day, just so they could get the publicity. I'd be making calls with Hollywood stars sitting next to me."

"Who'd you get?" Percy asked. "Charlie Chaplin?"

The young, wealthy white men from England's home counties fist-bumped each other.

"Oh, because I'm old, Charlie Chaplin, I see what you did there, very good. You both forget I've been doing this a lot longer you."

"He's gonna start reading *Death of a Salesman* in a minute."

"Good book," Maxwell said, "especially the ending."

At the next table, Donatello, the Teenage Mutant Ninja Turtle, turned so quickly and unexpectedly, his shell knocked Leonardo's bottle out of his hand. Beer splattered across the floor, but the bottle didn't break.

"What did you do that for, you tit," Leonardo said. "I've got to take this back later and there's beer all over it."

"Sorry, mate, I wanted you to see this, have a look."

Leonardo took his colleague's phone. "What is it?"

"It's those murders, the expat banker ones," Donatello said. "They've given him a nickname on Facebook."

Percy turned around. "What is it?"

"The IKEA Killer," Leonardo said, reading from the phone. "Because he always needs a screwdriver."

Percy and Thomas laughed. No one else did.

"This Facebook page says it's just the latest, extreme example of foreigners coming here and taking whatever they want and doing whatever they want," Donatello said, taking back his phone. "This guy is starting a petition for Singapore to cut back on all its foreign worker quotas. It's had more than 50,000 likes already."

The volume dropped around the tables filled with ice buckets of beer and champagne. Donatello pocketed his phone.

"This is hardly going to make us any more popular, is it?"

Maxwell sipped his beer and savoured the death of a party.

Chapter 26

THE rain pecked at the window in the psychiatrist's office. Its rhythms had always hypnotised Low. Monsoonal storms took him back to nights spent camping at East Coast Park before National Service, drinking warm Anchor beer and talking shit. The rain reminded him of a life before. He missed the innocence. Sitting opposite, Dr Lai sensed her patient's distraction.

"You like the rain?"

"I love the rain. It's the only good thing about our weather."

"Why?"

"Scrubs the place clean for a while."

"And then?"

"The cockroaches come back."

Low had plasters on two of his fingers and there were small cuts on his hand. "Have you hurt your hand?" Lai asked.

"Obviously."

"You're quieter today."

"Hmm." Low slouched down in the chair and gazed up at the ceiling. "Got cobwebs up there. Should tell the cleaner."

"OK. Anything else?"

"Also got gecko shit in one corner."

"Anything apart from the state of my office?"

"Not really."

"Did you resolve your issue with your friend that you mentioned last time?"

"Not really."

"Is there still a problem?"

"No problem. He's dead."

Low never took his eyes off the ceiling. For once, Lai was grateful for her patient's contempt. She needed a moment to compose herself. She took too long.

"Gone quiet now *ah*? You never knew is it?"

"Was he the one, I mean, in the papers?"

"Yep, second victim of our new IKEA Killer. The *IKEA* Killer. I must admit, this Harold Zhang, the IKEA Killer, that was brilliant. He always needs a screwdriver, fantastic, not too *cheem*, not too simple, just nice."

"But I read all the papers, English and Chinese."

"*Wah*, bilingual, very good, must make your parents very proud."

The psychiatrist ignored the insults. "They said the victim's name was . . ."

"*Aiyoh*, not going to say his name was Dragon Boy, are they? You blur or what?"

"Your accent changes slightly with your mood."

"Is it?"

"Yes, it's more . . ."

"Real?"

"I was going to say natural. You think you're not real?"

"I know I'm not real."

"Unless you're Ah Lian?"

"*Wah lan eh*, psychiatry for beginners, is it?"

"I don't know what you want me to say."

"Nothing."

In a childish display of petulance, Low folded his arms and

closed his eyes. Lai pushed her fringe behind her ear. She pursed her lips, uncomfortable with the inspector's silence.

"I'm sorry about your friend."

"Why? You didn't know him."

"He was your friend."

"So?"

"That's sad. It's sad when someone close to us dies."

"I used him."

"Is that how you feel?"

"That's how it is. I pimped him like a . . . a . . . *xiao mei mei* and now he's dead."

"So your mood is low right now?"

"You went to university for this? Yes. This is a low. I had the high meeting with Dragon Boy and chasing the case, but now he's dead and I'm nowhere near the case, so this is a low. You can complete your bipolar checklist now, throw the guinea pig back to your bosses."

"My bosses?"

Low sat up for the first time, his eyes blazing. "You give reports to different departments now?"

"What?"

"Chua."

"I don't understand."

"Anthony Chua, the deputy director of CID. He's overseeing the IKEA Killer case, the case I am not a part of. He's the deputy director I do not really work for. And yet he knows all about me now, thanks to you."

"If you are impugning my professional integrity, inspector, we can end this session now and refer the matter elsewhere. Look. I file a single report and it goes through the usual channel, no more, no less. They were the terms of our professional relationship from the beginning. You were referred to me after your undercover operation and I was asked to report my findings to your department. You knew this. I knew this. Nothing has changed. Who then has access to that file after that is out of both our hands. Don't you often say that everyone has a file in Singapore? Why do you seek to antagonise even those who want to help you?"

"We don't help each other. We service each other. Like prostitutes. We all do it, every day. Do you have name cards?"

"Name cards?"

"Yah, name cards to give out at your meetings and seminars."

"Yes."

"Why?"

"To tell people what I do."

"Exactly. Pimping yourself."

"Networking."

"Pimping. Those name cards are our special services. Remember last time, when prostitutes wrote their numbers on toilets and phone boxes? Now, no need, we give out name cards instead. This is my name, my number and my special service. If you have a special service that I can use then maybe we can pimp each other. We don't know this person. We don't like this person. We just use this person. We're all the same. The one who died first, the prostitute, she was the only honest one. She admitted what she was. We pretend. We call it networking. It's whoring. We're all selling our special service."

"You're drifting away from your original point again, finding it hard to focus, presenting a confusing argument, speaking fast and aggressively. We've been here before, haven't we? Bipolar patients veer between light and shade quickly. It's black or it's white, high or low, good or evil. At the moment, you're struggling with the death of your friend. That's understandable. But in your case, you go lower, deeper, and the emotions dredge up something darker, and this loathing, both for yourself and others, engulfs your mind and body. You struggle to reason and you struggle to find any energy. But it will pass."

Low examined the doctor's unblinking eyes. She really believed this stuff. He noticed the pink rubber case on her desk. "Is that an old iPod?"

Lai frowned. She had no idea where her patient was going with this.

"Yes, I still keep it for running. It's lighter, less bulky."

"Reminds me of this guy's radio. They had to keep me overnight once at Changi."

"The prison?"

"No, the airport. Of course, the prison."

"OK. The prison."

"Was picked up with some of Tiger's guys doing some, anyway never mind. I ask to follow them inside, just overnight, to keep it authentic. Also they talk cock more inside, you know. Everyone's scared so they're trying to act bigger. This other guy, he's already inside. He sees that one of my guys has a small radio. My guy had taken it inside for the English football scores on BBC World Service. The other guy wants the radio. My guy says, 'fuck you.' That's it. Finish. About one hour later, the other guy comes back and says, 'OK, never mind,' and asks to shake hands. My guy sticks out his hand. The other guy cuts his throat with a homemade razor. My guy bleeds to death on the floor. The other guy walks out with a five-dollar radio."

"Why?"

"Because he wanted the radio," Low said, slouching in the chair. "Life and death are simple. It's only people like you who complicate things."

Chapter 27

DEEP inside the pub's bowels, Maxwell buried himself at a table and watched the images of his dead lover and drug dealer occasionally appear on the TV screen. Penny Black was the ideal spot to hide out in the open, a white face among white people pining for a Ye Olde England that never existed beyond the dreams of the disoriented expat. Nostalgia was an addictive drug and the cravings came in all shapes and sizes. Maxwell had satisfied his with Dragon Boy's little silver packets. His compatriots fed their addiction with overpriced Guinness and fish and chips. The pub's walls were covered with the tacky indulgences of the confused traveller. In any other context, cheap prints of London's skyline and red buses and pillar boxes appealed only to the most superficial tourist. Through rose-tinted glasses, they were images of home.

Penny Black's jukebox was always tuned to flashback. The sounds of premarital sex, baggy jeans and long blond hair went down well with the Guinness. The pub took the piss with the prices, but knew they could because the menu was priceless. They sold the elixir of youth in a pint glass.

The bankers came to remember, but Maxwell didn't want to remember. He used to be one of the boys. Now he was the Fat Controller. He rubbed his cheek again. The rouge had been removed in the toilets, but he knew it was still there.

"Sorry, mate."

The pointy end of a rucksack had clipped Maxwell's shoulder. He turned slowly. The offender was in his early 20s in a white, creased Bintang Beer vest, easing his bulging backpack onto a barstool. He had handmade beads and bracelets around his wrists and neck, the ones that Balinese street peddlers sold to middle-class students seeking to find themselves during gap years by exploiting South-east Asia's poverty tourism. The guy's hair was blond and his reddish arms and neck betrayed the farmer's tan of the new-age backpacker. He came to explore authentic Asian culture. He didn't just come to get laid on Patong beach.

He didn't have to. The guy's partner stood across from Maxwell, already sitting on a stool, her tatty rucksack hidden beneath a round table. Her cropped mousey hair accentuated her blue eyes and the cut jean shorts made her legs appear longer than they actually were. There was little make-up and no designer labels. Maxwell recognised her immediately. She was old money getting down with poor Asians, discovering a world beyond her own with the family credit card before settling down to an event management job in London. They used to be easy meat for Maxwell on rugby away days; a routine lay between blue bloods before she went back to pretending among the poor people. But they always came back to men like Maxwell and Mr Bintang Vest in the end. The poor people were frightfully entertaining, until it came to paying the bill at LeVeL33. Bankers could be bores. But they always paid the bill.

"It's all right," Maxwell said. "You on holiday?"

"Yeah, just a stopover in Singapore for a couple of days before, you know."

"Thailand?"

"Yeah, Thailand, Cambodia, Vietnam and then a week in

Goa."

Maxwell took in their scruffy beach attire. They were so achingly cool, so hip and original, following the same path taken by a million backpackers before them.

"You should spend more time in Singapore," Maxwell said, standing up and joining the pair at their table, pulling his baseball cap a little lower.

"Well, we thought about it," the girl replied. "But when we looked it up on the Net, it didn't seem to have as much nightlife, as much Asian culture as the other places."

"You're in a British pub, with a British menu, drinking a pint of . . . what's that?"

The girl blushed. "Cider."

"Drinking a pint of *imported* Strongbow cider."

She giggled. "Yes, you're probably right."

"No, I was exactly the same when I first arrived." Maxwell offered his hand. "I'm John by the way."

They shook hands.

"I'm Wendy."

The boyfriend leaned across the small table. His peeling nose glowed. "Simon."

"Good to meet you both. Let me buy you a drink."

"Ah, there's no need for that, mate," Simon interjected.

Wendy said nothing. Maxwell faced the girl. "I see you're the smarter one in the relationship. You know you've got a long holiday ahead of you, the beer is much cheaper in Thailand and the prices here make you want to cry."

"It is bloody expensive here," she conceded.

Maxwell waved at the barman. "Same again for me please and two pints of *imported* Strongbow cider. Stick it on my bill."

His new friends were impressed by the gesture.

"That's really kind of you, thank you," Wendy said.

She leaned over the table to move the empty glasses. Her loose-fitting vest flopped onto the polished timber. Maxwell moved around the table to stand beside Simon. Wendy had breasts like Aini.

"So what have you done so far in Singapore, Simon?"

"Ah, we went to Haji Lane, the Arab quarter, you know."

"Good. Very attractive part of Singapore."

"We went to the SkyPark at Marina Bay Sands."

Wendy pulled back her vest as she stood up. "That was a rip-off. It was *20 dollars* and once you get up there, there's nothing except the view."

Maxwell nodded. "It's a common complaint. I always tell people go to the bar up there. It's called Ku De Ta, or Ce La Vi, or whatever they're calling it this week. The prices are a joke, 20-odd bucks for a beer, but at least you get the beer and the view. At the SkyPark, you're just paying for the view."

"God, I wish we had met you yesterday."

"Well, you've met me now."

"What do you do here, John?" Simon asked.

"Oh, I'm the expat cliché. I help to make an obscene amount of money for a broking firm and pretend it's a real job to make me feel better."

"Yeah, we had read on some sites today about that stuff," Wendy said.

"About what?"

"Singapore's huge wealth causing a rich-poor divide. I thought Singaporeans were all rich."

"They are the only ones who count. There are only two classes here—those who have money and those who don't."

"That's dreadful."

"It is."

Wendy smiled at the older Englishman. His hair was receding

and he was obviously overweight, but his broad frame was still there and he had *something*.

The barman left the drinks on the table.

"Thanks mate," Maxwell said. "Right, well, cheers guys, here's to your stay in Singapore."

They raised their glasses.

"Singapore," they chorused.

MAXWELL'S mood had improved. He was a little unsteady on his feet as he made his way back from the toilet, passing the Victorian sketches and paintings along the walls. The last few hours had been the most fun he'd had in weeks. They had *listened* to him. His opinions on Asia, the global economy, the banking industry and even western democracy's failings compared to Singapore's soft authoritarianism had actually resonated. He touched his cheek again. The rouge had definitely gone now. So had the Fat Controller. Talek Maxwell was back. Even Penny Black's opiate of the expats was taking hold. Nostalgia surged through his body. His walk turned into a swagger as he made his way through the white faces towards their table.

His new friends were waiting idly, reading their phones. Their glasses needed refilling.

"All right?"

"Yeah, yeah, all good," Simon said. "Here, let's get a photo together."

Simon raised his phone for a selfie. Maxwell threw up an arm.

"No, no, please, not for me."

"What's the matter?"

"Oh, it's just that, look, between us, I'm putting all this down to expenses. I can bill the company tomorrow. Say I was meeting a client. We claim everything over here. But if they see I'm on Facebook the next day, I've had it."

"We won't tag you," Wendy insisted.

"No, better not, just in case."

While the other two snapped a selfie of themselves, Maxwell called out to the barman. "Same again, please."

The trio sat at Maxwell's table. "You don't need to do this," Wendy said.

"No, it's my pleasure, really. It's been good fun."

Maxwell saw Simon was still tapping his phone. "You're not uploading your photos already, are you?"

"Of course not. I'll use the Wi-Fi at the hostel later. I'm reading this link about these Singapore murders. We saw them in the newspapers on the plane coming over. I didn't think Singapore was like it."

"No, it's taken everyone by surprise here," Maxwell said. "Singapore *isn't* like that."

"They reckon he's a white guy."

"An *ang moh*."

"What's that?" Wendy asked.

"Oh, *ang moh* means white guy. Well actually, a taxi driver told me it meant 'red hair', but that's what they call us over here."

"You speak Chinese?"

"Me? God, no. I just know a few of the local swear words, in case I hear them being said about me. Learn the swear words. Listen out for '*ang moh*'. If someone puts the two together, you know you're in trouble."

"That's a good idea."

"You should do it when you're travelling."

"I will."

The barman left the drinks on the table. Wendy gently elbowed Simon in the ribs. "Put the phone away now."

"Sorry, it says here that the guy killed a Singaporean and a prostitute."

Maxwell suddenly saw Aini's face beside him on the pillow, pushing his greasy hair behind his ear, whispering to him, telling him he was special. He wanted to push his pint glass into Simon's throat.

"What do you mean a prostitute?"

"That's what it says here. She was a whore."

"Simon, don't be so derogatory. *Jesus.*"

Maxwell recognised the dismissiveness immediately. The men at the table were from different generations, but shared the same ingrained condescension. Old world values came with the old school tie. Women always had a place, a role to play. And some played whores. Not Aini though. Never Aini.

"It's funny. You used a nationality to describe one and a profession to describe the other."

"How do you mean?"

"You said one was a Singaporean and one was a prostitute."

"Did I?"

"He was just being a knob," Wendy said.

"What did the other one do?" Maxwell asked.

Simon appeared confused by the question. "Which one?"

"The Singaporean one."

"I think it said he was a drug dealer."

"Yes, he was. It's quite interesting, really."

"I didn't think about it. If you're a drug dealer or a prostitute, you're taking your chances here, aren't you?"

"I really wouldn't know. I know that prostitution isn't illegal. But certain drugs crimes come with the death penalty. So there's a clear distinction here."

"Still, I can't think of anything worse, as a woman, I need a shower just thinking about."

Wendy's unexpected comment surprised Maxwell.

"Worse than a drug dealer?" he asked.

"He's selling drugs," Wendy said. "She's selling *herself*."

She spat out the words. Her contempt was real, her ignorance even more so.

"That's true. But there's the other argument, isn't there? Drug dealers destroy people. What is a prostitute's only purpose really? To give other people pleasure; single people, lonely people."

"Fucking dirty old men," Wendy muttered.

Maxwell finished his drink and remembered what it was like to be their age again, to be so sure of one's convictions, to know everything.

"You're probably right."

Maxwell wiped his mouth with the cuff of his white shirtsleeve. He was still wearing his Fat Controller shirt. He hadn't entirely disappeared after all.

"This is all getting a bit too serious. You're supposed to be on holiday," he said, drumming his hands on the table. "Who wants another one?"

"Yeah, if you don't mind," Simon mumbled. His eyes were already closing.

Maxwell checked the time on his phone. "Better yet, my colleagues have got a table at Pangaea. I said I'd join them later. Fancy coming?"

Simon and Wendy giggled like school kids. "To Pangaea? Are you serious?" Simon gushed.

"That's the one on Marina Bay, right, in that glass pavilion thing?" added Wendy.

"That's it, the world's most expensive nightclub."

"But we haven't got that kind of money," Wendy said. "We couldn't possibly . . ."

"It's all on the company," Maxwell interrupted. "It was our big annual charity day today. We made a fortune for good causes so we're celebrating."

"Bloody hell," Simon blurted out. "That would be sick."

"Yeah," Wendy agreed.

"Right then, we'll just have to pop by my place first, because I want to change my shirt and then we'll be straight in. We won't even have to queue."

"Fantastic," Wendy said.

"Yeah, cheers, John."

"It's no problem. It'll be something for your Facebook page anyway. Right, let's have another drink first. I fancy a cider now, haven't had one since university."

Maxwell moved slowly through the Penny Black crowd, squeezing past Ben Sherman shirts and sunburnt faces. He leaned against the bar and waited for the barman. He smiled back at the attractive couple, but his eyes were cold.

Maxwell had already decided to kill them both.

Chapter 28

DR Gary Choo always ran along Mandai Road. He followed the same route and routine five days a week. He parked his Toyota Prius outside his veterinary centre, warmed up in the car park and set off on his daily workout just before sunrise. With the pre-dawn breeze on his back, Dr Choo cherished his invigorating pre-surgery run. Vets in Singapore caught glimpses of the best and worst of humanity. He treated the coiffured poodles, chauffeured to surgery in a maid-polished Mercedes for their regular pedicures. He euthanised the stray cats found in drains with their tails hacked off. He primped the rich. He put down the poor.

So he ran. He covered the long, interminable stretch of Mandai Road that carved a tarmac trench through the forest, with the cicadas almost drowning out the seven-seaters crawling along the Seletar Expressway to get snoozing children to school at such an ungodly hour.

Dr Choo veered left to stay on Mandai Road, avoiding the crematorium on the other side. He didn't need to think about the cremated when he'd be tipping the ashes of dead pets into tiny ceramic urns throughout the day. He always trod lightly through the nature reserve, not wishing to disturb long-tailed macaques.

At Mandai Lake Road, Dr Choo turned and retraced his steps. Occasionally, he jogged along the winding Mandai Lake Road to the Singapore Zoo's entrance, but he had started later this morning and needed time to return and shower before opening his surgery. He always saved the favourite part of his run for the final stretch, deliberately avoiding it on the way out. The raised rock bund that acted as a dam between Upper Seletar Reservoir and the golf course gave him a cool, unblocked view of both the expansive reservoir and the forest. This morning, he ran beneath a handful of fading stars as he trudged towards the eerie image of the rocket-shaped viewing tower that illuminated the horizon.

With less than a hundred metres to go, Dr Choo pulled off his vest and sprinted towards the tower, his perspiring, gleaming torso twisting with every stride. He touched the side of the tower, a silly, superstitious tradition, and turned off his stopwatch. He pushed a couple of fingers into the side of his neck and was pleased with his recovering pulse rate.

Dr Choo was leaning against the rocket tower and stretching his quads when he spotted the graffiti scrawled across one of the viewing tower's pillars. The sun had not yet risen, but the crescent moon provided just enough light to make out the red ink. He found the torchlight function on his phone and read the graffiti:

The Ang Mohs are the men that will not be blamed for nothing.

Despite the clumsy use of a double negative, the graffiti ended with an incongruous full stop. Dr Choo examined closer. The vet knew what it was immediately. In the darkness, blood could appear quite black. Being a responsible citizen, he unlocked his phone and took some photos for his Instagram account. And then he called the police.

Dr Choo was about to give up when the call was finally answered.

"Hello."

"Hey, hello, is that Yishun police?"

"Yah."

"The one near Sembawang Road?"

"Yishun South NPC."

Dr Choo bit his bottom lip. His country's service standards shamed him.

"OK, I found some really bad graffiti."

"What's your name *ah*?"

"I'm sorry?"

"Your name *ah*, sir?"

"Don't you want to know about the graffiti?"

"Need your details first."

"Lucky I'm not having a heart attack, eh?"

"Come again?"

"Never mind. It's Gary Choo. Dr Gary Choo, I run the veterinary centre near here, at the corner of Mandai Road and Sembawang Road. Do you need my blood group?"

"No need."

His country's perennial struggle with sarcasm embarrassed him.

"OK, you need to do something about this graffiti because it's quite xenophobic and it's been written on the side of the rocket tower. And there might be something else there."

"The rocket? Where are you, sir?"

"Upper Seletar Reservoir. The small park there with the lookout tower."

"Oh, that one *ah*."

"Yes."

"OK, sir, I'll write this down."

"Are you going to send someone down? It's racist and it's written on a protected building."

"The rocket?"

"Exactly. And I think there's something else on the wall, it looks like blood."

"With the graffiti?"

"Yes."

"Could it be red paint? It's still dark there, right?"

"I know what blood looks like. I'm a vet. Are you going to send someone here?"

"Yes, sir. Can you see anyone around?"

"Now?"

"Yes, sir."

"Well, no, it's 6.30am. It's just me I think."

"Anyone fishing? That side usually got overnight fishermen."

"You think they'll graffiti the tower and then go back to their fishing?"

"No, sir, they might have seen the vandals."

Dr Choo suddenly felt foolish.

"Oh, right, I see, sorry *ah*. I'll look around, cannot see anyone, it's always deserted at this time, very hard to reach without a car . . . cannot see anyone fishing on the wall over there, only got my car in the car park, no one in the playground; it's too early, sometimes see PUB workers on the water, in their blue boat, but cannot see anyone . . . oh wait, sorry, how come I never saw them just now."

"What?"

"There's a couple sitting on the bench, under the shelter."

"OK."

The officer was barely listening.

"Yah, yah, over by the reservoir, that small field near to the water's edge, got a small shelter. There's one couple, looking at the reservoir. Shall I go over and ask them?"

"OK. Look, I'll see when someone is free to come and take a look."

"Eh, they look like *ang mohs*."

"OK."

"Strange *ah? Ang mohs* here at this time."

"Anyway, I've got your report and . . ."

"Excuse me, sorry *ah*, did you see anyone here just now, at the tower . . . oh no . . . oh, no, no, no."

"What?"

"They're dead."

"What?"

"They're dead."

"Who?"

"These two *ang mohs*, on the bench, it must be their blood on the . . . their chests, they've been stabbed. Oh my god."

"OK, sir, stay there. Don't touch anything, OK. We are on our way."

Dr Choo had seen many corpses in medical school, all sorts of species in various states of decomposition, but he'd never seen anything like this before. The dead couple looked so serene, so *beautiful*.

Wendy and Simon had slumped towards each other on the bench, their heads almost resting on each other's shoulders.

They were still holding hands.

Chapter 29

UPPER Seletar Reservoir Park was small and had been closed off for at least an hour, but Chan was still having trouble controlling the chaos. He was out of his depth and the older, cynical investigators knew it. Too many people crowded the tiny green space. Beyond the restricted area, the reporters did as they were told, naturally, and held off on the questions and flash photography, but the citizen journalists were having a field day. Joggers, dog walkers and a foreign army of gardeners, cleaners and plumbers had gathered to snap the police marquee covering the shelter. It was all over the Facebook feeds that the two dead bodies were *ang mohs*, but no one had managed to get a really good picture yet.

Decent cloud cover was sparing the corpses further indignity, blocking out the sun and delaying the decomposition, but the humidity played havoc with Chan's inferiority complex. Sweat cascaded down his back. He couldn't undo any more shirt buttons without looking like a lounge singer. He hadn't brought a hankie with him either, a rookie mistake. Hankies were old-fashioned, but still less humiliating than barking orders from a drenched face. He was already struggling to stay afloat. He didn't need the humidity to drown him.

"Ah, Detective Inspector Charles Chan. There you are."

Chan could've kissed Professor Chong. The pathologist's booming voice reiterated the younger man's rank. He was effectively underlining Chan's authority. Chong was on probation once, too, sent to Toa Payoh to investigate those graphic murders. He came equipped with a unique intellect, but not the experience. The textbooks never prepared him for the sexually abused, battered bodies of children. He heard the mutterings of the misinformed and ignored the homophobic jokers asking him to explain his whereabouts at the time of the killings. He was a probationary pathologist and he was gay. The victims had been children. So the murderer had to be Chong.

Obviously.

He never forgot the public humiliation. And he still visited those children in his dreams.

Chong gently touched the arm of the perspiring inspector. "Come. Show me your crime scene."

Chan pulled back the flap of the police tent and both men ducked inside.

"My word, they were a handsome couple," Chong said.

"Yeah, young too, on holiday, by their clothes and the tan lines."

"Indeed," Chong said, pulling on his latex gloves. "What else?"

Chan pointed his notepad towards the victims' chests. "One stab wound each, no other obvious injuries and not much blood, so they died elsewhere."

Chong peered over the top of his glasses to examine the bench and the grass around the victims' feet. "Correct."

"And, er, obviously, the previous victim, the loan shark, was found on the other side of the reservoir, with a similar stab wound. I mean, that one had other injuries, also, but the stabbing at the same place; unless it's a copycat, it's got to be the same guy,

"They've been told so many times already not to take photos," Chan said.

"We live in the age of the voyeur," Chong sighed. "If we do not take photos, we do not exist."

Low crouched and focused on the graffiti. "*The Ang Mohs are the men that will not be blamed for nothing,*" he said. "And this full stop is their blood obviously."

"It's not checked yet, but it's blood, obviously," Chan said.

"Obviously."

"I'm sure I've heard it before," Chong said.

"This sentence?" Chan asked.

"Yes, but I can't pin it down."

"It's not one of your bloggers is it, Stanley?"

"No *lah*, but it is the sort of blur shit they'd say. But this is different, clumsy in a different way. *The Ang Mohs are the men that will not be blamed for nothing.* It's upside down, saying they will be blamed for something. It's *ah*, what *ah*?"

"A double negative," Chan declared, feeling pleased with himself. "Two negatives in one sentence turning it into a positive."

"That is correct," Chong nodded.

"*Wah*, not bad *ah*, Charlie. You'll be deputy director next. He couldn't make a double knot with his shoelaces."

"It's too lame to be a double bluff," Chan wondered aloud, "to say I hate *ang mohs* because I am one, cannot be that."

"No. You did well with the double negative, Charlie. Quit while you're almost ahead."

Chong took out his phone and started typing. "I know this expression—*the men that will not be blamed for nothing*. I'm positive that I've read it before."

"What are you doing?"

"Google."

Low rolled his eyes. "Going to solve the case with Google

now, are we?"

"We just might, Inspector Low. I've found it."

The pathologist read out the search results. "The Jews are the men that will not be blamed for nothing, with Jews spelled j-e-w-e-s, written on the side of a Whitechapel road beside a piece of a leather apron in 1888, allegedly by . . . Jack the Ripper."

"Jack the Ripper?" Low repeated. "We're looking for Jack the Ripper now, is it? Is the Boston bastard Strangler involved as well?"

"Does the unimaginative invective ever become as tiresome for you as it does for everyone else, inspector? Look at the phone. Read it, man."

Low read out the Wikipedia page entry. "On the night of September 2, 1888, Jack the Ripper committed two murders in the same night . . ."

"Two murders in the same night," Chong emphasised.

". . . Police at the scene found a bloodstained apron near the crime scene."

"Bloodstains near the crime scene." The pathologist jabbed a chunky digit towards the blood-spattered full stop on the side of the rocket tower.

Low glared at him for the repeated interruptions. "Near the apron, on the wall, blah, blah, blah, written in chalk, was '*the Jews are the men that will not be blamed for nothing.*' It was rubbed away quickly, avoid anti-Semitism, blah blah blah, some say it was Jack the Ripper, others say it was just coincidence because there were xenophobic slogans all over East London at the time."

Chong took back his phone. "I don't want to do your job for you, gentlemen, but you've got two white victims, killed on the same night, with a sharp object, beside xenophobic graffiti at a time when our own multiracial city is suffering xenophobic strife."

"Shit," Chan muttered.

"*Aiyoh*, you buggers watch too many movies. Chong, how do you know this?"

"The graffiti?"

"Yeah."

"Back in my university days. The Whitechapel murders were the Holy Grail for budding pathologists, the biggest manhunt in history, one of the earliest uses of forensic analysis. It's a landmark case, studied on every basic pathology course."

Chan jumped in. "So he's a pathologist then? He's a resident pathologist who knows where and how to kill someone with a sharp object?"

"Don't talk cock, Charlie. You think a college professor in a tweed jacket can take down Dragon Boy, is it? No offence, professor."

"None taken. I'm inclined to agree."

Low shut out the gossiping officers and thought about the graffiti. When he had studied at the London School of Economics, Jack the Ripper was a cult character among Londoners, a genuine tourist attraction. England's warped sensibilities had always fascinated Low. In Singapore, the white collar ruled. The labourer was a lost cause, a source of national and family embarrassment. Only intellectualism earned admiration. Respect came from textbooks. Paper qualifications were the sacred scrolls of a society's success. But in England, the reverse held true. Anti-intellectualism could be rewarded with fame and fortune, chat shows and newspaper columns. Policemen were pariahs and murderers were made men; an exclusive club filled with best-selling authors and celluloid heroes. To be a killer was to be a king. And no one killed like Jack the Ripper. They paid to follow in his footsteps, literally, every day, on the walking tours of East London, to revisit the crime scenes, the pubs and the sites of the leather apron and the anti-Semitic graffiti. In Singapore, it was all about the punishment. In England, it was the crime itself that captivated. True crime. And Jack the Ripper was one of their own, a local boy made bad, to be ogled for all time, the eternally evil celebrity. In his long cloak, deerstalker hat and black leather gloves, Jack the Ripper held out a malevolent hand to every school kid. It was Boy's Own stuff, a hypnotic bogeyman beyond compare. No other country had a monster like Jack the Ripper.

"You little bastard," Low said, standing up. "This is rubbish. *Ang moh*, not *ang moh*, racist, not racist, it's all a waste of time. He's just playing with us, writing scary shit on a wall for fun. You're right, Chong. Only two kinds of people would know about this, right or not? And he's not a pathologist. No. This shit is his passport. This fucker is from London."

Chapter 30

THE Minister of Home Improvement's phone hadn't stopped ringing all morning. The British High Commissioner had relayed concerned messages from the British Prime Minister. They had offered full consular assistance. In the politest of terms, the Singaporean Minister pointed out what the British could do with their assistance. The days of bowing and scraping for the old colonial master ended decades ago. It was an equitable relationship or it wasn't a relationship at all. Besides, Singapore saved its bowing and scraping for when it was absolutely necessary. And these murders had nothing to do with China.

Their images appeared again on the TV on the far wall of the Minister's office. The media had soon found images of them on Facebook. They had been backpacking their way along the Lonely Planet path. Every pit stop had to be recorded for their Facebook friends. There were dozens of photo albums—on beaches, in bars, barely dressed and mostly drunk, with bleary eyes and sun-kissed faces. They were young, photogenic and Caucasian. They were a media dream and the Minister's waking nightmare. He oversaw the crime stats and also had a hand in promoting Singapore's image with potential investors. This case helped neither. He now had a serial killer focusing on the wrong skin tones.

His phone rang again as Deputy Director Chua knocked and

stuck his head around the door. The Minister waved him in, happy to avoid another qualified offer of assistance.

Chua nodded towards the trilling phone. "You want to answer that first?"

"No, no, I know what they want anyway."

The Minister pointed at the TV. An attractive, Eurasian news presenter was reporting from the cordoned-off crime scene at Upper Seletar Reservoir Park. The Minister admired her taste in clothes. She had an appealing locket that stopped just above her plunging neckline. She looked like a perk of the job. And the Minister had been working exceptionally hard. But he saw the photo of his daughter on his desk, smiling at him, and returned to Singapore's serial killer.

"They know what they want on TV, deputy director," he said. And I know what I want. A name, followed by a swift arrest and conviction."

Chua awkwardly sat down.

"Understood, sir. We've got Technology going through Facebook feeds. There's a CCTV camera at Boat Quay, between a McDonald's and Penny Black, the expat pub, that has footage of them walking beside the river, so we're speaking to the staff there. We're getting closer. He's getting sloppy. He didn't dump the bodies in the water. So Professor Chong has more to work with in pathology."

"Need anything else?"

"I need the media to pull back. Driving us crazy for updates."

"Ah, digital media was always going to make this happen. It was so much easier in the old days, wasn't it? I still remember when the media lines were clearly demarcated, when I first came in, back in the late 1990s. The masses had the print media and the Internet belonged to an intellectual minority. Now we've got the masses driving the media angles online. The sheep are chasing the shepherds. It's very troublesome. OK, I'll speak to the newspapers. Tell them to step back from the case and wait for your releases."

"It's not really them. It's the websites, the bloggers. We've now got *The Singapore Truth* site saying we only care about this guy now he's killed *ang mohs*."

"And he's right."

Chua was shocked by the Minister's candour. Such cynicism was way beyond his pay grade. "Well, sir, I can assure you it doesn't make any difference to us."

"But it does to them," the Minister said, gesturing towards the TV again. "The killings confirm every stereotype to our paranoid western friends. To the ignorant, it's another example of pretty, white people dying in a backward Asian country filled with mopeds and dead dogs. And to the educated liberals irritated by our economic success, it's a chance to gloat. You can almost hear them penning their commentaries now. *You see, Singapore? Where did your soft authoritarianism get you in the end? It's no safer there than it is here. You have crime, but no freedom. At least we still have freedom.* The fact that the killer appears to be a Caucasian weakens their argument, but it hasn't taken an edge off the gloating. Western backpackers knew they had to be careful on Thai beaches, but now they're not even safe in draconian Singapore. The western media is positively feasting on the irony."

"So what can we do about it?"

"Catch him. At least our shared goal is a simple one."

"We've never had a case like this since Adrian Lim."

"There's no religious angle to this one, right?"

"No, we don't think so."

"Good, there's an election coming."

"Yes, sir."

"Just settle this case quickly. My door is always open. This one cannot persist."

"Yah, a serial killer, I never expected anything like this."

"A serial killer who kills Caucasians is the problem. Westerners in other countries will empathise with the cultural proximity. He's killed two of their own. You'll have the whole world following your case now."

Chapter 31

"THEY call it missing white woman syndrome." Low was slumped back in the chair, his jaw resting on his chest. "Do you know what that is?"

"I've heard of it," Dr Lai replied.

"Of course you have," the inspector said. "You know exactly what it is. We have to go through this . . . this dance at every session, this ritual, with me playing the social leper, and you playing the healer. When deep down you know, you must know, that it's all rubbish, that you need me to take care of them, because they are sicker than I'll ever be. We both know that. But you can't admit that. You must believe you can heal the sick with your lithium."

"We don't heal. We treat."

"I'm sure that makes you feel better when the salary clears every month."

The psychiatrist's office was clean and mostly bare with a vase of fresh flowers on the desk and a couple of neatly folded newspapers beside her daily planner.

Low found the newspapers amusing. "You brought in the papers today?"

"They gave them to me at the MRT station."

"No, they offered them to you outside the MRT station, but

normally you don't take them. I've never seen them here before. You don't want the ink smudges on your fingers and clothes, not when you can read the latest news on your phone and avoid the risk of opening out a newspaper and brushing against a stranger on the busy train and blushing through your make-up, right or not?"

"I just picked up the papers to be polite."

Low rubbed his hands along his jeans. His doctor had noted the absence of shorts and vest, his usual, antagonistic attire. The policeman was wearing his jeans and a smarter, almost clean, T-shirt, his work attire, ready to go into battle, reaching for another high. He was already probing and insulting her. His mania was taking hold again. There was nothing like a serial killer to make her incorrigible patient feel alive. Lai squeezed her thighs together. His interrogations felt like violations.

"No, you didn't," Low sneered, still rubbing his thighs. "You picked them up because two pretty white people stared back at you from the front pages. Their toothpaste smiles caught your gaze. They didn't look like the usual faces on our front pages, right or not? People like them don't get murdered, not in Asia, not in Singapore, not even in the movies. Those are the rules. The black guys get killed. The Latinos and the Chinese definitely get killed. We always get killed. We're either the IT guy or the triad gangster and we're lucky if we even get a name, let alone make it until the end of the show. But white women are angels."

"That's not why I took the newspaper, no."

"Of course it was."

"But there is research to suggest that the idea of a 'damsel in distress' is often Caucasian, and sometimes blonde," Lai admitted. "The popular imagery is often fixed in childhood, coming from our exposure to predominately western folk stories and fairytales—*Cinderella*, *Rapunzel* and more recently with *Frozen*.

Social scientists have highlighted the phenomenon, particularly in the US, of media coverage focusing more on cases that involve missing young white women from affluent backgrounds, compared to other ethnicities and social backgrounds."

"And why do you think that is?"

"Well, based on the research . . ."

"No, forget the research. What do *you* think?"

"It's not relevant what I think."

"Yes it is. If you tear up all your theories and pull back the curtain, you see what we really are. You know what we are. We are racist. Even after death, we're still racist. We rank people, skin colour, economic background, even in death. Hundreds die in Iraqi car bombs all the time, it's a footnote. A few people die at the Boston Marathon, it's an international tragedy. A little white blonde girl goes missing on holiday, it's a front-page story for years."

"Yes, I'm aware of that. It's sometimes called the hierarchy of death."

"There you go. You buggers have even got a term for it. The hierarchy of death. Bloody hell."

"That obviously bothers you."

"Of course it bothers me. *Wah lau.* My Technology team are all working overtime right now, cannot go home to their families, working their balls off. You know why? Racism. They are working round the clock to feed our racism."

"I don't understand."

"Look. Every Facebook page, every photo, every newsfeed ever visited, every aspect of social media that was uploaded or read by our dead *ang mohs* is being analysed right now."

"Because they were murder victims."

"Because they were *white* murder victims. We've got American and Australian media covering the case now. Why? They weren't from either country. We've got New Zealand and Canada offering their condolences. Why? We've got the Government giving us more men. Why?"

Lai frowned at her ranting patient. "Singapore has a serious killer. He has killed four people."

"Please. That one was obvious. Once he killed the second one, no point in stopping."

"OK, let's assume what you are saying is true. Yes, institutional racism is commonplace. Yes, the human mind still struggles with inherent prejudices. I have read studies that show Israeli deaths get twice as much media coverage as Palestinian deaths. The evidence is there."

"Exactly."

"But is this anything new? I know how capable and intuitive you are as an investigator. None of this should come as a surprise to you. And yet, the aggression is obvious. Why do you think that is?"

Low rubbed the stubble on his chin.

"Because I asked those bastards to get me involved once my boy was involved. And they told me to stick with the bloggers. When he died, when that fucker stuck a screwdriver through his heart, they didn't give a shit. A *Singaporean*. And they didn't give a shit. Now I sound like a bloody blogger, but fuck it, it's the truth. Dragon Boy was doing it for me, helping me to catch this bastard, and for what? He died for nothing. He's been sliced up for the autopsy, cremated and gone. But those two, on your newspaper there, passing through with Daddy's credit card, gave this country nothing. And look at us, look at the whole country, running around like headless chickens."

"So really, this is about Dragon Boy."

"No *lah*. It isn't about Dragon Boy at all. That's the point."

Chapter 32

AT the front door of Maxwell's apartment, a young Malay man pulled off his motorcycle helmet and tapped on the door with a gloved knuckle.

"Just coming."

The courier took the pizzas from his heatproof satchel and waited expectantly. The girl in the office had said the double cheese pizza delivery was a *mat salleh*. *Mat sallehs* usually gave a tip.

Maxwell opened the door. He was wearing only boxer shorts. His stomach flopped over his waistband like a loose tarpaulin flapping in a storm. "How much was it again?"

"Er, $34 with the garlic bread, sir."

Maxwell went through the notes in his wallet. His TV played loudly in the background, catching the delivery guy's attention. He rubbernecked over the fat white guy's shoulder.

"You watching my TV, there?"

"No, no, sir."

"It's OK. What do you think of it? Sixty-five inch, curved, 4K."

"Damn *shiok*, boss."

"Yeah, she always liked that TV. Anyway, what was it, $34, right? Hey, let's make it an even 40."

"*Wah*, thanks man."

"No problem, have a good night."

The delivery guy felt like he owed the generous tipper something. "Terrible ah, on TV."

"What's that?"

"The two *mat sallehs*. Sorry, I mean the two, er, Caucasians on the news. Very sad."

"Yes, it was. I heard it's four people altogether."

"Is it?"

"Yes. Anyway, thanks for the pizza."

Maxwell closed the door. He didn't want to say or do something the delivery guy might regret and he had found the cigarette smell nauseating.

But his mood had improved in recent days. The media's hypocrisy had entertained him. The Penny Black pub had been packed with potential eyewitnesses so he knew it was only a matter of time. He was determined to enjoy himself.

After a couple of slices of pizza, he returned to his repair job in the kitchen. Earlier in the day, he had bought a new plug socket plate to replace the blackened, scarred one. He worked quickly with his yellow Phillips screwdriver. He couldn't bring himself to throw it away, or even clean it properly. There were still traces of what he had lost. The first two screws went in easily, but the third proved trickier, requiring real force in the wrist to drive through the incomplete thread.

Whistling his favourite Britpop tunes from the 90s, Maxwell was about to start on the fourth when an unattractive, sweaty Chinese guy filled the screen. The harsh camera light did the guy no favours on Maxwell's 65-inch TV. Ugly people didn't belong in high definition. Maxwell read the crawler beneath the man's perspiring armpits:

Breaking news—Anti-foreigner rally planned for Speakers Corner.

On screen, Harold Zhang blinked in the stinging lights, ignoring the uncomfortable beads of sweats attacking his temples like bluebottles around a horse's eyeball.

"This is too much already," Zhang said to the reporter. "Singaporeans are scared of this serial killer. But the Government is only scared when this serial killer attacks foreigners. So we must gather to make a real statement."

Maxwell smiled. The idiot on TV had a point.

Maxwell turned to the laptop on the breakfast bar beside him and found *The Singapore Truth* homepage. He now had the site bookmarked. He was curious to see what the repugnant fool had to say this time. He left the final screw for the time being. Instead he reached for another slice of pizza and opened Zhang's latest blog posting:

WHITE MEN CAN JUMP ALL OVER SINGAPORE

Two ang mohs are killed and now the Gahmen wakes up. Two ang mohs are murdered and the Gahmen decides they cannot tahan already. Four people killed, but only the last two count. Two white people are better than two brown people. Two foreigners are better than two Asians. What about Singaporeans? Heck care lah. What about the first foreigner? Heck care lah. She was a prostitute only. But we are the whores already. We are being screwed every day.

Maxwell stopped reading the drivel. As expected, Zhang's only salient point was lost in the xenophobic whining. But that didn't particularly bother Maxwell. He only ever wanted the moron to push buttons on his behalf and he found the headline mildly amusing. But the uncouth "whore" references were too much, so unnecessarily rude and undeserving. There was no need to prolong the pain.

Chapter 33

ZHANG and half a dozen comrades with neatly parted, oily hair stood together on the makeshift stage. The sun's relentless rays filtered through the trees at Hong Lim Park and cast them all in an unforgiving light. When they joined hands and raised their arms aloft to salute the crowd, they revealed the sweat rings beneath their armpits. The applause was generous, but soft. The crowd was small, almost lost in Chinatown's tiny green lung. Committed activists waved xenophobic placards, calling for foreigners to go home. Tattooed Chinese gangsters posing as legitimate political opponents screamed, "true Singapore for true Singaporeans" whenever the chance presented itself. This was Speakers' Corner, the island's tokenistic nod towards free speech. The location was handy for many Singaporeans. Many came to Chinatown for the cheap shopping and food. Speakers' Corner was a convenient, quiet shortcut to the MRT station.

Zhang's colleagues retreated to the rickety plastic seats at the back of the stage, wiping their foreheads as they sat down. Their self-appointed leader moved towards the lectern. He grinned at his wife, sitting with his colleagues over his shoulder, at the edge of the stage. Li Jing crossed her legs and ignored him. That was all the encouragement he needed.

"I see your posters," he began slowly. "We will pick out

prizes for the best posters later, but I see them. Singapore for Singaporeans. Foreigners go home. Keep our jobs here. Protect our borders. They all say the same thing. We are strangers in our own country. We go in a shop or take a bus and we cannot find anyone who speaks our language. But we cannot say anything. We cannot say anything at all. If we speak up, we are whacked by our own government. If we speak up, we are xenophobic. If we complain got no space, we are racist. We complain got no job, we are ungrateful, typical Singaporeans; always complain, no perspective, strawberry people, bruise so easily.

"But I'll tell you this. My friend on stage, who will speak later, middle manager, got qualifications and experience. He was replaced by a PRC. Now he's a taxi driver. Also up here, got one lady, work in a shopping centre for 20 years, the same department store, replaced by a Filipino. They say her English was not good enough. She never smiled enough. They say her salary and CPF make her too expensive. Now, she helps her cousin at his coffee shop. Is Singapore helping these Singaporeans?"

Zhang paused for the muted indignation. The crowd was pitiful, the lowest yet. The anti-government novelty was wearing off. Heated anger was hard to sustain in an air-conditioned nation. Not everyone had Zhang's resolve. Not everyone was married to Zhang's wife.

He nodded at the roars of dissent, privately counting the numbers. He figured around 500 had turned up, maybe 200 were rubberneckers, 200 were hardcore supporters, 20 or so were hooligans looking for a fight on a lazy Sunday afternoon and the rest were journalists, undercover officers and patronising tourists wandering through to catch Singapore's nascent democracy in action. Zhang would record at least a thousand in his blog later. The mainstream media would go no higher than 300 and their respective audiences would be none the wiser.

Zhang glimpsed over his shoulder at his wife. She was reading her phone. Perfect.

I'll get your attention now.

"They say citizens come first, always come first and we do. First for National Service, first to take our CPF, first to take our jobs," he shouted, pausing until the last of the easy laughs faded away.

"And now first to take our lives. Now we know where we really live, right? This monster, this IKEA Killer, is like nothing before. He kills a prostitute. Nothing. She's a prostitute. She doesn't count. He kills a Singaporean, definitely doesn't count. Then we find out he's an *ang moh*. Last time we bring in foreigners to take our jobs, now we bring in foreigners to take our lives."

A smattering of boos filled the heavy, humid air, but a dissenting voice shouted, 'Bullshit'. Other mocking jeers could clearly be heard. Zhang had overreached. The dissenters were probably plants, scattered among his followers by undercover officers. Or they could have been tourists and expats. He had spotted one or two in the crowd. Or they could have been bleeding-heart liberals, with their overseas degrees, foreign ideals and wishy-washy philosophy. They bothered him more than the foreigners. But the boos were a misstep. In a crowd this small, Zhang's GoPro cameras would almost certainly pick up the negativity. The booing had just lengthened his editing process.

"OK, OK, this killer is a one-off. But he is an *ang moh*. And now, he has killed two *ang mohs*. And now everybody is here, the foreign media is here. The newspapers are here. There are TV cameras here. It's not about us anymore. It's about them. It's not about our dead Singaporean. It's about *their* dead foreigners. Two dead *ang mohs* holding hands at Upper Seletar and now everyone gets excited. Now the *Gahmen* say they will do anything to catch the killer, more police, more money, more everything. Who are they doing this for? For us or for *them*?

"I'll say one more thing, OK, one last point, and yes, it's controversial. But this IKEA Killer is a monster. He must be stopped. And we support the police in catching this man, doesn't matter where he is from. But he showed us what we already know. For 50 years, we been told we *need* foreigners, cannot survive without foreigners, got no natural resources. Our economy would collapse without foreigners. What does it tell us? Foreigners are more important than us. All our lives, we hear the same message. Foreigners are more important than us. That's what it means. That's what they are really saying. And now, at a time when our country is scared, when we must all be helping each other, we are still getting the same message. Even in death, foreigners are more important than us. Frankly speaking, I hope the police catch this animal. But he's told us something that I think we already knew. Dead or alive, we don't count anymore."

Zhang brought his wife to the front of the stage to acknowledge the applause. The event's other speakers flanked them on either side. Zhang waved to the crowd. "Should sell quite a few T-shirts today," he whispered to his wife.

"Didn't think racism was that popular," she hissed, waving to the crowd.

"The truth always sells. In the end."

In the middle of the crowd, Low scooped out the last of his buttered sweet corn from a polystyrene cup. He thought about his dead *kaki* and tried not to laugh. Dragon Boy was many things, most of them unpleasant. But he was never a national martyr. Now he was a poster boy for unhinged nationalists. In truth, the gangster was not in the least patriotic, always selling his services to the highest-bidding capitalist. In that sense, he was an authentic Singaporean. Tiger had been the unswerving patriot, loyally committed to both the flag and the biggest crime syndicate in the country.

But Low had seen enough. The diatribe was as dull as expected, but he had at least gleaned something from the tiresome blogger's rant. How did Zhang know the victims were found holding hands? That was never made public. Being attractive, white and dead was enough for the tabloids. Singapore didn't need the handholding adding to the melodrama.

Low pulled his cap lower and eased through the crowd, his eyes always pinned to the feet of passing strangers. He brushed past a broad-shouldered man and made his way back to the temporary sweet corn stall. There was always time for a second cup before returning to the office.

The man with the broad shoulders glared at the runt scurrying past in the baseball cap, but continued to applaud Zhang and his wife on stage. He put his fingers between his lips and whistled loudly.

When the clapping stopped, he waited for the crowd to shuffle towards the best poster competition being held on the field.

And then Maxwell slowly made his way to the stage.

Chapter 34

RAGE weakened most men, but Low was a rare exception. He knew that. So did his employers. The leash was short, but it was still there. They couldn't cut him loose. They needed his anger and so did he. Fury fuelled him. It blew the clouds away and allowed him to think clearly. The only man who matched Low in this regard was Tiger. There was little to choose between them. Low caught the old loan shark in the end, but the inspector never kidded himself. He had the law on his side. Nothing else.

Chan wasn't blessed with such a dubious attribute. Low watched carefully as the younger inspector made his way through the coffee shop crowd. The zip on his trousers was partially undone and the back of his shirt flapped over his belt. His matted fringe stuck to his forehead and his puffy eyes sagged. The recent promotion had aged him. Low channelled the inner loathing, both for himself and his quarry, until it consumed him and propelled him forward. Most men succumbed to the weight of expectation, to the horror, in the end.

As he put two cups of *teh tarik* on the table, Chan looked like most men.

"Eh, Charlie, you OK or not?"

Chan didn't bother to correct his old mentor. "I'm fine. Why?"

"You look like shit, man."

"So would you if this was your case."

"I always look like shit."

"I was being polite."

"No need." Low sipped his drink. "This *teh tarik* damn *shiok*."

"It's Geylang."

"That's why."

"I did my first police cadet work here."

"Everybody did at some point, right?"

"Crime capital of Singapore."

"Sex capital of Singapore."

"Yah."

Chan's gaze drifted past the packed coffee shop tables and street traffic. "Started simple with the prostitutes, aggressive soliciting in the coffee shops. Then moved on to the pimps, *wah*, the real scum. Selling fake virgins from Cambodia and Vietnam. Then move onto to the brothel owners, the *towkays* . . ."

"And then move on to Tiger."

"That was you, not me."

"What's your point?"

"It never, you know, *stops*."

"Of course, otherwise we'd be estate agents. Come on *lah*."

Chan faced Low directly. "He's not going to stop, is he?"

"No."

"Until I catch him."

"*We* catch him."

"How?"

"How what? How we catch him? Same as always, man. He fucks up or we win the lottery."

"Yeah, and everyone's a detective now. Everyone is telling us how to solve the case, online, overseas, everywhere."

"Balls to them."

Chan concentrated on stirring his tea. He hesitated before

speaking.

"I'm sleeping on the sofa. Well, I'm not sleeping at all. I'm lying on the sofa, whenever I go home."

Low nodded. "Yah, I been there."

"You never been married."

"No, but I been there," Low jabbed his forehead. "Probably why I never got married. They say don't take it home, right? Don't take 'it' home. I am the 'it'. I can't take me home to anyone."

"It's happening to me."

"No, it's not. You're just having a shitty case. This guy picked your probationary year to kill four people. It's not your fault."

"The IKEA Killer," Chan whispered.

"I know, right? The IKEA Killer. I could kill that blogger."

"Good name though."

"Great name. Always needs a screwdriver. Brilliant name. The bastard."

"How was the rally?" Chan asked, eager to talk about something else.

"Ah, the usual shit. But someone's definitely leaking him information. You never told anyone about the *ang mohs* holding hands right?"

"Of course not."

"He mentioned it on stage."

"What? How?"

"How you think? Greed. The uniforms get paid shit, cadets even less. You remember last time. Overworked and underpaid. Now it's even worse, everyone's anti-government, everyone thinks the newspapers are shit and these bloggers are gods. Everyone's online, moaning, leaking and hacking. The world's upside down, man."

"Are you serious?"

"You think they're happy earning $2,000 a month to scratch

their balls at crime scenes? Zhang makes more with one blog."

"It's not helping us though, is it?"

"Ah, doesn't matter anymore. Everything is about this case now. You get the lab report back from Chong?"

"Yah, the blood on the full-stop was theirs. The grass was damp, so got some footprints, but with gardeners there every day and construction workers renovating the rocket tower, will take some time. Hair and fibre confirm it's the same guy, blondish Caucasian, but the wounds were cleaner this time."

"Of course, he's getting quicker, more precise. He's experienced now. How's the search going?"

"It looks like they were at Boat Quay, witnesses are coming forward now. We're checking CCTV. A description should come through soon. We're doing interviews at all the expat bars and hangouts, banks and trading firms around the Singapore River and Marina Bay. Been told to tread carefully. Chua keeps saying, 'Not every expat is a murderer, you know.'"

"Fuck him, worry about our guy. He's getting sloppy. He'll be picked up on CCTV around Boat Quay. You almost know enough already. He's a white-collar expat, working in the CBD area with a decent, well-paid job, probably in the Blair Plain area. Knock on doors around there."

"Why?"

"He's not dumping them in a taxi. He's got a car for that, except for the first one, that was on foot, local, fleeing the scene of the crime, cannot drag a body from a car right beside a coffee shop that was open at the time. And he's English."

"Ah, your Jack the Ripper theory."

"Balls to you, he's from England OK, probably London, or near London. Look for a heavy, blond English guy with money and a car and living near the CBD."

"That could be half of Marina Bay."

"You want me to point out someone in the street, is it?"

"I wish you would."

Low felt sorry for Chan, but also envied him. The puppy-dog eagerness to appease and impress unforgiving masters remained. He knew that his friend was desperate for fresh insight. But Low had nothing beyond the obvious. So he spoke slowly, hoping that the words carried greater gravitas than they deserved.

"Go home to your wife. She's pregnant, angry and confused. Kiss and make up. And try and rest."

"I need to go back to the office."

"No point. Might as well go home and recharge the batteries first."

"What for?"

"So you can be fresh when he kills again," Low said as he finished his tea.

Chapter 35

ONE or two stragglers spotted Harold Zhang running across Hong Lim Park. The grassy field was reasonably small, but he laboured to cover the distance. Most of the crowd had left, wandering across to People's Park Complex for a cheap dinner as Speakers' Corner returned to its natural state: silent and ignored.

Zhang struggled to stabilise either his heavy breathing or his thumping heart. He wasn't fit. He loathed physical exercise. Only his fingertips enjoyed a daily workout, tapping out his foaming rants at the keyboard. She had never liked exercise either. She had never bothered with her diet either. Friday night trips to Katong for curry *laksa* had been a happy tradition since their initial fumblings of courtship, a bowl of something hot and spicy and then a cuddle at East Coast Park. They were the happiest days of Zhang's life. His desk job was monotonous and the salary poor. He was unknown, even on his office floor, but he was loved at home. At least, he *felt* loved.

And he adored her.

Australia changed everything. Suddenly, *laksa* was replaced by lattes. The mahjong table was shoved in a cupboard, swapped for Pilates and a yoga mat. Their old, happy lifestyle now embarrassed her. Money was less important than quality of life, whatever that was. She wanted to be *happy*. She wanted surfers and sunsets. She wanted to live in a love song.

In a puerile act of rebellion, Zhang went to the opposite extreme. He ate more and exercised even less. He founded a mahjong and poker group with other displaced Chinese expats and gambled away whatever money the couple had left. He started a blog mocking the shallow, fickle hypocrisy of Asians seeking a western utopia that didn't exist. The blog exploded. Advertisers besieged him. He found fame and fortune by screaming in front of his laptop. His self-diagnosed therapy earned him a second act. He became a cult hero for the disenfranchised, a mouthpiece for the oppressed and a rallying cry for closet racists. His sudden wealth made their return to Singapore inevitable. He had saved her from herself, from her woolly-headed ideas about lifestyle choices and rat races. He had taken her away from *him*, that bastard surfer. Zhang couldn't compete with him physically, so he killed him off with a keyboard. And she hated him for it. He had saved his marriage, but lost her love forever. Zhang could live with the trade off.

But he was paying for his lack of fitness now. Adrenaline propelled his chubby legs, but his clogged arteries were failing him. He wiped away salty stinging tears of sweat, but it didn't improve his vision. He stumbled towards the incongruous blue and white two-storey building at the edge of the park. Zhang seemed to remember the preserved property once being a post office, but he wasn't sure. The sign above the Kreta Ayer Neighbourhood Police Post bounced before him, swaying from side to side like a ship's horizon line. Zhang often mocked the oxymoronic irony of the neighbourhood police post. The Kreta Ayer station was built in a field, surrounded by hotels and shopping centres. There was no neighbourhood, but there was Speakers' Corner. The police post had ringside seats for the boys in blue and their binoculars. Zhang couldn't speak without consulting the authorities first for a permit. Zhang couldn't speak without always being surrounded. He was General Custer in a Chinatown field, outflanked at every turn.

But Zhang needed them now. He felt the blood on his fingertips. He really needed them now.

He couldn't run for much longer. His legs were shaking and his hamstrings tightening, screaming at him to stop. His arms flopped to his sides. He couldn't keep them up, couldn't raise his fists, couldn't wipe away the falling stars obscuring his view of the police station, couldn't keep going, but couldn't stop. His wife kept him going. His wife allowed him to push past the pain.

Screw your Pilates, screw your yoga, screw your surfer dude and screw you.

Zhang ran up to the glass door, pushed hard and lost his footing. He was falling, tumbling, his knees smashing against the fading, cream-coloured tiles. There was more blood now, blood on his knees to go with the fingers. Grabbing one of the blue chairs for support, he got up. His breathing had been replaced by a harsh rasping that scared him, but he couldn't stop. He reached out towards the counter aggressively. Staff Sergeant Razali Othman instinctively stood up. The small police post was quiet and orderly and representative of the society Zhang was so keen to ridicule. The waiting area was empty, a stuffy, nondescript room with rows of blue seats. But now Zhang needed the tools of state he so often mocked. He wanted his share of Singapore's law and order.

The officer looked at the crumpled, bleeding, middle-aged Chinese man staggering towards his polished counter. Without thinking, he went for the holster, placing his hand over his Taurus Model 85.

"You OK, sir?"

"You know who I am," Zhang sputtered, using the last of his

strength to stand up straight.

The officer leaned over his counter, not taking his right hand off his holstered gun. "No, sir."

"Don't bluff. I put on the show outside. Harold Zhang. *The Singapore Truth.*"

The officer blushed. He didn't expect to meet a celebrity today. "Mr Zhang. Yes. You OK or not?"

"Read this."

Zhang threw a crumpled note onto the counter and then lurched sideways, catching himself against the side of a chair, correcting himself, eyes drooping, before flopping into the seat.

The officer read the handwritten note.

Dear Mr Zhang,

Your show was painful. Now get ready for mine.

Yours truly,
The IKEA Killer

P.S. Love the name.

The officer dropped the damp note on his desk. He didn't want to get the blood on his fingers.

Chapter 36

STANLEY Low powered along the footpath, his younger, fitter colleague struggling to keep up. Their impromptu dash from the car park to the adjacent Kreta Ayer Neighbourhood Police Post defined their personalities. Charles Chan, lagging behind, moved like he was treading water, almost drowning in his own anxiety. He didn't want murderers and mayhem. He craved paperwork and his Punggol apartment. He wasn't a bad investigator. On the contrary, he was diligent, brave and committed. But he disliked uncertainty and chaos. He wasn't used to either. He was Singaporean.

"Slow down, Stanley," he croaked, his throat pulling, his mouth drying.

The first of the evening's dog walkers stepped back to allow the inspectors to pass. Behind the police post, the anti-immigration stage was being dismantled. The discarded leaflets and xenophobic banners were being swept up by foreign workers, the irony lost on everyone except the foreign workers earning less than minimum wage. The last of the anti-immigration activists made their way across the field, discussing the success of the rally and making preliminary plans for the next outdoor event. They ignored the platoon of foreign workers clearing up the mess they had left behind.

"Balls to you, Charlie. Faster *lah*."

Low was flying, gliding across the concrete, his feet barely touching the ground. He relished the kaleidoscope of colours dazzling before him, his brain fizzing like champagne, toasting his own brilliance. He was the Lone Ranger, the man in the white fucking hat, ready to ride in and save the day. Low lived for these moments. And these moments kept him alive.

He was reaching for the door, gripping the handle, one more step and he was in, ready for his cowering blogger, his cornered prey, his stepping stone to catching a madman. The IKEA Killer was about to kill again. And he was going to kill Harold Zhang; two birds, one stone.

Low was at the desk, fists pressed against the surface, glaring into terrified eyes before Chan had reached the police post.

"OK, man, where is he? Bring him out here."

Low was shouting. His bipolar condition came with only two volume settings—loud or mute. The voice had no middle ground. Nor did the man.

"Er, who?"

The young officer appeared utterly distraught.

"The Jade Emperor. Who do you think? Harold bloody Zhang. Get him out here."

Chan almost fell through the door, breathless and drenched in perspiration. "Tea, *prata*, Geylang, Chinatown in 20 minutes cannot make it."

"*Yah lah*, never mind that now."

Low raised a hand to silence his colleague and turned back to the wide-eyed boy in the blue uniform with polished buttons. "Get him now."

"Er, sorry *ah*, I need to see some ID first. You know, security, just in case, you are . . ."

"What? The killer? You think we *ang mohs* is it? Where did

you study, the Braille school?"

Low pulled his ID from his wallet. "Look, there you go, Captain *Kiasi*. I'm Detective Inspector Stanley Low from Technology and this is Charlie Chan from the 1930s."

"Stanley," Chan interrupted.

"*Yah lah, yah lah*, OK, sorry for the sarcasm, Officer . . ." Low peered at the nameplate. "Razali Othman. *Wah*, you're double screwed *ah* with a name like that in Singapore. Cannot be prime minister, cannot run the police force. But you can get me Harold Zhang."

"He went home already."

Low heard an explosion behind his frontal lobe. He clenched his fists until the knuckles turned white. Through gritted teeth, his sarcastic smile came out all wrong, horrifying the policeman and alarming Chan. The inspector instinctively moved towards Low to protect Othman, but his sudden move had the opposite effect. Now the teenager had two inspectors towering over his desk, crushing his confidence.

Low spoke slowly. "Why did you let him go home?"

"He asked if me he could go home. And then he just left."

Low was incredulous.

"Oh, is it? So if I ask to have sex with your sister, you'll say yes?"

"He said he was scared. He said the note was handwritten and left on the stage."

"Where is the note?" Chan asked.

"Uh it's here under the desk."

"Take your time," Low said, as Othman found a pair of leather motorcyclist's gloves to put on. "The killer's got all day."

The uniformed officer laid out the note carefully on the counter. "Mr Zhang came in all scared, waving this note. He had blood on his fingertips, from these blood streaks here on the note.

They were still wet when he came in."

"So the note was written just before," Chan said. "Why take such a risk?"

"Don't know. And then?" Low snapped.

"Mr Zhang got jittery. He was sweating, scared, running around, kept looking out of the window, saying that the killer was outside, waiting for him, shouting all the time. He was out there right now. So Mr Zhang said he had to get away."

"And then?"

"I asked him to wait, have a cup of water while I called CID, obviously I knew this was serious."

"Obviously."

"But he just got too distracted and left while I was on the phone."

"And then? Why didn't you chase after him?" Low asked.

"I couldn't."

"Why?"

"Cannot leave the police post unattended, sir."

"You are the only officer working today?"

"No, sir."

"So where were the others?"

"Outside. Our boss told us to watch the rally."

"*Aiyoh*, these buggers. If you were asked to think out of the box, would your head explode?"

"Sorry, sir, but my orders were to . . ."

"This isn't Nazi Germany. You're a policeman. Think for yourself."

"Leave him, Stanley," Chan said.

"Leave him? This idiot sends a guy back out into the arms of our serial killer and we're supposed to do what exactly? Give him a promotion?"

"He was scared, sir, thought the killer was waiting for him,"

Othman muttered.

"He was inside a fucking police post."

"I'm sorry."

Low eyeballed the chastised officer. "No, now you're disappointed because you let him go. When he's dead, then you can be sorry. When he's been stabbed in the heart, then you have my permission to be sorry."

"How long have you been in uniform?" Chan asked, pursuing a different tack.

"Nine months already."

"*Wah*, nine months," Chan continued. "That's quite a long time, no? After nine months, they had me out in Geylang chasing pimps and bookies."

"Yah, I done that already."

"So you got some experience, man."

"Yah."

"Yah, so it's a bit surprising that you didn't wait for us first. He was obviously in danger and not thinking straight, but you let him leave."

Othman fiddled with one of his polished silver buttons. "Yah, that was a mistake. But he was so scared. He said he was easy to recognise around here. Everybody reads *The Singapore Truth*, but nobody knows where he lives."

Low's eyes widened. "*The Singapore Truth*?"

"Sir?"

"You mentioned his website, *The Singapore Truth*, no one else did, but you brought it up."

"I don't understand, sir."

Low nodded. "Everybody reads *The Singapore Truth*, you said. I know Inspector Chan doesn't. I do only because I have to, even though I'd rather stick mahjong tiles up my arse, but you said everybody reads *The Singapore Truth*. What you mean is, you read it, right?"

"Well . . ."

"It's OK. It's not a crime to read it, yet. I'm sure the Obscenity Act will find a loophole at some point. But you read it. Your friends read it. I'm sure the guys here read it. You're his target audience, his demographic. You're a bit younger maybe, but you're in a dead-end job, only got basic diploma, no degree, so not much prospects, right? *The Singapore Truth* says what you're thinking, what you're saying to your *kakis* in the coffee shop. It's true Singapore for true Singaporeans, right? You can't say it in uniform, but you can read it, you can share it with your private account. You heard him out there on the PA system. The foreigners taking *your* jobs, *your* money. Last time it was just the *mat sallehs*, but now everyone is doing it, right or not? But you can't say anything. You can't say a word. You are part of the silent, seething majority who no longer have a voice. You complain and you're a xenophobe. You complain in that uniform and you're fired."

Othman took half a step back. "No, sir, that's not true. I'm not a racist, sir."

"No, you're not a racist. You're really not. You're just angry, like three million other citizens being squashed in their own country, but you can't say that, only Harold can say that. And if I got my tech guys to check your phone and maybe the computers in this office, his site would be frequently visited, right?"

Othman said nothing.

"Of course. But I don't care about that. My problem is when you saw Harold Zhang burst through your door, talking cock, you didn't see a crazy old Chinaman, you saw a celebrity. And your brain turned to *ice kachang*. You didn't concentrate. You were star-struck and you let him go. And now you've got to live with that. That's your punishment. Because your hero is going to die tonight."

Chapter 37

ONLY the strawberries and cream were missing. Chan watched the verbal tennis being played between his boss and his friend, his head moving from left to right like a courtside umpire. But he never interjected. He was aware of the career-ending repercussions of questioning the CID's deputy director. And he never interrupted Stanley Low, not when he was like this. Rabid dogs do not appreciate being poked with a stick.

Anthony Chua stood behind his desk in a pitiful effort to retain his authority within his own glass cubicle. The Major Crime Division was supposed to be investigating leads, chasing witnesses at both the Speakers' Corner rally and Penny Black, hunting down CCTV footage. But Chua saw them, sneaking peeks above their computer screens, interpreting the body language, trying to lip-read. Chua's glass cubicle demarcated his authority, an imposing monument to his shiny nameplate. But it was also a goldfish bowl. Everyone watched while he went around in circles.

"Look, I'm not interested in your relationship with Harold Zhang," he said slapping his hand on the desk to intimidate Low. It didn't. "You had no right to be there. And as for you inspector, if you seek input, you come to me. You don't go to this, this, blogger hunter."

Low chuckled. "Eh, not bad *ah*. Blogger hunter. You make that one up yourself?"

"You want to be fired?"

"Yes. Every day. Can you fire me? No. So let's save time. Let's do what we did in science class when I was in primary six. I'll get my dick out. Then you get your dick out. Charlie can measure them, then we move on with our lives. Can?"

Chua was astonished by his anger. The thought of violence had always appalled him. He was a scholar, not a fighter. He grew up with textbooks, not tantrums. He was smarter than that, better than that, *bigger* than that. Violence was the last refuge of the feeble-minded. They fought on the playground concrete because they couldn't fight in the classroom. Chua was raised to believe that. Chua *knew* that. But now he was fighting himself, waging an internal war to hold back, to suppress his emotions and deny himself the illicit, unbridled joy of ripping the inspector's face off.

"No, no," Chua said slowly, breathing deeply. "I'm not going to do that."

"No dick-measuring?"

"No."

"Good, because mine looks like a lady's lipstick."

Chua sighed. "Tell me about Harold Zhang."

"Harold Zhang? OK, five or six years ago, he was nothing, *ikan bilis*, waste of time. A middle manager, earning $3,000 a month, kissed all the right arses and still got retrenched. He says he didn't, says he left the job to follow his wife to Australia, but he did. We checked with the company. Then he goes to Australia and of course he hates it, cannot get a job because of their Australians-first policy—the same thing he wants here by the way—so he ends up doing odd jobs, really demeaning stuff. Some people call him 'Chink' at the shopping centre and suddenly he misses Singapore, especially after his wife starts shagging a surfer. So now he loves Singapore and Singaporeans, but really hates foreigners. So he puts the two together in a blog and gets rich on racism."

"Why are you watching him?"

"Why you think? He gets too many hits in the wrong places. He panders to the darkest corners of the electorate. Every country has got a Harold Zhang, but ours is too small for someone so big. He's a . . . a . . . what they call it, Charlie?"

"A social media influencer."

"Exactly. So the *Gahmen* don't like him, the mainstream media don't like him, anyone with a brain doesn't like him, but he gets half a million hits a day and most of them are voters."

"So he will get taken down at some point."

"Definitely."

"But he still keeps going."

"Of course, his story is simple. It's love and betrayal. He loves his wife. She betrayed him. But he can't stop loving his wife. So he can't stop hating her."

"So it's the foreigner thing?" Chan asked.

"For the killer? Don't know. He's not been political so far, it's been pretty random."

"He cannot be a political killer," Chua said. "That one definitely cannot."

"It's not. You're an *ang moh* and you kill two Asians and two *ang mohs* to make a statement? Please *lah*. Doesn't make any statement except if you're colour blind."

The silly joke made Chan smile.

"Hey, show some respect please, inspector," Chua said. "As far as we are concerned, Harold Zhang is still alive."

Low nodded towards the clock on wall. It was 8.15pm.

"Love your optimism."

The deputy director's phone beeped. "Yah, hello . . . Oh hello, Minister. Not yet, sir. We've heard nothing. He hasn't gone home, sir. We've got officers outside his apartment and his family members . . . Actually, sir, I got that information from Technology. Yes, that's right. Er, yes, sir. He's with me now."

Chua grimaced. "Yes, sir. I'll tell him, thank you, sir. I'll keep you updated."

Low was already standing up. "And I suppose I can get whatever I need?"

Chua sighed. "It seems you have a friend upstairs."

"No, I don't. He hates me just as much as you do."

Chua tried to come up with a pithy comeback, but Low had already left his office.

Chapter 38

THE razor swished through the foamy water. Maxwell tapped it against the side of the sink and continued shaving. The fitted cabinet above the sink had a mirror door, allowing Maxwell to admire his handiwork. He had tidied up. The towels were neatly piled in the corner, the water streaks wiped from the tiles and the bottles returned to the stand in the corner of the shower cubicle. That's how she had always tidied up. It was a common trick of the casual cleaner. Stack everything into neat piles: towels, bottles, books, remote controls, everything. The image instantly gave the illusion of a tidy home and an organised, fastidious cleaner.

Wiping the soap from his neck, Maxwell bounced along the corridor and into the living room, humming along to the blaring music. The song was the same, the only song he played now.

Tonight, I'm a rock 'n' roll star.

Maxwell threw the towel over the bamboo pole suspended from the ceiling in his laundry. He was naked, all 120 kg of him, standing at 1.9 m tall, broad-shouldered, chest out, balls swinging. Sometimes the maids saw him when they were hanging out the neighbours' washing. Most of them blushed and turned away. A few giggled. But one or two continued to stare. He drew them in. His nakedness was flypaper. He signaled for them to join him later, any time, at their convenience. They always came.

It was so easy, a joke. There were no restaurant reservations, no inane small talk before and after movies, no childish fiddling in the back of a taxi, no leaving the house, just a tentative knock at the door and a sheepish grin, a brief introduction and a quick tour. There's the apartment, there's the bedroom, that's the time, mind how you go.

Maxwell wandered into the kitchen, his naked body enjoying the air-conditioning. He had scrubbed the sideboard and replaced the plug plate on the kitchen wall. She would've liked that. He took his yellow Phillips screwdriver from the drawer and scrubbed it gently with a green scourer. He wasn't fussed about the handle. Indeed he found the tiny red flecks comforting. But he liked the silver shaft to shine.

The living room TV was switched on, but with the sound turned down. The music took precedence, especially now. Maxwell had tried to convince her of the merits of Britpop, but to no avail. She had adored those unbearable power ballads, forever singing along to a ghastly nursery rhyme from Richard Marx or Whitney Houston. She had believed in love songs. She had believed in love.

Maxwell held up the screwdriver against the kitchen's fluorescent lights. He still wasn't satisfied. He returned to his scrubbing, working slowly and carefully, making sure he didn't touch the pointy end. The screwdriver was already an impractical tool. He didn't need it to be further blunted. He had thought about using something else, but couldn't bring himself to get rid of the screwdriver.

It didn't seem right.

On the TV screen, Harold Zhang appeared over the shoulder of a young Chinese woman. She was reporting from the anti-foreigner rally at Speakers' Corner. The camera zoomed in on Zhang. He was in full flow on stage, foaming and sweating.

Maxwell considered turning up the TV, but changed his mind. He'd heard it all before.

He turned up the music instead, the bass line thumping along the walls of his apartment. The naked Caucasian sang along with the music as he made his way towards the TV in the living room.

Tonight, I'm a rock 'n' roll star.

Maxwell stood in front of the TV as the camera panned across the crowd. He tried to find himself, but the camera cut back to the reporter. Not surprisingly, there appeared to be no mention of his letter. Flipping the screwdriver in his right hand, he used its handle to scratch his testicles. The humidity drove him to distraction.

Maxwell smelled the screwdriver. He was relieved. He could only pick out LYNX shower gel. She had once complained that his extra weight made him perspire more. Fat people smelled worse, she'd said with her usual lack of tact and nuance. But he smelled just fine. And the screwdriver was clean enough. He would listen to the song one more time and then get dressed.

Maxwell was ready to make amends.

Chapter 39

THE other diners registered their displeasure with the slurping. Zhang was being deliberately loud with his *laksa*, lifting the bowl to his face, licking the curry around the sides and ignoring the dribble stains on his chin. Li Jing always loathed the slurping, saying he sounded like an old Chinaman, particularly after they returned from Australia. Everything irritated Zhang's wife after they returned from Australia. Mostly, she hated the slurping.

But she wasn't here.

She used to be. When they were younger, they always came to Katong for the *laksa*, the best in Singapore. They held hands under the table and wiped each other's foreheads with tissue paper. They fed each other *tau pok* chunks and discussed their futures. Li Jing talked about getting married and backpacking across Asia. Zhang talked about saving enough money for their first apartment. In the end, she relented. She sided with her future husband. Safety first. They put her travel ambitions on hold and saved enough for a deposit. But there was never enough time, never enough money, until Li Jing came up with the ultimatum—Australia or divorce. Zhang supported his wife's juvenile travel dream and she thanked him by sleeping with a surfing instructor.

But they'd shared some good times over Katong *laksa*.

Zhang settled the bill and headed off into the balmy night

air. He dashed across East Coast Road, ignoring the families enjoying dinner together. Smiling couples and giggling children strolled beneath the restored shophouses, glowing in the neon shop signs. Zhang had wanted children, but she was never sure, always deliberating, always procrastinating. He had reminded her that her biological clock was ticking, that he needed time to find a good maid, that they had to think logically and rationally about the role children played as care givers in their old age. But Li Jing struggled with rational thinking. She had filled her head with whimsical notions of travel, exploration and quality of life. Zhang had tried reasoning with her. How would they enjoy quality of life without children and maids to look after them?

Zhang was halfway along Joo Chiat Road when he thought he saw something. The street was dark, but no less busy and reasonably well-lit. He was certain he saw *something*. He stopped at a traffic light crossing in Marine Parade and waited. He kept looking over his shoulder, but wasn't sure why. He was uncomfortable. The road was filled with cars and buses, but he felt lonely, exposed.

Perhaps it was her and his intended destination.

As he skipped down the stairs towards the illuminated underpass, he stopped again. The tunnel that linked Marine Parade with East Coast Park evoked warm memories. She had always clung to his shoulder, seeking his masculine reassurance, his white shirt providing a security blanket. Singapore's underpasses left her feeling isolated and vulnerable. Once inside, along the tunnel, beneath the expressway, there was nowhere else to go. The walls closed in. Zhang had always manipulated her apprehension, stealing a hug and maybe a squeeze of one of her breasts. In those moments, she needed *him*. The underpass turned their relationship upside down. In later years, he used the underpass as a political tool, reminding her that such places were never safe in Australia, with their urine-stained, graffiti-filled walls and homeless beggars. Li Jing grew tired of the sermons and the nostalgic trips to the seafront faded away. But Zhang never forgot them. They were before *The Singapore Truth*, before the blogs and the exhausting ranting, before the money and fame, before the metamorphosis. He was a happy man. He was a simple man. It was enough for him. It was never enough for her.

Zhang stopped in the middle of the underpass. It was his favourite part and her worst. She was equidistant from either end, always walking quicker, always squeezing his arm. He leaned against the tiled wall and closed his eyes.

I still love her.

I still bloody love her.

He took out his phone and dialed. There was no answer. She was busy.

Reaching the other end of the underpass, Zhang hesitated before climbing the stairs. He heard the distant echo of footsteps. He was alone in the tunnel. The footsteps drifted away. Zhang wasn't sure. He wasn't sure of anything.

He was up the stairs quickly, surprising himself with his sprightly eagerness, across the path and towards the faint white lines in the gloominess. Perspiring, gleaming runners made their way through East Coast Park, their presence spoiling the mood, breaking Zhang's concentration. They made him think of part-time surfing instructors with peroxide hair.

Soon he was across the path and through the grass, treading carefully to avoid the snaking tree roots, taking his shoes and socks off, following the soothing, rhythmic sounds of the encroaching tide. The container ships lit up the dark horizon line, their twinkling lights competing with the few stars visible in a polluted sky. Zhang felt his feet sink and his heart soar as he made it onto the beach. This was the beach—*their* beach—where they went after *laksa* every Friday night. This was where Zhang's world began and ended.

He hurried across the sand, stopping only when the water washed across his feet. He heard something behind him, but he didn't care now. Nothing was going to spoil his moment. He was where he wanted to be, right here, right now. With his hands on his hips, he tilted his head back slightly, allowing the sea breeze to catch his face. There were definite footsteps now, but it didn't matter.

Zhang closed his eyes and replayed his favourite images.

She was there, gliding across the sand, walking towards him, stroking his hair in the moonlight, kissing him, fondling him. They were lying on their backs, under the stars, oblivious to the sand, to strangers, to prying eyes. They were grappling, pulling, unfastening, opening, connecting; losing their virginity, right there, on the beach—*their* beach—forever.

Zhang heard something, but didn't turn around, didn't open his eyes. This was his moment. He would not be denied, not now.

"Well Mr Zhang," said a voice behind him. "I'm ready when you are."

Chapter 40

LI Jing deleted the missed call message. She wasn't interested in him, not tonight. Stirring the melting ice at the bottom of her glass, she smiled at the birthday party in the corner of the bar, away to her right on the raised, carpeted lounge area. A Caucasian guy blew out the candles on a cake as his friends and their partners applauded. They downed a round of tequilas and called the waiter over for refills. The kid quickly arrived with the bottle. He was aware of the socio-economic make-up of the birthday party. He was on for a decent tip. Li Jing caught the eye of the birthday boy. He was handsome, in his mid-20s, with a trendy, gelled hairstyle and an expense account. Li Jing raised her empty glass. He nodded his gratitude and turned away. He still played the numbers game. The older Chinese woman had a decent body, but no longer played in the premier league.

Li Jing wasn't hurt. She understood the rules. In Australia, she was a slim, attractive Asian novelty. In Singapore, there was too much competition, even in one bar. But she kept coming back to No.5, mostly with friends, sometimes alone. The cocktail bar in Emerald Hill reminded her of better times; the clientele, the music, even the menu made her think of him. It was a guilty pleasure. Not that she had anything to feel guilty about. There was no pleasure left in her life. Her husband had seen to that.

But she was still young enough. Her favourite cocktail dress accentuated both her slender legs and long, black hair. There was still time. She hadn't given up on the pursuit of pleasure just yet, not entirely.

She watched as he returned to the bar from the toilet, still adjusting his zip. He wasn't perfect. He certainly wasn't a surfer. But he wasn't Harold Zhang either.

"Thanks again for the drink," she cooed.

"Ah, that's all right," he said, taking the stool beside her at the long, wooden bar. "It's no fun drinking on your own."

The flirting had the subtlety of a sledgehammer, but Li Jing was happy to play along.

"It's an unusual name, really."

"Talek? Yes, I suppose it is. That's why most people call me Maxwell."

Chapter 41

THE darkened, empty room didn't particularly bother Zhang, but the air-conditioning did. He was certain there were two machines, one either side of the table, blasting at his face. He had raised an arm to feel the cold air against the back of his hand. The fans were on swing mode, oscillating. No matter where he sat, the rattling units found him. Whenever he stood, a metallic voice ordered him to sit down again. Initially, Zhang shouted threats and promised blogs, writs and public shaming. But he soon piped down. It wasn't the draconian orders and archaic interrogation ploys that bothered him. It was the indifference. Stripped of his laptop, he was unprotected, nothing, a ball of wool for the big cats to amuse themselves with. Two air-conditioning units demonstrated real power. Zhang could shout and scream and bang his feet. But he couldn't turn the machines off.

Suddenly, the fluorescent tubes were flickering to life, buzzing and blinking and filling the room with light. Two Chinese men, one young and smart, the other older and scruffier, opened the door. They carried coffee cups and folders. Zhang was shielding his eyes, still cowering from the unexpected brightness, squinting through the gaps in his fingers at the photographs being spread out across the table. The scrapping chairs stung his eardrums. The two men sat and sipped their coffees. They said nothing.

They stared. They sipped and stared. The older one, with coarse features and deep, black bags beneath his eyes, kept smiling. The younger one betrayed no emotion. The older, grinning one scared Zhang more.

"I want to know why I'm here," Zhang muttered. "I'm the victim here, OK? You see that letter or not? You cannot do this to me. I want my lawyer."

The two men said nothing. They sipped and stared.

"I know how this works, OK. You think I'm blur, is it? I know you watch me. I know you follow me. I know you bring me here, give me air-con, cannot eat. This is what? Revenge for you, is it? I *tekan* you, now you whack me is it?"

They sipped and stared.

"What, you think I scared is it? You know you cannot touch me, not now, I'm too famous already. Too *atas*. Cannot bully me, no one can bully me anymore. You know who I am or not?"

"I know exactly who you are," said the older Chinese guy finally. "You're a fucking idiot."

Zhang was immediately silenced. The quiet, calm contempt in the other man's voice terrified him.

"Now. Let me tell you, Harold *chee bye*, who we are. This is Detective Inspector Charles Chan and I am Detective Inspector Stanley Low. And do you know what we have?"

Zhang didn't answer.

"We have a blank canvas to catch your IKEA Killer. You know what that means? We have the authority of the Home Ministry to do whatever it takes to stop this man before he kills again. So we are no longer just police officers. We are the Singapore fucking Government."

Chan turned away so Zhang couldn't see him giggle.

"And you are a real double-edged sword for us, or for me," Low continued. "We've got to stop him killing, but it would

appear that he wants to kill you. That's understandable. I want
to kill you. Every ounce of my being wants to scoop out your
eyeballs with chopsticks and piss through the holes. You have
blown this case up, you have rallied racists against us, you have
turned a domestic case into an international incident and you
have somehow managed to make a serial killer even madder than
he was in the first place."

"I was doing my job. I am a political blogger."

"You are a piece of shit, still pissed off that your wife got
shagged by an *ang moh*."

"How do you know? I mean . . ."

Low leaned forward. "I know everything. I know you went to
Australia last time but couldn't make it. I know your wife wanted
to leave you, but you forced her to come back to Singapore
because you threatened to expose her on your blog."

"I would never . . ."

"Please. She had a new job, a new life and a new partner, why
else would she come back to you?"

"Singapore is our home."

"No, no, no, you came back because you couldn't take being
a minority, being a second-class citizen, not even a citizen, but a
temporary visa holder, only one step up from a refugee, from boat
people. Bloody *boat people*. And they treated you like boat people
didn't they, Harold? Called you names, didn't they Harold? Never
got that in Asia, did you Harold? Not in Singapore, where you are
part of the majority, where you benefit from our unspoken racial
hegemony every day, right Harold? Of course, we can't say that,
can we Harold? Not officially. Got to convince the neighbours
and what's left of our indigenous population that we're all equal,
got to say that our 75 per cent racial majority is to preserve our,
what, Asian values? Our Confucian values? But we can't say that,
can we, Harold? Everybody wants to, but we can't. We can't say

we love our racial hegemony like a warm security blanket because that seems wrong, doesn't it, Harold? The whites in Australia can't say it. The Malays in Malaysia can't say it. And the Chinese in Singapore definitely cannot say it. So we pretend we like multiculturalism, when what we really like is being the majority race, the safety in numbers. And you didn't have it in Australia, so you came home to get it back, to protect it.

"You went after the foreigners because they were the easy target. Too many foreigners taking our jobs, too many foreigners celebrating their foreign national days, too many foreigners shagging our wives, but only *your* wife was being shagged. You turned the people in this country against one another because an *ang moh* screwed your wife. You turned a serial killer into a race war because an *ang moh* screwed your wife. If this bastard does kill you, we should give him a National Day Award, you twisted piece of shit."

Zhang struggled to find some words. "I don't have to, you can't talk to me, you can't, no way, not like this."

"Yes he can," Chan said, finally joining the interrogation.

"Why?"

"We're the Singapore Government."

"I said that already," Low objected. "You stealing my lines now?"

Chan rolled his eyes. "Please. Every undercover officer says it during an arrest. Makes them feel like a big shot."

"Is it? Bastard. I thought I was the only one."

"No *lah*, but he's right," Chan said, gesturing towards his partner. "And you can make fun of us in your blog, you can whack us at your rallies, but without us you'd already be floating in the reservoir."

Low recognised the frustration in the young inspector's voice. Chan was becoming a better policeman and that saddened Low.

Of the two, Chan was always the better man. It was difficult to be both.

Zhang sat back. "So why did you pick me up?"

"He was at your rally, obviously," Low said, spreading the photos across the table. "We've been through these photos of the crowd, but we mostly focus on the crowd around the stage, the volunteers, you know, the real idiots."

"Who took these photos? ISD? I knew it."

"We got these from Facebook, moron. Need Internal Security for what?"

"So?"

"He's not in these photos. No *ang mohs* there. Probably waited outside and came in at the end, so we want your cameras."

"What cameras?"

"I work in Technology. I monitor your shitty site. You use GoPro cameras on the crowd, so you can edit later and make the crowd look huge."

"We didn't record this time."

"Yes you did. I saw your guys set up around the stage on tripods. I was there. But you haven't put up the videos because the crowd was lousy, right? Even you cannot edit enough to make it look like a big crowd. So you give us the cameras."

"I'm not sure who has them, maybe one of the volunteers."

"If we don't have them by tomorrow morning, you'll be charged under the Sedition Act."

"What for?"

"Whatever we like."

Chan opened an envelope and pulled out a photocopy of the handwritten note.

"The lab is looking at the blood stains on the letter, but let's assume it's genuine. Why you?"

"Don't know."

"*Your show was painful. Now get ready for mine,*" said Chan, reading from the note. "What does that mean?"

"My rally, what? He was there, right?"

"He brought the note to the rally. It was prepared elsewhere. He wanted his message to be clear to you. You're his target."

"I know, OK. I used him in the blogs, said that it was typical, got foreigners killing foreigners, now got foreigners killing locals and foreigners. Locals cannot feel safe and protected in their own country. I been saying this all along what?"

Low looked up. "What? What did you say?"

"I said locals cannot feel safe anymore."

"That's why. You did say that. I remember now. You got a big spike after Dragon Boy. That's when it really took off, after Dragon Boy and then the *ang mohs*, because they were good-looking, but Dragon Boy was the turning point."

"Because he was local. It's obvious."

"But it exploded after the *ang mohs*. They're not local, didn't even work here, just backpackers."

"Yah, so?"

"You didn't care that much about the Indonesian girl, not at first."

Zhang shrugged. "She was a prostitute."

Low's mind spun. He visualised the cogs turning, the mice on the wheel. He counted them and watched them run.

"No, no, no. She wasn't a prostitute."

"She was what? She was a whore."

"She was his. She was *his* prostitute, the only one not found at the reservoir, the first one, the messy one, probably an accident, he didn't mean to do it. She was his girl, maybe his only girl. But you never knew that. You kept calling her a prostitute. I read those blogs. You got more vulgar as you got more hits, the names got worse: prostitute, hooker, whore, drip-feeding the masses your disgust for her profession. But she wasn't a prostitute, not to him. You kept insulting his woman, getting nastier and nastier as your hits went up. You attacked her. You attacked your wife. She was another Asian girl with a rich white guy. And you hated her. Those blogs got nastier, you never even used her name in the end. The prostitute, your wife, what's the difference, right? Both were whores, both were disgusting. Even the *ang mohs* you called by name, and Dragon Boy, Lee Kok Wah, you even used his name. But she ended up just being a prostitute, just like your wife. She wasn't even a person any more. She was just a whore. Read me that line again, on the note."

Chan looked confused. "The line?"

"The line, the line, about pain," Low said, grabbing the photocopied note. "*Your show was painful. Now get ready for mine.* He's not talking about the bloody rally. He's talking about your blog. Your blog is painful. You kept calling his woman a whore. You've hurt him, now he's going to hurt you in the same way. His pain is going to be your pain. He's not going to kill you. He's going to kill your wife."

Chapter 42

THE phone vibrated on the long bar, lighting up as it edged towards Li Jing's glass. She went for the glass instead, finishing the Rémy Martin, before banging the glass down against the polished timber. Through droopy eyes, she admired the raucous birthday party up on the raised platform. They were singing now, hitting one another with cushions and playing drinking games, making a mess on the Persian carpets; locals and foreigners, lost in the moment, just as it should be, as it used to be for her.

"They're certainly having fun," Maxwell said.

"It's the *ang moh*'s birthday."

Li Jing was slurring slightly. Both picked up on it. Both pretended to ignore it.

"Sorry, not *ang moh*. It's the . . . what is it . . . it's the Caucasian's birthday. I almost forgot there."

"It's OK. I don't mind *ang moh*, lah."

"*Wah*, you speak Singlish is it?"

"No, I just put *lah* at the end of all my sentences."

"Ah, it's OK. I got Chinese friends who do that. The rich ones. Try to talk like *ah lians* outside, so they don't sound like spoilt brats."

Maxwell knew exactly what an *ah lian* was, but couldn't possibly reveal how he knew. He played the dumb foreigner instead.

"*Ah lians?*"

"Oh, *ah lian* is like a, what *ah*, like a kind of gangster for a girl, no, more like a gang member, a girl in a street gang."

"I know what you mean. In every country, it's the same. In England, we have mockneys. My old school friends, private school friends, they all became mockneys."

Li Jing frowned, seeking further explanation.

"Like a Cockney, someone who's working class from London. They pretend to be like them, like poor common people."

"Yah, almost the same."

Maxwell shook the ice in his glass. "It's funny. It's changed again now. When all those Guy Ritchie movies came out, everyone spoke like a gangster and swaggered down the street like a monkey."

Li Jing giggled.

"But now, thanks to our private school system, poor people can't afford to make movies or music anymore and now we've got Benedict Cumberbatch to thank for making posh people cool again. When I was in England, my people were cool in Asia. Now I'm in Asia, my people are cool in England again. I've always been in the wrong place at the wrong time."

"Yah, I understand that," Li Jing muttered. "Well, here, it's very clear, never changes. If you have money, you are always welcome. And if you are poor, you are nothing."

"Which one are you?"

"Ha. Me? I'm in the middle. Does that make me one of your, what do you call it?"

"Mockneys."

"Yah. I'm a mockney."

Maxwell raised his glass. "And I'm an *ah lian*."

As Li Jing laughed, Maxwell ordered two more cognacs.

CHAN'S car was already rolling out of the parking space when Low opened the door and jumped inside. The older investigator was on the phone, talking quickly.

"*Yah lah*, his home, get the local police post to wait outside. I was there before, but that was two hours already, yah, correct . . . Speak to Harry Lim at Technology, the new guy, but quite good. Ask him for Zhang's file, got all the addresses inside. Cover them all, especially her parents, she stays over sometimes, yah, got an old flat in Queenstown . . . *Yah lah*, something like that. Cover her office, nearest MRT, bus stop, taxi stand. And double check the reservoir OK? Everything, and do it now, OK? . . . Well, get off the phone then."

Low held onto the dashboard as Chan took a sharp right, running a red light and ignoring the droning horns of braking vehicles.

"OK, we'll go to their place first, then see how," Low shouted over the accelerating engine. "Come on, Charlie, move."

On the back seat of Chan's car, Zhang curled into the foetal position. He was quietly weeping.

Maxwell hoped he was nodding in all the right places. He had never been much of a listener. He was from a privileged background. People usually listened to him. He caught the barman's attention and pointed towards the empty glasses, careful not to turn his head away from her watery eyes.

"He thought I would be impressed by the money," Li Jing said, clutching the glass against her chin.

"Most people are."

"I know, I know, especially in Asia. It's an Asian thing, get a steady job, put a roof over our head and then that's it, finished, you know."

Her phone flashed again.

"You're certainly popular tonight."

"It doesn't matter. See?"

Li Jing switched her phone off. Maxwell toasted her decision.

"But I had the same with my partner," he said. "She didn't see me. She only saw my skin colour. She saw my wallet, another rich white man in Asia, but she never really saw *me*."

Maxwell's tears surprised him. He convinced himself he was a good actor. She certainly believed him, patting his hand on the bar.

"And it didn't work out?"

"No. She left me."

Maxwell couldn't stop the tears now.

"I'm so sorry," Li Jing whispered, still holding his hand.

Maxwell took a deep breath.

"And now, what? What should I do now? My friends say I should go home. Go where? I am home. Singapore is my home. I love Singaporeans. I love Asians. And yes, I'll admit it. I love Asian women. I see them for who they are really are, not for what society tells them to be. I don't see state-sponsored, baby-making machines or a signature on a housing loan. I just see . . . I don't know. I don't know what I see, but I know I don't see any of that."

Li Jing smiled as she sipped her cognac. "My husband sees a *prop*."

"A prop?"

"A prop for his traditional family model, his Asian values, his damn rallies. That's what I am."

"Rallies? Wow. Is your husband a politician?"

Li Jing almost choked on her drink.

"He wishes."

LOW was already out of the car, running across the void deck.

Two uniformed officers stood in front of the lift doors, blocking his entry.

"I'm Detective Inspector Low, Technology," he barked, producing his ID. "Well, is she at home or not?"

"Er, no, sir, got officers in their apartment now, it's empty," said one of the perspiring policemen.

"Fuck." Low kicked the green dustbin beside the lift. "Right, you, let us know if anyone comes OK. Don't close one eye. No talking cock, no falling asleep. You see anyone you don't like, shoot them first, interview later. OK or not?"

"Yes, sir."

"OK. Good luck."

By the time Low returned to the car, Chan was leaning against the open driver's door, talking quickly on the phone. Zhang hovered next to the door, walking in small circles, mumbling to himself.

"So how?"

"Nothing," Chan replied, tapping his phone against the car roof. "Got police here, at parents place, her workplace, the MRT over there. Nothing. Her neighbours said they think she came home after the rally and then she went out again. Don't know where."

Low moved quickly around the side of the car, the adrenaline seeping through his pores. He was on autopilot, navigated by the mania. His euphoria directed him towards the grumbling, weeping mess of a man.

"Where the fuck is she?"

Low saw his hand grab Zhang's throat. He was squeezing, watching the pink blotches appear on that grotesque, bloated face, his veins burrowing through the flesh, looking for an escape route.

Chan separated the men to save them both.

"Stanley, enough already."

"It's OK," Zhang whimpered, rubbing his neck and coughing loudly. "This is my fault. I know that."

The three men slumped against the car. Zhang sobbed quietly.

"She's going to die, isn't she? He's going to kill her, because of me."

"We need to find her," Chan muttered.

"I don't want her to die. Please." Zhang grabbed Low's arm. He was shaking now. "I don't want her to die. She's my wife. She's my life."

Low said nothing, but he heard the pain. He loathed Zhang, hated everything about him. But the primal despair was beyond his reckoning, beyond his understanding. Unconditional love made the pain absolute.

Low examined the broken man. "You really love her that much?"

It came out as a question, but was really an observation, the inspector thinking out loud.

"You didn't see each other after the rally, right?"

Zhang wiped snot across his cheek. "No, she always leaves just before the end, won't take photos or shake hands, never wants her colleagues to see too much of her on Facebook the next day."

"You told her about the letter."

"No. When I went home, she wasn't there, so I went for *makan*, before you stopped me at East Coast I've been calling, so many times already, but she never answered. She never talks to me after my rallies."

"Because she hates them."

"Hates me."

"Yah, probably."

Both men stared at Low.

"No, no," Low said. "After the rallies she does, definitely;

hates that world, wants to get away from it, away from you, wash it off her clothes. Remove the dirt, the grubbiness of you and those speeches. Where could she go to get away from you?"

"Anywhere. Her parents' place?" Zhang suggested wearily.

"No, we looked there already," Chan interrupted.

"No, no, not enough. She wants to get away from that life, that whole life, everything you do or touch, everything you came back for."

"No.5."

It was almost a whisper, barely audible. The policemen looked at each other.

"What was that, Harold?" Chan asked.

"No.5. It's a cocktail bar."

"And?"

"She goes there with her colleagues sometimes. Also when we argue. She knows it pisses me off because expats like the place, especially Australians. Men like *him*."

"Where is this place?"

"Er, not sure, I never go there before."

Even Chan was losing his cool. "Harold, try to think, OK?"

"Yah, it's near Orchard, she told me before, behind Orchard."

"Around Scotts Road?"

"No, the other side. The old side, with the shophouses."

"Shit, I know the place," Low said. "Emerald Hill. It's Emerald Hill, right?"

Zhang nodded. Chan was already in the car and starting the engine.

MAXWELL signed the bill and added a $50 note, making sure both the barman and Li Jing saw it before closing the leather-bound folder. In one smooth move, he pushed the bill towards the barman and a large cognac, the last of the night, along the bar to his right. Swaying on the stool, Li Jing greeted the glass like a long-lost friend. Her maternal, warm smile was fixed in place by a dozen cognacs, but her heavy eyes were pulling in the opposite direction. She focused on the glass as if it were a distant, blurry object being spied through binoculars. She grabbed it with both hands and swallowed hard.

Maxwell left his drink untouched. "I think that's enough for us tonight."

"It's not fair. You're not even drunk."

Maxwell grinned. The waistline and the hairline had both deserted him, but he still had the impudent grin. She had always complimented his smile in the past.

"Are you kidding? I'm flying."

"But you're just sitting there."

"Ah, but when I'm sober, I'm falling off the chair and singing rude songs."

Li Jing snorted. "You're funny."

She leaned towards him, her hair brushing against his shoulder. Maxwell edged away.

"Can I ask you something?"

"Anything you like."

"Why do you stay with him, your husband?"

Li Jing's shoulders slumped.

"Because he's my husband," she said, raising her glass. "Good Chinese wives stay with their husbands. Good Chinese husbands go to massage parlours and keep mistresses in Batam. That's what we do, our wonderful Asian values."

"No, that's not really true, surely, not anymore, half of my office is divorced."

Maxwell took her hand and placed it gently on the bar, wrapping her hand in his.

"You can leave him, really."

Li Jing pulled her hand away. "Every day I want to leave him. Every night I say I'm going to leave him. Then in the morning, I see his eyes. He's broken, like a lost little boy. He should hate me, really, really hate me. I hate me. But he still loves me. It's in his eyes, every morning."

"Are you sure? After all that's happened? Because I had great plans for us tonight. This was only going to be the beginning. You wouldn't believe what I've got in store for you."

Li Jing chinked her glass against his. "My loss, eh?"

"Oh well, if you say he still loves you."

"He does."

"You're absolutely sure?" Maxwell asked, his blue eyes sparkling through Li Jing's drunken haze. "There only has to be a little doubt, just the tiniest inkling that he doesn't love you anymore and tonight could be very different for us."

"I'm sure. But he does. He does love me."

Maxwell downed the rest of his drink.

"Such a shame. You really are a kind, beautiful woman. He should realise how lucky he is."

"Ha. That's never going to happen."

Slowly and very gently, Maxwell caressed Li Jing's smooth cheek with the back of his hand.

"I'm sure he will."

EMERALD Hill was old and new Asian money in a single, quiet street. A nutmeg plantation owner established the enclave and opulent, terraced houses soon followed. They were family-owned and passed through the generations, old money propping up old properties. Chan parked his car outside one of the gazetted homes and the three men ran towards the other end of Emerald Hill, towards the shopping behemoths and the international bars. The fresh vomit along the sides of ceramic plant plots provided the smell of new Asian money.

Low was ahead of the other two men, sandwiched between the historic, elegant homes on either side. The No.5 bar was on his right, a two-storey Peranakan shophouse propped up by new money. The DJ's set-list reeled in locals, expats, tourists and prostitutes, all seeking a profitable night out. Three strides took him through the silver tables outside the bar, along the timber-decked terrace and past the smoking couples huddled together beneath nicotine clouds, and he was in.

He was up on his toes, craning above the pogoing crowd. The late hour had robbed the clientele of their inhibitions. The booze granted courage if not rhythm. Up in the lounge, on a raised second tier, a Caucasian guy in a birthday hat was covered in streamers and having his shirt pulled off by a couple of young Malay women. Designer beer bottles were being raised to the ceiling as too many red faces toasted their corporate omnipotence in a foreign land.

Low was pushing drunks aside, brushing away authentic Ralph Lauren shirts and fake Louis Vuitton handbags. One or two considered a confrontation until they saw the Chinese guy glare back at them. The eyes had it. They always did.

At the bar, the same bar, the same spot, Low leaned over and tugged the barman's shirt at the shoulder. When he pulled back, his arm knocked a glass on the bar, the same glass, *her* glass.

Chapter 43

"Oi, don't touch me," the barman shouted, already making eye contact with a no-neck doorman in a black suit.

"Eh, not now *ah*, Tom Cruise," Low said, flashing his ID. "Is there an *ang moh* in here with a Chinese girl? A big *ang moh* guy, maybe blond hair and the Chinese girl in her late 30s, early 40s."

"*Yah lah*, of course."

"Where?"

The barman waved his arm at the crowd. "Everywhere."

"Eh, don't be a fucking joker, OK."

Chan and Zhang squeezed their way through to the bar. Low grabbed Zhang.

"Give me a photo."

"What?"

"A photo of your wife, in your wallet, your phone, come on."

Zhang didn't hear the inspector, focusing instead on the crowd, dancing, bumping, grabbing, molesting; local on local; foreign on foreign; local on foreign. He was a stranger in his own country. His wife was a stranger to him.

She missed Katong laksa for this?

"Maybe she never come here," Zhang mumbled. "She probably never come here. Maybe she go home already. Can call home right?"

"Zhang, give me the fucking photo."

"What photo?"

Zhang was drifting away, smiling at the crowd.

"Bastard." Low shoved his hands into Zhang's pockets, groping for a wallet, spinning him around, patting him down. "Fuck *lah*, where's your wallet?"

The scream from outside stopped everyone.

The scream bled through the bar. It brought down the beer bottles and beat out the bass lines.

The scream turned off the party. It made the topless birthday boy feel the air-conditioning for the first time.

The scream shook the barman's hands. It dropped the bucket filled with Tiger beer and sent ice cubes skating across the floor.

The scream sent the men with black suits and no necks running from their posts. It silenced the smokers and ended their flirting.

The scream forced Low to look away from Zhang. It pinned his gaze to the polished timber beneath his feet.

The eyes always have it.

And poor Zhang didn't need to see what he already knew.

Chapter 44

A CROWD had already gathered around Li Jing's crumpled body by the time Low arrived. Emerald Link was a nondescript side street between the majestic homes, a short cut for delivery trucks and students of the nearby international school. The high wall on the side of a property overwhelmed the Chinese body lying on the pavement. Her blood was still trickling along the kerb. The bystanders looked on in horror, not sure what to do next as the doormen from No.5 tried to keep order.

So they took lots of photos.

Low made his way to the front of the crowd and snatched the nearest phone from a Chinese girl young enough to be his daughter. The gawkers cowered as a shower of broken phone pieces bounced off the wall and fell over their heads.

"OK, next person who takes a photo gets arrested," Low shouted. "Now everyone except the club doormen, go back to the bar and wait to be questioned."

He pointed at the men in black suits. "I want you here to keep them out until the police arrive. The rest of you go back to the bar and wait for the police. I want to talk to the people who found the body. Who screamed?"

A petite Filipino woman in high heels and a cropped top sheepishly raised her hand. She was still crying. She had watery, panda eyes and black streaks of make-up down her cheeks.

"You're the one who found her? Right, the police will talk to you first. Everyone else, back to the bar, do not leave, do not go home and do not upload any photos. We will monitor OK. We will find your Facebook accounts and we will find you. Now, go back to the bar."

Murmurs of dissents soon gave way to shuffling footsteps as customers reluctantly turned their backs on the night's unexpected entertainment. Emboldened by their intoxication, a small gang of young Chinese men hovered, testing the boundaries of the skinny, plain-clothes policeman. Low stepped towards them. The doormen considered intervening, but thought better of it.

"Ah, you want to play is it," Low said, putting a hand on his holstered gun. "Want to test me right, OK, let's play a game. You stand there. No problem. And then I shoot you for disrupting a criminal investigation. Can?"

Low pulled his gun and prodded it against the nearest belligerent face, resting the muzzle on the bridge of the gang member's nose.

"So how? Want to stay or not?"

Low pressed the gun against the flesh between the Chinese kid's eyes, forcing him to step backwards. The doormen swallowed hard but couldn't swallow their impotence.

Low jabbed the gun into the guy's forehead each time he spoke. "Go . . . back . . . to . . . the . . . bar."

The last of the gang were leaving the scene when Chan arrived. A doorman raised a trunk-like forearm towards his throat.

"No, it's OK, he's with me," Low said. "Can come through."

Both inspectors crouched beside Li Jing. In the darkness, she appeared to be sleeping, resting peacefully on her side. Chan dabbed at the blood on the pavement with his forefinger.

"This hasn't congealed yet. This only just happened."

"Yeah, I know. Where's Zhang?"

"Having a whiskey. Got security babysitting him until the police arrive. You touched anything yet?"

"No *lah*, no one has, which is good."

Chan placed a hand on Li Jing's arm. "She's not cold yet."

"Poor bastard."

"No *lah*, I mean not at all. She's still warm, the blood is still dripping, look. This only just happened, Stanley. Maybe 10 minutes ago, maybe only five minutes ago."

"Fuck, we just missed him."

The wailing made both men jump. It was the wounded, anguished cry of a lost child.

Zhang had finally decided to come and see his wife.

Chapter 45

NO.5 was quiet now, the only noise coming from Low as he hurried through the hushed crowd. The DJ had turned off the music and conversation was subdued and stilted. Even the birthday party had fizzled out, the guests staring at their untouched tequila shots. Only Low was switched on, alive to the possibilities of a fresh breakthrough. The body hadn't even gone cold. He was almost on the scent.

That fucker was here. Ten minutes ago. He was in this bloody room.

Low was sashaying quickly, his movements almost balletic, twisting shoulders to avoid the drunken zombies, stepping sideways to avoid people crying over spilled blood. He was at the bar, leaning across that gleaming timber, shouting loudly. The barman had been there in the street just now, a face in the crowd, staring at her face, her death mask, contorted in pain and fear.

You never forget your first.

Low certainly hadn't. It was a domestic case. A cheating husband had taken his wife's dignity so she took his beloved baby daughter. She had grabbed the little girl and jumped from the eighth floor of their apartment block, hoping for luck in the afterlife. When Low first saw what was left of her skull, scattered across the void deck like a thousand tiny pieces of eggshell, he knew she wasn't going to get it. Nothing came close to those early nightmares. When he thought of crime and punishment, with its bottomless pit of human depravity, he thought of dead mothers and babies.

That's why he went for the barman. Low recognised the mournful gaze and the hollowed eyes. Li Jing was the barman's first corpse, a corpse that came with a crushing caveat. The barman had witnessed life and death in less than 10 minutes. His nightmares would last longer.

"She was here right, just before," Low said.

The barman nodded, pretending to scoop out the detergent smudges on the inside of a wine glass with a tea towel.

"Where was she in the bar?"

"There."

"This stool next to me," Low exclaimed.

"Yeah."

"So I'm . . ."

The barman nodded again. "He stood right there, maybe 15, 20 minutes ago."

Low pulled back from the bar, as if it were radioactive.

You were here. You were standing here, mocking me, bastard.

Fingerprints would be needles in haystacks, lost in the puddles of beer splashes and wiped away with sodden tea towels.

The sudden burst of energy was making it hard for Low to breathe, to hold on to the reins. "What did he look like?"

"Er, big guy *ang moh*, light hair, like brown or blond, but quite *botak* already, quite fat actually."

"Fat?"

"Yeah, in a shirt can hide it one, look like a big guy, like a sports guy, but definitely fat one."

"You got CCTV, right?"

"Yeah, of course."

"I want everything from your boss. How did he pay?"

"Er, credit card."

Low held out his hand.

"Oh, yah. Shit." The barman found his receipts beneath the optics and glanced through. "Yah, yah, he paid credit card, only just, so it's near the top."

The barman peeled off the receipt and waved the small, white piece of paper in the air. His shock was giving way to triumphalism. The woman at the bar had been pretty. He wanted the monster caught too.

Low took the receipt slowly, savouring the sensation, allowing the euphoria to take over. These rare moments gave him reasons to live. He needed these moments not for their highs, but to hang on to them during the lows.

He turned it over.

"Talek Maxwell. That's his name? Talek Maxwell."

Low was already on his way towards the raised, carpeted area. The receipt drove the mania, but it wouldn't last. He had to sustain the high with another hit, to hold off the descent. He was so close now. Another hit might be enough, another high to keep him tuned in.

Low leaned in to the subdued party spread across the Persian carpet. He faced Birthday Guy, the man of the hour, the previous hour, before the screaming had started. Now he was an empty shell in an expensive shirt, like everyone else in the bar.

"Hey, it's your birthday, right," Low said, talking quickly, almost incoherently.

"Er, yeah, why? Who are you?"

Birthday Guy shifted his weight to the other side of the cushion. The chilled, seated area with low tables and oversized pillows created a Zen vibe and sore arses.

"I'm Detective Inspector Low. Some of you saw me outside

already, but you never come outside, right?"

"No, it's my birthday."

"Happy birthday. What's your name?"

"Mark."

"How long you been here, Mark?"

"Most of the night. We came here straight from work."

"Great. And there's how many in your group, five, six?"

"I think there's eight of us."

Low took in the party: four white male faces and four brown female faces, all drunk, all sheepish.

"Take out your phones, all of you."

The drooping faces around the table hesitated.

"Now."

Reluctantly, they complied. Low went for Mark's phone. "Show me your photos."

"Why?"

"Say 'why' again and I'll arrest you for being a public nuisance."

"Excuse me, officer. I'm not being a public nuisance."

"You will be when I drag you down the street by your balls, now show me your photo gallery."

Mark unlocked the phone and handed it over. Low scanned the gallery before throwing the phone on the table.

"Bullshit."

"What?"

"Where's the other one?"

"What?"

"The phone, bastard, the phone. That one got photos of your family. Your family is not here. This is your other family, right? That's fine. I don't give a shit. Two families, two phones. Give me the other one."

Mark pulled a second phone from the other pocket in his trousers and handed it over.

"You guys think you're so clever, so original, but I see you guys every day. I see you women every day. Normally you entertain me. Give me target practice, but today I don't care. Today, I just want photos. I bet it's not even your birthday today right?"

Mark fiddled with his other phone.

"Right?"

Mark shook his head.

"Nope, of course not. You'll have the nice family meal next week, maybe Raffles, maybe Marina Bay, put up the photos for your friends back home, show them your all-year tans, show them how successful you are in your hot, sunny country and then they can look at you from their freezing country and hate you a little bit more, right? Ah, look at this. Lots of party photos. Look at that one."

Low held up the phone for Mark and his friends.

"Got your shirt off in that one. And that one got tequila shots, and that one got this one kissing that one. Ooh and that got you molesting that one. And there you are, behind your secret birthday cake ready to blow out your secret candles at your secret party."

Low froze.

He had found them.

They were over the right shoulder of the idiotic *ang moh* blowing out the candles. She was closer, sitting on that stool, turning away from the camera, her long black hair flowing down her back. But he was facing her, facing the camera, standing in that spot. His face was blurred, but still recognisable. He had his hand on hers, smiling at her, reassuring her, telling her that everything was going to be all right. Low checked the time stamp above the photo. She would be dead in less than an hour.

Low ignored Mark's whining about his private property and returned to the bar, shoving the phone in the barman's face.

"That him?"

Shock stole the barman's voice, pulling it deep into his stomach. He felt nauseous. He had served them minutes ago, a lifetime ago.

"Is that him?"

The barman managed a slight nod but nothing more. He had seen the poor woman alive and dead. Being told to look at her for a third time was torturous. And he couldn't look at him. He didn't need to. Both men had exchanged smiles when he'd accepted a $50 tip. He would never forgive his obsequious gratitude. Their brief encounter had forever sullied the barman's soul.

Chapter 46

PROFESSOR Chong waited for the uniformed officer to stop being bored long enough to lift the crime scene tape. It was unbecoming of Singapore's leading pathologist to duck under a tape like an overweight limbo dancer, particularly with all those onlookers with Instagram accounts. Chong's most famous cases had already been serialised for local television. The last thing he needed was a Vine video of his belly sticking out.

"Thank you, officer," he said regally, strolling beneath the raised tape, his shoulders pinned back, marching towards his latest kingdom.

Aside from being called to another murder in the small hours, Chong was in surprisingly good spirits. His self-imposed celibacy had ended and fewer people cared. The thought of a planned trip across Europe, as a belated honeymoon, made him desperately happy. His private life had always been a lie. Now it only needed to be discreet and mostly overseas.

Despite his girth, Chong was soon passing the sweaty uniforms and the sleepy investigators. To his surprise, the CID deputy director was already there, talking to Chan and Low. The older inspector was jittery, gesticulating wildly, his eyes flickering in the darkness. Chong recognised the symptoms. Stanley Low was a rather textbook bipolar patient—and everyone knew what had happened to him after the Tiger case. Professionally, it was quite something to behold. Chong had never seen a mind so malleable, so willing to bend itself out of shape and morph into something else entirely. But Low just couldn't put himself back together again. Chong wasn't sure if he ever would.

Low had his hand out, grabbing Chong's and shaking it vigorously. The pathologist couldn't recall the inspector being quite so frantic before.

"We got him, professor. We got the bastard," Low said.

Chong was taken aback.

"You've arrested a suspect?"

"No *lah*, *wah lau*, she's still on the pavement. But I got a name and a photo. Know who he is and what he looks like."

Low held up the confiscated phone to show the photo.

"That's him? The birthday boy? But his hair seems too dark, surely."

"No, behind, look behind, over his shoulder."

Chong lifted his glasses and squinted. "My god. Is that him?"

"That's why. Right there. Just an hour ago. Hour plus maybe. Next door in the bar."

"And that's the victim?"

"Yeah."

"The poor, poor girl."

Chong shivered in the heat. The proximity, the hair's breadth between life and death unnerved even him.

"Sometimes we forget they were living and breathing shortly before we found them."

"And we were already on our way here. Missed him by 10 or 15 minutes, got police stopping cars and taxis all over Orchard, roadblocks on both sides," Chan said. "But he's gone already."

"We don't know that for sure," Chua interrupted, joining the conversation. The deputy director extended his hand. "Hey, professor. Thanks for coming so fast."

"No choice, dear boy. What's the name?"

"Li Jing, 41 years old, Chinese Singaporean, married to Harold Zhang, the blogger."

"No, no, I meant *him*."

"Well, if he was using his own credit card," Low said. "Talek Maxwell. I don't know what Talek is, sounds like an Indian name."

"No, I'm pretty sure it's British," Chong said.

"Never heard of it."

"I think it's a rather posh name, a public school name, like a Tarquin or a Benedict. Talek Maxwell. It's rather catchy, isn't it?"

Chua coughed.

"Yes, well, time is pressing. Let's see." Chong dropped his kit beside the body. He ripped open a cellophane bag and pulled on his gloves, avoiding the risk of contamination until he was beside the body. Fresh corpses promised a real treasure trove. He switched on a small, pocket torch. The glare revealed Li Jing's fragility. A pulpy, sad face stared back at him.

"These red marks around the mouth, some swelling and bruising coming through."

"Yah, saw that, more brutal this time, *ah*?"

Chong shook his head.

"Not quite. Maybe even the opposite. His biggest enemy on this occasion, my dear boy, was not his victim, but the clock and the location."

"Had to be fast," Low muttered.

"Precisely. His screwdriver must work quickly. He's not using his apartment, nor is he using the reservoir to clean them up. He is exposed this time. Look at the cheeks and chin. That's a pressed hand mark, held for a long time."

Chong stood up to act out the execution. "The facial swelling indicates a more brutal killing, but this was actually cleaner and quicker than the previous killings. One hand, a strong hand, covers her mouth and pins her to the wall, looking at the wider red mark across her chin, a probable left hand. We already know he's right-handed from the previous incisions. The left hand covers the mouth and holds her still, the right hand, a really forceful powerful hand, pushes the screwdriver through her heart. And he removes neither, easing her down the wall. You will find hair and fibre on the wall, I'm sure. Then he drops beside her in this position, still crouching over here, waiting for the fight to dissipate. And it's done in less time than it's taken me to tell you. Did you find her like this?"

"Yah, pretty much," Chan said. "On her side, with her back almost against the wall."

"Did anyone touch her hair?" Chong asked.

"No."

Low nodded. "He straightened it, right?"

"It certainly looks very neat and parted considering how she died."

Low crouched beside the professor. "This wasn't really about her. It was about her husband. He was hurting the husband. She was a means to an end, a quick killing to make a bigger point. His problem was not her, so doesn't want her to look violated. It was quick not just out of necessity, but also respect for her. He had to do it, had no choice, had to, but he didn't have to particularly enjoy it. He didn't want to enjoy it and didn't want to prolong her suffering. He stayed with her until the end, right?"

"That's hard to tell."

"No, no, he did. It also works for him. Anyone passes in those few seconds, he's just a white knight helping a drunk local. An *ang moh* crouched over a passed out pretty girl? Can see that every night in Orchard Road. Stayed with her, sat beside her, listened to her and when he was sure, checked the street and he was gone."

Chua wasn't convinced. "But it's such a risk, Orchard Road at that time, got people everywhere?"

"Doesn't care anymore," Low said, rising slowly to his feet. "He's already made his point. He could've paid with cash, but he paid with a credit card. He's ready to be famous now."

"That's not happening," Chua insisted. "Not making a hero out of this guy, not now, got a foreigner killing famous locals' wives, no way. We know what he looks like. We know his name. No way we go public."

"You have to, no choice."

"Why?"

"Because he won't stop this until you do. It's not about the bodies anymore. It's about making a statement."

"You think we're gonna promote his crusade? Are you mad or what? I am not giving this man the oxygen of publicity. We take his oxygen away, on the end of a bloody rope. That's it."

"Just give him what he wants. Make him famous and we'll catch the fucker."

"We'll catch him anyway. He'll be in an interrogation room by midnight."

"Really *ah*? You wanted me to go after Zhang, when I knew it wasn't about him. It was about his wife. You only think literally. And I'm telling you to take your literal, dunce cap off and realise he's making a statement with each killing. That's all he wants to do now."

"So you wanna put him on TV and make him a star?"

"No, basket, I want him to stop killing people."

"Then catch him. Now."

"I nearly did. I missed him by 10 minutes because instead of thinking like you, I thought like him. It's called deduction. You should try it, instead of sharpening pencils."

"It's called insanity."

Low was in the deputy director's face, peering into the blood-streaked corners of tired eyes. "What did you say?"

Chan stepped between them, edging them apart, his back against his superior officer, his hands pushing his friend away.

"Don't do this. Not here. There are too many people watching."

"And Miss Li Jing is still here."

It was Chong, still crouching beside the forgotten victim.

"I realise that our profession thrives on ego and self-respect. But maybe, right now, hers is worth a little more."

Chapter 47

AT 6:15am, the Minister of Home Improvement was already in his spartan office. He yawned loudly, but that was to be expected after his Bukit Timah run to the hill's summit and back. His pre-dawn runs sustained him through the stressful periods. He focused only on keeping pace with his security, reminding them daily that age was no barrier. The TV on the wall in front of his desk was already on, with an attractive reporter speaking at the Emerald Hill crime scene. The volume was off. The Minister already knew what the talking prop was saying. She said whatever his Ministry told her to say. Life was so much simpler with calm exteriors.

The Minister picked up the coffee cup that was placed carefully on a coaster near his daughter's framed photograph. She was so photogenic in the black and white portrait, inheriting her father's genes. It was always in the genes in the end. They couldn't be taught or bought, only passed down, the most priceless of family heirlooms.

"Send him in."

The Minister sipped his black coffee. He needed the caffeine. So did the deputy director. He looked terrible, unwashed and unshaved.

"Thanks for seeing me, sir," Chua said, taking a chair. "I came straight here."

"I can see that. Maybe shower here before you leave. For the media later."

"Yes, sir."

"So, how?"

"Professor Chong says it's the same guy."

"I know that, Chua."

The Minister struggled with Chua's generation of department heads. They made him question the government's education policies and he abhorred questioning his own policies. But Anthony Chua was not only a very literal man. He was neither here nor there. It was a given that scholars came with the academic tools and not the street smarts, but the latest batch fell between two stools. They grew up in affluence, depriving them both of the resilience required to get by and the resourcefulness needed to solve problems. Everything was a click away on a computer. They proved to be marvellous project managers, but less intuitive. It was hard to think on one's feet when one was always sitting down. There were few rotten apples left in the Minister's orchard. They were all homogenised and sterilised, palatable and safe. But their guts had gone, or mostly gone.

"What is Inspector Low doing?"

The Minister's mention of the man's name stung Chua like an angry hornet.

"He's working on the leads, sir."

"And?"

Chua knew there was no point in lying. The Minister had informers everywhere.

"He's got a name and a photo of the suspect, sir."

The Minister almost suppressed the smile. He gripped the arms on his executive chair. The man he loathed more than any other had at least vindicated his decision to include him in the investigation.

"So you're going to arrest him?"

"Yes, sir, hopefully today."

"Outstanding news and perfect timing. The election is coming."

"Yes, sir."

"Excellent. Excellent news. I want to know as soon as an arrest is made."

The Minister sipped his coffee and straightened the photo frame on his desk.

"Yes sir, it'll be a joint operation between Major Crime and Low's Tech team. We'll get all the information we need online, home and office details and then we go."

"What's his name? The suspect?"

"Er, Talek Maxwell, sir."

The Minister put down his coffee cup. "*Aiyoh*, is he Indian? I thought he was an *ang moh*."

"No, he is sir. They say it's an old British name."

"Didn't Low say he was British? Something about the graffiti on the rocket tower?"

The deputy director squirmed in his seat. "Yes, sir."

The Minister shook his head, swallowing his begrudging admiration for the unhinged policeman. "That guy, *ah*?"

"Yes, sir. Exactly. That's why I contact you first, sir. Want to ask your authority for something."

"It's your case."

Chua understood the low, flat tones. It was his case until an arrest was made. Then the case belonged to the Minister. But if the case went unsolved, well, it was the deputy director's case.

"Understand, sir. But Low wants to go public with Talek Maxwell's identity as the main suspect, you know, like asking the public to look out for this man, if you see him to contact the police."

The Minister leaned back in his seat. "Why should we alert the suspect that we know his identity?"

"Exactly my point. But Low thinks that this guy's motive is some sort of statement. He wants to be famous or something."

"They all want to be famous. No, arrest first. Then we can make a big splash in the media. Never the other way round. No point. The island is too small. Where can they go? Have you told ICA already?"

"Yes, sir, all immigration checkpoints, first thing, sent over name and photo to the ICA myself, straight from my phone, before I left the crime scene."

"Then there should be no problem."

"I agree, sir, actually. But just to be clear, I want to, well, just in case."

"You want to protect your position. I understand." The Minister really did. Chua's generation was all the same. "You came to me and I agreed. Suppress his identity until an arrest is made."

Chua shifted his weight in the chair.

"But just in case, hypothetically speaking, he attacks someone else, someone who might have known if we'd released the information first . . ."

"You're going to arrest him today, right? In the next couple of hours?"

"Yes, sir, putting the teams together now."

"Good. Now consider what would happen if we did reveal his identity now. First, he would go into hiding, obviously. But more importantly, we would confirm that a white man had just killed another Singaporean, an attractive Singaporean woman. A foreigner had murdered the wife of Singapore's most anti-government blogger. What would that do?"

"Make people angry, sir."

"People are always angry. No, it would make Harold Zhang a martyr."

Chua saw the obvious flaw in his boss' argument. He heard his own voice run away from him.

"But, sir, sorry *ah*. She's already dead, right? So he's already a widower. So he's already a martyr, right?"

"Of course. The backlash will reach the blogs by breakfast. The reaction will be poisonous. But there's a quick antidote."

"When we arrest him."

"Exactly," said the Minister, opening a diary on his desk. "OK, I've got lunch in town, so if we can synchronise, I'll schedule the press conference for around 11.30am, 12pm latest. Then we can make the Chinese evening press. Let them gorge on all the gory details at the tabloid trough. Possible?"

Chua started to get up. "Yes, sir."

"OK then. Let's see. It's not even 6.30 yet. So you can grab a quick shower here. Take your breakfast. And bring me Talek Maxwell by lunchtime."

Chapter 48

THE 12 officers of the Major Crime Division ignored the perspiration. Their bulky, protective uniforms had made the heat unbearable in the van earlier. They now stood in the lift lobby of a low-rise condo in Blair Plain, the gentrified, affluent side of Chinatown. There were nods and smiles to each other. Neither disguised the tension.

Low ushered them away from the lifts, gathering them in a small corner. A neighbour came out to watch the free drama being played out in her corridor, but an armed officer soon directed her back into her apartment. She was ordered to lock the door.

Low examined the men. They were younger than him, mostly Chinese and Indian, with a couple of Malay faces in the determined crowd, presumably to keep the quota counters happy. He sensed the nerves.

"*Relak lah,*" he whispered, holding a Taurus at his side. "No one ever got whacked by a screwdriver, OK."

The confident nods pleased him. In a way, Low envied these men and their apprehension. Their reaction was appropriate. Once the natural fear mixed with their programmed training, they would be quick and decisive. Low's nerve endings tingled. The joy overwhelmed him. His mind had been a series of colourful explosions all morning. The office had hacked Maxwell's

Facebook account, finding photos of his condo, his workplace parties and his women. A single call to Immigration and another to the Ministry of Manpower gave the police everything: Maxwell's full employment history, his movements in and out of Singapore, his academic qualifications and schooling, his medical reports and even his blood group. Singapore's stat boards and government agencies often infuriated Low. But their paperwork was exemplary. Within an hour, Low had assembled two teams for him and Chan. Both men had wanted Maxwell's home address and flipped a coin. Chan lost. Chan got the stockbroking office at Marina Bay. Both men knew he wouldn't be at the office today.

An hour later, Low was in the back of the van, briefing his men, detailing possible scenarios. He spoke too quickly. The words ran away from his sentences. He wasn't always coherent, but his enthusiasm proved infectious. The younger officers didn't see the insubordinate, intolerable middle-aged inspector. They saw Ah Lian. He was the man who took down Tiger. He was their case study in theory classes on undercover operations. They were privileged to share a stage with the Method Man. Superior officers and team leaders deserved loyalty and respect. But only Low deserved awe.

Clearly, he lived for these moments. And so did they.

The officers checked their weapons a final time and glanced across at their colleague's ballistic armour. They were equipped for most outcomes, except the one on the other side of the oak door. Singapore's last serial killer was hanged before some of these men were born. Talek Maxwell was a case study for the next generation. The officers' actions today would be studied tomorrow. They had read about dozens of serial killers. They were about to face their first. Once they kicked in the door, their training became obsolete.

Low was satisfied with the team's preparations. He was ready.

They would just have to keep up.

"OK, ready to catch this bastard? He's killed five people. Bloody *chao ang moh*."

The smiles turned to grimaces. Low nodded to the officer at the head of the unit, holding the battering ram.

A second later, Low was in the living room, his pistol raised to eye level, following the other officers, in two rows of six. The men were scattering in pairs, kicking open doors and shouting, loudly but calmly. Low moved swiftly through Maxwell's large apartment, on the shoulder of another officer. He took a right down the corridor, then another into the bathroom, then a left into the second bedroom, filled with dusty gym equipment. He was checking a wardrobe, rifling through the tailored suits and designer shirts, making his way through the sizes, watching Maxwell grow bigger and fatter in his own cupboard.

Another left and he was back in the corridor, sliding along the wall and into the master bedroom, passing the neatly made king sized bed and the Chinese oil painting on canvas. In the walk-in wardrobe were more suits and trainers and rugby boots still in boxes, along with a rugby ball on the floor, unblemished and untouched, the symbolism obvious, the wealthy, private schoolboy gone to seed.

Louder now, less subtle, the heels on Low's shoes tapped along the polished timber floor. But their banging failed to silence his throbbing temple. Low was sinking as he drifted along the corridor, past the second bedroom and the second bathroom, back in the dining room and towards the marble-topped island in the kitchen. His men confirmed what he already knew, shouting the same word, over and over again, like a verbal machine-gunning.

Clear. Clear. Fucking clear.

Maxwell wasn't home.

Low was already on the phone, waiting for hope that wasn't

coming. He checked the time. Either way, it would be over.

"Eh, Charlie, how? *Yah lah*, same here. Don't know *leh*."

Low leaned on the marble-topped island in the kitchen. The euphoria was slipping away. The adrenal dump was coming. He would tire rapidly and need to rest. As he absentmindedly rubbed his hand against his stubble, enjoying the scratchy friction, he turned his head towards the wall. He noticed the plastic plug plate on the wall was crooked. There was a screw missing.

And then he saw the blood.

Chapter 49

THE conference room at the Home Ministry was full of restless journalists. It was almost 12.30pm. The news couldn't be positive if the Minister was keeping them waiting. He needed to make the evening newspapers just as much as they did. Captured serial killers were great for business. Unkempt cameramen adjusted their tripods as Eurasian reporters checked both their complexion and their accents in a compact mirror, mouthing their rehearsed introductions carefully.

The late arrivals were inevitably western journalists. Asian reporters were already in their seats, heads down, scribbling furiously and scrolling their phones, secretly pleased to have the British tabloids in the room. The slovenly, red-faced white men with their shirttails flapping over bulging waistlines would ask the questions that they couldn't. The locals would still get the quotes without the private dressing down the following morning. In a fiercely independent, post-colonial nation, middle-aged white men could still drive the news agenda.

The scampering of Chinese men in white shirts and black trousers around the raised platform indicated that the Minister was about to enter. The Singaporeans in the room immediately fell silent. Western writers would continue to chatter until the Minister stood behind his lectern. It was a puerile point of principle.

The Minister entered from the left side of the stage, moving quickly towards the lectern and clutching his notes. He was an engaging, charismatic orator. His public debating schooldays and his tertiary studies overseas had served him well. The grey patches around the ears added to the gravitas. He went through the same education system as his Cabinet colleagues, one that favoured obedient children being seen rather than heard, but he had always taken great pride in enunciating clearly and concisely. He had little difficulty code switching. He was fluent in Mandarin. National Service left him with conversational Malay and his Singlish was invaluable at the hawker centres on the campaign trail. But he found the local patois of the street to be vulgar and boorish. There was no place for it in press conferences or parliament. He often enjoyed watching the YouTube mash-ups of British politicians dropping their medial consonants to connect with the kids. Singapore had no need for such transparent pandering to the chattering classes. Eugenics prevailed. The cream always rises to the top in Asia.

The Minister surveyed the crowd before speaking: locals at the front, foreigners at the back. He needed a face to focus on and found one seated half a dozen rows back. She was Chinese, pretty enough for a reporter's byline, not pretty enough to introduce movies on HBO; young enough to still be cynical, old enough to recognise the fragility of her rice bowl in the Singapore media. She wouldn't ask any awkward questions. She would be his eye line.

"Good afternoon, ladies and gentlemen," he said. "As you are already aware, a woman was found earlier this morning. She died in terrible, tragic circumstances."

Hands were already going up in the room.

"Was she the wife of the anti-government blogger Harold

Zhang?"

The Minister adjusted his notes on the lectern. He knew who the questioner was and his publication; a publication previously banned in Singapore. Since Lee Kuan Yew's funeral, they had all gotten louder, brasher. They poked away with their blunt sticks and presumed the animal was mortally wounded. Of course it wasn't. It was just morphing into a different beast to cope with a changing terrain.

"I'll take questions at the end, but as I was talking about the victim, yes, she was the wife of Mr Harold Zhang. My thoughts are with Mr Zhang's family and Miss Li Jing's family. Out of respect for both families, I will say nothing further on either Miss Li or Mr Zhang other than— as you would expect—counselling services have of course been extended to Mr Zhang.

"But this is not a time to talk politics. This is not about the Government. This is about a destructive force, a man determined to scare us, intimidate us and destabilise our society. He is challenging the values that we hold dear as a nation—law and order. But he will fail. He is trying to unravel the very social fabric of multiculturalism that has knitted this country together for more than 50 years. But he will fail."

The reporter's hand went up again.

"Yes, but are you any closer to making an arrest? Can you now confirm that he's British? And if so, could he escape and return to his own country?"

The Minister inhaled sharply to hide the rage. Rage was unprofessional. Rage was undignified. Rage was rude. He glowered up from his speech. It was the same Caucasian reporter from the same, slighted publication. Of course it was. The Minister checked his notes again and peeked at his watch. His daughter would be waiting for lunch, but there was still time.

There was always time for batting practice.

"We are closer to making an arrest, but our investigations have been hampered—and will continue to be hampered—by unnecessary intrusions and interruptions. We will bring this man to justice, soon, but he is feeding off the social unrest that is being sparked by a number of media organisations. The focus has been on his skin tone and his passport. There's been a similar fixation with the background of his victims, whether they were local or foreign, Asian or Caucasian, rich or poor. These discussions have not been helpful, nor have they been relevant, either to me, or the investigating officers. Our only interest is finding this individual and ending these horrific killings. I would assume that our interests would be the same as your interests. Would I be right? Would your publication's interests be the same as ours?"

The crimson-faced reporter turned away. The Minister returned his gaze to the young Chinese woman sitting near the front.

"But I am pleased to report that we made a tremendous breakthrough today, a real breakthrough in the case."

The Minister took a sip from his water, waiting for absolute silence.

"In light of recent investigations, we believe we know the identity of the suspect and an arrest is imminent."

Every arm in the room went up. The silence gave way to chaos. Everyone was shouting now, all decorum was lost.

"What's the suspect's name?"

"Will you release an image of the killer?"

"Is he still in Singapore?"

"Are Singaporeans safe in their own country?"

"What's his name?"

"Tell us his name so we can warn Singaporeans."

The Minister raised his arms to hush the crowd. He wanted to elaborate on the last point.

"Officers have assured me that their investigations are at a critical juncture. To reveal his identity now could jeopardise the manhunt."

"But what if he kills again? What if he kills again because future victims were not aware of his identity?"

The questioner troubled the Minister. She was clearly Singaporean and genuinely fearful. He couldn't have her demoted for being afraid, particularly if her views were representative of other voters.

He sipped his water again.

"I understand your concerns. I very much do. But what we need now is calm. We need the police departments to be left alone to do their jobs. We do not need panic on the streets with countless cases of mistaken identities. Let me assure you again. The police know who he is and where he is. The only person in Singapore who should be afraid is him. We are onto him. I want him to know that. It's not our job to glorify him. It's our job to catch him. And we will. Soon. Thank you."

The Minister ignored the shouting voices and left the conference room.

Chapter 50

"NO. No. No. No."

Maxwell was stretched out across the rear leather seat of his Porsche, his phone on his chest, rising and falling slightly with each angry breath. On his phone screen, the Minister left the stage and the live news coverage returned to the studio. Seated behind a curved desk, two news anchors discussed the implications of the Minister's press conference, waffling on about national security being more important for the country than a sensationalist naming and shaming announcement and some other utilitarian bullshit. Maxwell shook his phone.

Sod your security issues. Take me back to the Minister. Where's the Minister?

Maxwell accepted he was taking a crazy risk, but he no longer cared and had little left to lose. He was working on the principle of not seeing the wood for the trees. He had once watched a TV movie where a carjacker stole civilian vehicles from a police station car park, working on the assumption that it would be the last place that anyone else would think of. The thief was eventually captured and shot by police in the final reel, but this was Singapore, a land of literal thinkers. Maxwell figured he had half a chance.

With his aviator sunglasses on and his baseball cap pulled

low, he peered through the rear window. Across the busy road, the assembled media moved quickly to get into position outside the Home Ministry building. Cameramen checked their lenses and reporters straightened their ties. A polished, black Mercedes pulled up outside the lobby. Burly men in white shirts stood either side of the car.

The Minister was on his way.

Ducking beneath the rear window, Maxwell used his camera phone to zoom in on the car. He could follow proceedings without being spotted, particularly when the Minister's car drove away.

Suddenly, the Minister appeared on Maxwell's screen. He slid his fingers across the panel to further zoom in on the handsome Chinese face, snapping a photo just before the Minister disappeared into the car. Maxwell didn't need the photo, but he couldn't help himself.

He waited for the Minister's car to pull away and then sat up quickly. He squeezed between the front seats and started the engine. He signalled and pulled out into the traffic. There was a U-turn up at the next junction and he needed to hurry. He changed lanes and caught his reflection in the side mirror. He was smiling now. He was so happy, so, so happy.

It was almost over.

Chapter 51

DEPUTY Director Chua kept a neat department. He hired extra cleaners to vacuum carpets and polish desks; tidy offices, tidy minds. Rows of partitioned cubicles housed men in identical white shirts staring at computer screens.

Low was running past them, shaking off Chan's arm and making for the deputy director's glassy cocoon. His office symbolised his elitist position; isolated and detached from reality, buffeted from the real world, Low's world. Low kept moving along the production line and the endless rows of automated uselessness. The cubicles, the coffee cups, the computers, the pressed white shirts, the cubicles, the coffee cups, the computers, the pressed white shirts; it was the iconography of sleep-deprived middle management, artificial stimulants to wake up artificial minds. Low loathed them all. And they hated him right back. They chased pay cheques. He chased his calling. Both sides usually won, but one side always lost in the end.

They were watching him now, craning their necks over their partitions, the minions following the madman. Floorboards creaking below the cleanest carpets, Low never trod lightly. Kicking the glass door open, its silver hinges rattling against the frame, he was in the deputy director's office. Already on the back foot, Chua was retreating further behind his desk, shrinking in his own kingdom, cowed by the inspector's anger. The visitor's chair on the other side of the desk was pushed aside, its wheels sliding along the carpet before clattering into a bookcase.

Only the desk separated them.

Ordinarily, that was more than enough in an Asian workplace, a physical and metaphorical boundary in the office hierarchy.

But Low wasn't an ordinary man.

"Why the fuck didn't he give Maxwell's name?"

Chua's eyes darted towards the outside cubicles. His glassy cocoon couldn't contain the voice. He had to reassert his superiority.

"Now, look. I spoke to the Minister."

"Fuck the Minister."

Chua was now staring at Low. So was Chan, unable to look away from this mess of a man.

"Stanley, come on *ah*," Chan mumbled.

"Please Charlie not now. This isn't about me or you or him or even Maxwell, it's about politics, right or not? If we had put out the *ang moh*'s name, this would already be over."

"He is a flight risk."

"*Wah lau*, what's he going to do? Swim to Malaysia? He's not going anywhere."

Chua raised an eyebrow at the inspector.

"It's happened before."

Low thought about punching the deputy director. The anger blurred his vision. He couldn't see straight. It ran away from him like a spooked horse. He had to hold on, stay upright.

"Ah, you want to play games now, is it? You want to play poker with me, scholar boy. Come we play poker. We let go who we choose to let go. You want me to name names? I've got a list as well you know. And my one is bigger than your one. I was CPIB when you were still playing with your stat boards. Still want to measure dicks, is it?"

"Yah. OK. Very good. Your gangster act is still damn solid, still the best *ah beng* in the police force. Well done. But if we give Talek Maxwell to the media, we create a nationwide panic."

"There's already a nationwide panic. We've got a serial killer. How much more of a panic you want?"

"Correct. So we must keep a calm . . ."

"Don't give me the Minister's calm exteriors shit. Heard it enough times already. This is bullshit. You should've let him have his moment. Let him be famous."

"If the Minister went public this morning then every *ang moh* in Singapore will suddenly look like Talek Maxwell," Chua said. "We know who he is. We can control this case. Otherwise, we got chaos and that's what he wants."

"He doesn't want chaos, he wants fame. He's already controlling this case. He put the *ang mohs* at the reservoir to send a message. He told us he was from London with that Jack the Ripper bullshit. He used a credit card and then left Li Jing out in the open, a huge risk. He wants to be famous now, the Jack the Ripper of Singapore, the Ted Bundy of Asia, the usual shit. The first one was an accident and he thought, *Fuck it, I'm dead anyway, might as well be worthwhile.* He just wants to be named now. That's it. That's all. And we wouldn't give it to him. And now it's worse."

"Why?"

"Because he knows he's on borrowed time. He can't hide in Singapore for long. He'll keep killing now until we catch him." Low pointed at Chua. "Everyone he kills now is your fault, OK. The blood is on your hands now. Not mine. Not Charlie's. You. Just you and the Minister."

"Fuck you, psycho."

The unexpected invective from his boss was Chan's trigger.

He was on his way towards both men, separating them before the pushing gave way to punching.

"Yeah, yeah, big man now, is it?" Low shouted over Chan's shoulder. "Think you got the Minister in your corner, is it?"

Chan shoved his friend hard in the chest. Low stumbled backwards, alarmed by the sudden aggression.

All three men were breathing heavily, listening to their hearts thumping. No one spoke. There was nothing left to say.

The ringing phone made each man jump. Slowly, Chua picked it up.

"Yah, what? . . . Really? . . . OK, OK, stay there. No, just stay there. I'll call you right back."

Chua seemed to return the phone in slow motion. He inhaled. He waited for his scrambled brain to join the dots. He wanted his voice to be low, almost monotone.

"You are not always right, Detective Inspector."

Low's eyes narrowed. "What?"

"That was the staff sergeant at Kreta Ayer Police Post."

"Yah, me and Charlie met him before. So?"

"Talek Maxwell just handed himself in."

Chapter 52

DEPUTY Director Chua and Detective Inspector Chan were experienced interrogators. They stayed calm on the drive across Chinatown, focusing on what they might say, how the initial interview would go. They remained composed when staff sergeant Razali Othman ushered them into the holding room of the Kreta Ayer Police Post. They even managed to restrain Low and order him to wait outside with the flustered officer.

Besides, this wouldn't take long. They would identify him, apprehend him and get him back to their department and their redoubtable interrogation tactics.

But Talek Maxwell disgusted them; disappointed them even. He was a sweaty, balding, slovenly white man. Singapore's entire police force and every relevant government agency had focused all available resources on *this*.

Both officers were married. Both men had relatives who hadn't walked the streets after dark for weeks. Both wanted to rip his eyes out.

Maxwell sat on the other side of the table, wearing his favourite Brooks Brothers chequered shirt and khaki shorts. She had always liked that particular combination, said it made him look like he'd just stepped off a yacht. The shirt also hid his girth. He wanted to adjust the waistline of his shorts; the belt was cutting into his belly, but the handcuffs would have made him appear clumsy.

He leered at the deputy director. Chan admired his boss' restraint, but privately wished that Low had been allowed to join them. The occasion called for a little civil disobedience.

"So Mr Maxwell, thank you for doing the right thing," Chua said.

The deputy director perused the passport and identity card on the table.

"It's certainly you at least. Now we must take you back to our office and conduct a proper interview there."

Maxwell leaned back in his chair and shook his head.

"Eh, you don't have a choice, OK?" Chan said, leaning forward. "We can drag you by your ankles into a police car outside now."

Chan felt the deputy director's hand on his.

"We don't want to do that, Mr Maxwell. It's still light outside. Everyone is a media photographer these days. But this is a small neighbourhood police post. It doesn't really have the facilities to keep you here."

Maxwell said nothing. He looked around the room. It was small and reasonably secure, but stifling. The officers had switched off the air-conditioning.

"Mr Maxwell. I'm going to ask you again to stand up and accompany us outside. We've got other officers outside, plus several police cars on standby. I don't know what you are doing. And frankly, I don't care. You are the only suspect in five murders and you are coming with us."

Maxwell yawned.

The bravado didn't impress Chua. He had survived a sadistic Indian staff sergeant during National Service, a rare staff sergeant who had risen through the ranks without using a silver spoon as leverage. He bullied the Chinese because they were the racial majority. He picked on scholars because they were being fast-tracked on fluffy pillows. And he bullied Chua because he was a Chinese scholar and overweight, forcing him to attend a long and humiliating weight-loss programme in Basic Military Training. But Chua rose to the challenge. It tested his firm beliefs in eugenics. They all did. Every day. The Malay drug addicts and the Chinese bookies, the PRC pimps and the South Indians killing each other with cheap beer bottles; they all strengthened his convictions. His DNA was inherently superior. He was, quite simply, a better man.

And this fat *ang moh* would only prove his point.

"You're tired, is it? All the yawning. That for me, is it? You want to show me you're not scared? I know you're not scared. If I killed five people, I would not be scared."

Maxwell crossed his arms and chuckled.

"OK, enough of this shit," Chan pushed his chair back. "Call in the other officers. Go fetch a blanket. We're not making him famous."

Maxwell cleared his throat. "Maybe you should stay here."

It was the first time he had spoken. Chua didn't move.

Maxwell slid his chair back. He was standing up. Chan was on his feet faster, hands gesturing towards the table.

"Woah, woah, woah, sit down, Maxwell. Now."

Chan had his hand on his gun, ignoring the incriminating sweat rolling past his ears and hoping Maxwell would do the same.

Maxwell raised his hands in the air slowly, but leaned forward, across the table and towards the officers. Chan flipped off the catch on his holster and grabbed the handle.

"Don't do this, Maxwell. We're not your suicide squad, OK?"

Maxwell's right hand moved towards Chan's arm. The inspector edged away from the table and went for his Taurus, one efficient move, chest-high; his hands remarkably steady.

"We are not going to kill an unarmed man in a police cell, OK? But I still got every right to blow your balls off."

Maxwell rolled his eyes.

"It's OK. I was just trying to check the time." He tilted his head, slowly, carefully, theatrically, to read Chan's watch. "Ah, not much time."

Maxwell returned to his seat.

"For what?" Chua asked.

"Ah." Maxwell frowned, as if searching for a distant memory. "No. It's gone."

"Enough already," Chua said, turning towards the door. "Let's get him out."

"You said five."

"What?" Chua asked, facing Maxwell, making no effort now to conceal his contempt.

"You said five people. Just now. You seemed *very* certain."

"You want to play games, is it?"

Maxwell pointed to the empty chairs opposite him. "You want to sit down?"

"Not really."

"OK."

Maxwell stretched out his legs under the table. Chan clipped the gun back to his hip.

"Are you saying there's more than five, Talek?"

"It's not *Tar*-lek. It's *Ta*-lek as in talent."

"Are there more than five, Talek?"

Maxwell shrugged his shoulders. "What difference does it make? When you're the personification of evil, yeah, I think that's what I was called in one of the more frenzied pieces in the local newspapers, the personification of evil; when you're the personification of evil, five, six, seven, they're just numbers. Once you get past the first one, they're just numbers, like being in the army, I suppose."

Chan sat down. "OK, you think you have some sort of leverage over us."

"The penny drops."

"You handed yourself in."

"Yes."

"Because you wanted to be caught."

"Exactly."

"Because you want it to be over."

"Not quite."

Chan examined the Caucasian's inscrutable face. He offered nothing. "We've been to your home and office."

"I'm sure you have."

"You don't really live near here. There are other police posts closer."

"I'm sure there are."

"You chose this police post deliberately."

"Very good."

"It's where you watched Harold Zhang's rally."

Maxwell tapped his wrist with his forefinger. "Tick tock."

"Have you killed someone else?"

Maxwell wagged his finger at Chan. "No, no, no. That's too much of a leap. Your reasoning was going quite well, but that was too much of a leap in faith, too big a gap in logic."

"What? I don't know what you want me to say?"

Chua leaned on the table. "Stop playing games."

"Who's playing games? I'm just saying that time is running out."

"For what?" Chua asked. "What do you want from us?"

"I want what you're going to give me anyway." Maxwell pointed at Chan's watch. "Just a few more minutes and I'll get exactly what I want."

"What's that?" Chan asked.

"This policeman of yours. Ah Lian. I want to see what all the fuss is about."

Chapter 53

LOW was aware that he was pacing the floor, going around in circles. The Malay kid's uncertain eyes followed him. The police post was too small, too nondescript to contain Low.

"Do you want anything, inspector?"

Staff Sergeant Razali Othman's voice startled Low. "What? No?"

Low was reaching for the door handle, pulling it, staring through the glass at the Chinatown traffic, a deserted Hong Lim Park on his left, a Speakers' Corner with no voices, just as Singapore liked it. The uniformed officers outside turned to address the door shaking. When they recognised the culprit, they pretended to ignore him.

"You locked this door, right?"

"Yes, sir, as soon as he came in," said Othman, standing up. "I only open it when you come with the deputy director, and then I lock it again."

"Well done."

"Thank you, sir."

"He never threatened you or try to run away, right?"

"No, sir."

"Tell me again."

"Er, he come in and close the door. He told me his name, but

I recognise him already. *Wah*, damn shocked I tell you, first time I pull my gun outside, well, outside training, you know."

"And he never reacted?" Low was treading the same path, going round and round in circles, not deviating.

"No, no. In fact, he said, no need gun, just put on handcuffs and make your phone call. He lift up his shirt, show me he had nothing, then sat down and put out his arms, basket, I was nervous, got no support, was the only one here. But I put on the handcuffs and put him inside, watching him the whole time."

"Relax, you're not on trial, OK. You did good. Tomorrow, you'll be famous. They'll make you the pin-up on their new 'Stop, Thief' posters. Very good. Now, never mind what you did. I want to know what he did."

"Nothing."

"What?"

"Nothing. He just sat there and waited. Told me to call you guys. Told me to relax. Told me he'd sit down at the table and keep his hands on the table, so I could see him. He told me he was no problem. And he wasn't. He just waited."

Low's head pounded. On the wall behind Othman's desk, the clock-ticking taunted him. He rubbed his right cheek until the stubble burned against his reddening skin.

This isn't right. We shouldn't be here. It doesn't end here. Tiny police post, idiot policeman, empty park, no one around, he doesn't finish here. He had time, hours, could've gone anywhere, seen anyone, killed anyone. He's always been in control, even after the first one, the disposal was improvised, but still smart; definitely in control for the second one, definitely after Dragon Boy—poor Dragon Boy, bastard—but it was Dragon Boy, after that, heck care lah. After that didn't matter, killing for fun, making a statement, leaving silly clues and playing games, giving his name at the bar—No.5 for number five, sick bastard—No.5 for number five, that's good, that's really

*fucking good, almost funny; that's a lucky break though, that was
her choice, not his, her hangout to see ang mohs and reminisce about
the good times in Australia. That was her choice, but his chance to
be caught, to be caught everywhere—on camera, on the bill, in the
street, on CCTV—time to finish one life and start another, become
a somebody, a name, a legend, just like all the others, a cliché, but
he's not, not yet, we didn't name him. So he names himself, walks in,
hello blur Malay policeman, my name is Talek Maxwell, serial killer,
superstar, you know who I am? Damn shiok, feels like an orgasm, but
no one else knows, right? Not yet. But now they do. Now we know
his name. Now everyone will know his name, but no need to wait,
five enough already; the blogger's wife's huge, that's it, finish, but you
waited for what? To kill more? To kill bigger?*

Low didn't hear the banging, not at first. His feet shuffled
around in circles, not listening to the thumping, not seeing
Othman standing up, his mouth open, finger pointing at the
door. The voice was muffled, bouncing back off the glass, not
seeping through. But it was getting louder.

"Low, open the door."

The inspector heard something this time, forcing him to
look up at the familiar face, the crying face, on the other side
of the door. At first, Low didn't move, struggling to sharpen
the dizzying, distorted images, the mosaic of emotions against
the glass, the clenched fist, the teary eyes, the suppressed terror.
Nothing matched. And there was that voice, distinct now, rising,
but disconnected.

"OPEN THE DOOR, LOW! OPEN THE BLOODY
DOOR."

Low was drifting across the floor, towards the dumbstruck kid
in uniform, one hand out, taking the key, retreating, on his heels,
finding the lock, turning, opening, the blast of sticky, damp air
in his face.

The wide-eyed inspector held on as the Minister of Home Improvement fell into his arms.

Chapter 54

THE other men struggled to look their Minister in the eye. It wasn't particularly ministerial to cry. It wasn't really Asian. Chua stood beside his boss, loyal and resolute, offering tissues. The two inspectors sat on the front desk, leaving Othman to babysit Maxwell in the next room.

The Minister of Home Improvement knew what his scrunched up, tear-stained face looked like, what it represented. He was weak, inadequate. Politicians didn't get caught crying in front of a camera unless national security itself was at state. This was a private matter that the Minister had now made public. But he didn't care. He really didn't care. Nothing else mattered. He blew his nose and straightened up, his eyes drilling holes through Low's skull.

"So how, Low?"

The inspector focused on Chua. "The deputy director won't let me sit in on the interrogation, sir. He says I'll make it personal."

Chua cleared his throat. "He knew one of the victims, sir, the second one, the pimp."

"Eh, he wasn't a pimp, OK, dipshit."

Chua raised a hand towards Low, registering his exasperation. "You see?"

"I'm not interested," the Minister said. "I just want my

daughter back."

The three investigators in the room exchanged the same edgy glances. Low shifted uneasily on the desktop. "Er, sir, you know *ah*, your daughter . . ."

"Don't tell me she's dead. Don't tell me that my little girl is dead. Can you do that, inspector? Tell me that you *know* that my daughter isn't dead."

Low looked away from the weeping father. "I can't do that, sir."

The Minister stepped forward; the man who'd aced every test, every exam, every job, every promotion and every national project, the man who'd never failed, eyeballed the inspector.

"You get in there and find out about my daughter. You give him whatever he wants, say whatever he wants you to say, but get me what I need. Did you hear the phone? Did you hear my little girl's voice? This cannot be the last time I hear her voice."

The Minister held up the phone and played the message, putting it on speaker. A frightened woman's voice echoed around the small police post.

"*Daddy, it's me. It's Gabriella. I'm . . . It's OK. OK. I'll say it. Please. I'll say it . . . Daddy, he was there after our lunch, waiting for me. He, erm . . .*"

The voice cracked and drifted off, replaced with soft whimpering. As he held up the phone, tears streamed down the Minister's face.

"*Tell him.*"

It was Maxwell's voice. Low's stomach turned on him. His throat was constricting, struggling to breathe.

"Daddy, he says his name is Talek Maxwell. You know who he is, Daddy. He's the . . ."

The voice was almost buried beneath the sobbing.

"*Tell him. Fucking tell him.*"

"*He says he's going to give himself up. He's going to a police station now, but he'll only speak to Ah Lian. Do you know who that is, Daddy? If you don't, Daddy, he's going to.*"

"*Going to what? Tell him. Tell your Daddy.*"

"*He's going to kill me like the others.*"

Her gentle crying stabbed the Minister through the heart.

Suddenly, unexpectedly, Gabriella was speaking quickly, her voice getting faster and louder.

"*Daddy, we're near the restaurant. I think he's got a Porsche and we're on the AYE and . . .*"

Her scream chilled the room, but was less terrifying than the silence that followed. The Minister held the phone, leaving the dead air hanging in the confined space. Chua hesitated before stepping forward.

"Sir, which restaurant did you have lunch with your daughter? We can check CCTV cameras and then trace . . ."

"Trace what?" Low interrupted. "The fucker is sitting in there already. He knows where the daughter is, no one else does."

Low sighed. He needed to buy time, a chance to descramble. "OK, must use the toilet first. The Minister must wait outside, cannot go in, obviously, cannot be involved."

"You want me to come inside?" Chan asked.

"I want you both inside," Low said.

The deputy director brightened. "Why?"

Low was already heading for the toilet behind the front desk. "To stop me from killing him."

The other men believed him. But he didn't. He didn't feel anything. And that concerned him so much more than meeting Maxwell.

Chapter 55

LOW splashed water on his face, but it made no difference. The pinkish blotches on his forehead remained. They were slight, barely noticeable, but weak spots nonetheless, the blood vessels bursting through to illustrate his apprehension. He dried his hands and dialled again; same tone; same voice.

"You've reached the office of Dr Tracy Lai. We are now closed for the day. Our opening hours are from 9am to 5.30pm. If you feel it is an emergency, please stay on the line for the following numbers."

Low hung up. The detective inspector's hands were shaking. He was trapped in Stanley Low's body at the wrong time. He needed Ah Lian, not this jittery wreck in the mirror. He wanted Tiger's boy back in the room, with his King Kong balls and Old Testament values.

He rang the number again.

"You've reached the office of Dr Tracy Lai."

"Fuck," Low muttered.

He knew she wasn't there, but he couldn't stop calling. Maybe it was her voice. Maybe it was her soothing authority. Maybe he had no idea what he was doing. Low struggled with the phone. His hands were still shaking.

STAFF Sergeant Othman found Maxwell's gaze unsettling. The

mat salleh had his head on the table, peering up at him. Othman had been instructed not to engage the suspect, not to speak to him unless it was absolutely necessary. So he focused on staying quiet by picturing the newspaper headlines, thinking about what he might say to the media. He was the man who caught the IKEA Killer. His parents would be so proud.

"You smoke right?"

Maxwell spoke with his chin still on the table. Othman didn't answer.

"I can tell by your fingers. Look at them. You're so young but they are already nicotine stained. Terrible. It's such a filthy habit. That's what often puts me off the Malay girls here, always smoking like chimneys. I know why you do it of course. It's about the only vice you're allowed, right? Can't drink, can't gamble, can't marry outside of the community, can't eat pork, can't eat at all sometimes and yet, somehow, smoking slipped beneath the radar. So you make up for it by going crazy on the cigarettes."

Othman concentrated on writing the next morning's headlines in his head.

"And the funny thing is, we love your women. Just love them. I'm no exception. The dark skin, the long hair, we cannot get enough of it in Asia. And yet as soon as you go anywhere near them, out come the cigarettes and the yellow fingers."

Othman wondered if the newspapers would want a photo of him in his uniform at the Kreta Ayer Police Post or at home with his family. There was the potential to be the next poster boy for the Malays. The Government was always looking for one, particularly in such racially sensitive times.

"Yes, I can't abide by the smoking in your community, can't go anywhere near it," Maxwell continued. "That's probably why I never killed any Malays."

Othman's newspaper headlines suddenly vanished.

"You did. The first one," the staff sergeant heard himself say.
Maxwell laughed.

"So I'm guilty already? No trial or anything."

Othman prayed under his breath, begging forgiveness and
hoping that his words weren't picked up by anyone outside.

"Anyway, it's not your fault," Maxwell insisted. "I wasn't being
specific. I meant to say Singaporean Malays. I didn't kill any local
Malays. When they come from overseas, it's completely different,
you know. They're poorer. Most of them can't afford cigarettes.
So they don't smoke. That's why I prefer foreigners. I won't fuck
a Malay woman unless I'm absolutely positive she doesn't smoke.
Does your sister smoke?"

Othman realised he was pushing a chair aside and heading
towards the table when the door opened. He stopped, horrified
by his intentions.

"Ah, that's a shame, I was starting to enjoy myself," Maxwell
said.

He sat up and pointed at the haggard policeman.

"You must be Ah Lian."

Chapter 56

THE small interview room felt crowded and claustrophobic. It wasn't built for a thorough interrogation. Chan stood at the back of the room, leaning against the wall with the deputy director. They sipped coffee they didn't want, but it was part of the routine. The air-conditioning unit rattled behind Maxwell, spitting cold air at his exposed neck. Low sat across from him, keeping his hands beneath the desk, just in case. The inspector recognised the other man's physical strength, his broad shoulders and upper arms more than capable of driving a screwdriver through Dragon Boy's scrawny chest. In fact, Maxwell's physique reminded him of Tiger, a rugby player gone wrong. But the *ang moh's* unblinking eyes held their focus, betraying neither fear nor resignation. They were still, lifeless eyes. The same eyes that had followed Low to the door when he'd visited Tiger for the last time. They belonged to a man who was aware of his fate and welcomed the downfall.

Low nodded at his coffee on the table. "You want some?"

"No, thank you, inspector."

"Good. You're not getting any."

Maxwell grinned.

"What?" Low asked.

"No, it's just a little obvious that's all, a tad too transparent. The cold air-conditioning, your immediate belligerence, my lack of legal representation; it's all a bit clichéd, isn't it? A bit too, I don't know, South-east Asian?"

"I don't give a shit what you think it is."

But Low was aware that he was acting, manufacturing his aggression. The spontaneity wasn't happening. There were no internal ripples. He was lumbered with calm rather than chaos. Dr Lai always stressed his worrying inability to turn off the mania with an internal switch.

Fuck that, I can't switch it on.

Maxwell was less than impressed with the shriveled policeman fidgeting in front of him. "I read you're the best policeman in Singapore."

"We're not here to talk about me."

"What would you like to talk about? Your holidays?"

"Where's Gabriella?"

"Who?"

"Where's the Minister's daughter?"

"Oh, is that her name? She just said 'Daddy' and cried a lot." Chan threw his empty polystyrene cup on the floor.

"Eh, screw you OK. Where is she?"

The deputy director grabbed his inspector by the arm, gently pulling him back. He said nothing. He didn't want to infer what everyone else in the freezing room was already thinking. Maxwell was right. Low was lost. This didn't even look a fair fight.

At the table, neither man moved.

"Why do they call you Ah Lian?"

"I'm not called Ah Lian."

"OK, you were called Ah Lian before."

"We don't have time for this."

"No, *you* don't have time. I have all the time in the world. Your Minister's daughter doesn't, but I do. Why Ah Lian?"

Low sighed, clutching his hands beneath the table. He couldn't stop the damn shaking. "Will you answer my questions if I tell you?"

"I definitely won't answer them if you don't."

"It means girl in Chinese, like a wayward girl."

"I know that."

"It was a nickname I was given before because they said I was skinnier than a boy, so I must be a girl."

"It was given to you by a gangster, when you were working undercover."

Low's eyes narrowed. "How you know that?"

"Google. It's a marvellous thing."

"So this is it, is it? You bring me in to tell me my life story, is it? Fuck you. I already know my life story. Play your games with them."

Low slid his chair back, rising quickly.

"Tick tock," Maxwell said. "If you leave, she dies."

Low squeezed the door handle. It stopped the shaking.

"She's dead already."

"Is she?"

"Yes."

"If you leave she is. I won't talk to them."

"Why you want to talk to me?"

"Dragon Boy."

Low saw the images in his head, a fuse being lit, spitting out sparks, heading towards a padlocked box, the fizzing intensifying.

"Dragon Boy?"

"Yes. He made me curious about you. He seemed to be rather fond of you. In fact, most of his last words were about you."

The padlocked box had a hole for the fuse to pass through. It was disappearing inside, getting noisier, sparking away in the darkness. The fireworks would be fabulous. They were already rumbling, spinning in anticipation. Low was on his way back, no longer slouching, his steady hand pulling back the chair, ready for the fucking fool on the other side of the table.

"Did he? What did he say?"

Maxwell was taken aback by the question's breeziness. "You really wanna know?"

"Yeah, what were my *kaki*'s last words about me?"

"He said that Ah Lian would get me. The great Ah Lian would catch me."

Low smiled. He was so proud of his old protégé. Tiger would be, too.

"He said that *ah*?" The inspector was shaking his head in admiration. "Blur like *sotong* that one, even at the end."

"But you didn't catch me, did you?"

"No, I didn't. Is that what this is? To prove a point, I never caught you because you were so clever. Is this why you put on this big drama, to show Dragon Boy was wrong?"

"I don't know."

"No, you don't know. So I'll tell you. Even if you kill all of us in here with your bare hands, go outside and kill the blur policeman and everyone in Chinatown, you still cannot make it with me and Dragon Boy last time. Dragon Boy could whack every gangster in Singapore and not even blink. You kill women. *Women*. You are nothing. We look people in the eye. We face them, man to man. Dragon Boy didn't play in the dark with screwdrivers. He had balls the size of fucking durians."

"Not anymore."

Low crouched lower to peer up at the overweight Caucasian. "*Wah*, not bad *ah*, that time you really sounded tough, *ang moh*. And you are tough, look at you, big guy. I read about you, saw some photographs. Big handsome man last time, wealthy family, popular, rugby captain, Captain Cock last time."

Maxwell sneered. "You never played rugby."

"No, definitely not. Too skinny. I was the other one, that one *ah*, the one who never got the girl. They all went to guys like you. And then when I grew up, I saw them still go to guys like you around Marina Bay. Must make you feel good right? Give you a nice big erection?"

Maxwell looked across at Chua and Chan. "Is he always like this?"

"Don't look at them, look at me. I'm the great Ah Lian, right? I'm the man who cut your balls off. And that's driving you crazy. It doesn't make any sense, right? At school, I'm the guy you push down the toilet. In the bar, I'm the guy who cleans the toilet. You own men like me. And then, when you show your power, when you're proving what a big man you really are, when you're sticking your metal dick through my boy's heart, he mentions me and your dick falls off. He mentions *me*. Even when you're being the big man, when you're sticking a screwdriver through his chest, he's talking to you about another guy. You're in the middle of sticking it in and he's screaming out another guy's name. He's cheating on you, ruining your big moment. And that's when you know you're nothing. He can't even remember your name, even when you're killing him, because you're nobody. You're nothing, a fat, bald nothing who kills women and tourists. And we will make you nothing. We will control the media until the very end. We will belittle you, humiliate you, make you the most fucked-up perverted piece of shit in history. We will make your rich family and your famous fucking school bury you forever. And when we're done, when the whole world has laughed at you, we'll give your little dick to the hangman."

Maxwell pointed at the clock. "Tick tock," he said, still smiling, but the fight was ebbing away.

Low got up to leave.

"Yeah, you said that already."

This time, the inspector slammed the door behind him.

Chapter 57

"HERE'S what I don't get," Low said, returning to the room with another cup of coffee for himself. "Why you just didn't kill the Minister's daughter?"

Maxwell gestured towards the clock above the heads of Chua and Chan.

"She could be dead already."

"I'm sure."

"I'm serious."

"I believe you. I really do. But why this way round? Normally, you want them to be found, at least the later ones. But the Minister's daughter, there's no body."

"Not yet."

Low sipped his coffee. "How are we going to find it?"

"I'm going to tell you."

"When?"

"When you give me what I want."

"Which is?"

"You tell me."

"Look, we did the riddles already. You got me in the room. I'm here. I'm sorry I fucked up your perfect murder with Dragon Boy."

"It wasn't a perfect murder," Maxwell interrupted.

"You want to talk about that one?" Low asked.

"Sure."

"Will it give you want you want?"

"It might."

"OK, what happened?"

The handcuffs chinked as Maxwell raised his arms to point at Low, his finger almost touching the inspector's nose. "You killed him."

Neither man moved.

"Put your hands down," Chan ordered.

Maxwell did as he was told. "Sorry. I realise what kind of threat a handcuffed man must pose to three armed policemen."

"Why did I kill him?" Low asked.

"You sent him after me, didn't you? Of course I didn't know that at first. It was only much later when I read the newspapers about his role in a criminal gang, this Tiger Syndicate, which was broken up by this undercover cop called Ah Lian, the same Ah Lian who was coming to get me. It wasn't difficult to figure out. I went to university, you know. Your dying friend was talking about you. But he was an accident, like the first one. We got into a fight and, well, he lost."

"Both in your apartment."

"Yes."

"But you dumped the bodies in different places."

"Yes, the first one I was improvising. The second one I thought it through."

"Upper Seletar Reservoir was a long way from your apartment. Weren't you worried about being stopped?"

"No one stops a Porsche in Singapore."

Low thought he saw something behind the sarcasm, but wasn't certain.

"But it was still a risk to do the same thing again with the backpackers."

"It didn't really matter by then."

"Because you'd already killed two."

"Exactly."

"But they were the first deliberate killings, the others were accidents. Why did you keep going?"

Maxwell yawned before continuing.

"Well, they really weren't planned. I'd had a shit day at work, our annual charity day, you know, let's make money for some poor people and feel better about our greed for a day. I have no problem with the greed. It's the pretense I struggle with. Anyway, after a terrible evening at Marina Bay, I popped over to Boat Quay and this couple started talking about the killings. They said something I didn't particularly appreciate and that was it."

"What happened?"

"Oh, I took them back to my apartment, said we were going on to Pangaea at Marina Bay. They were backpackers being promised free booze. It was hardly Machiavelli. I brought them in to freshen up and sent them off to the showers. I've got two at my place and they could barely stand by then. I did him first. I thought if I did her first and he came in, it might be more of a struggle. In the end, she never heard a thing. I did him then did her while she was still in the shower. She never heard a thing, too busy dreaming about the Instagram photos she'd get from Pangaea. And she was in the shower, so the water was cleaning her at the same time. It was very efficient. She had a terrific body, really. Hadn't seen a white body like that since university. But I never touched her, not in that way. I'm sure that came back in all your lab tests. It wasn't about that. I did have to hold her left breast, while I stabbed through the other one, but it wasn't sexual. Please make sure her family knows that."

At the back of the room, Chan picked the skin around his

forefinger until the blood trickled across his nail.

Low digested the information.

"OK, what was it about?"

"What?"

"You said it wasn't about sex. What was it about?"

"The, what was it, the hypocrisy," Maxwell said, pleased with himself for finding the right word. "Look at your media. I killed two people, one of them a Singaporean, a local, and there was hardly any reaction. You didn't take me or the victims seriously. But after the backpackers, my god, your post-colonial inferiority complex was truly laughable. Everyone went crazy. Suddenly you cared. Suddenly I was the most wanted man in Asia. And for what? For killing two Asians? No, for killing two white people. And yet, your hysterical media pointed the finger at *me*. I was the bad guy. Me? I think some serious introspective analysis is needed here. I didn't discriminate. You were the ones who discriminated. You cherry-picked my victims. I killed two Asians and I'm a bit of a nuisance. I killed two sun-tanned blondes and I'm a monster. A hardworking cleaner and a local Singaporean are nothing. But two lazy backpackers drinking their way around Asia are *somebodies*. Their killings count. Who decides this? Who adjudicates? Animals. And they point a finger at me?"

"Was that what the Jack the Ripper rubbish was all about? Your attempt at political comment?"

Maxwell laughed loudly. "Ah that, that was the pub, Penny Black. Have you been there? It's all Victorian London expat nostalgia. I was coming back from the toilet when I saw all these old photos of London and thought of Jack the Ripper. We studied him at school. Plus, I knew that the backpackers would make me more like him."

"How?"

"You need to kill at least three to be a serial killer. I checked on Wikipedia."

Low took another long, slow sip from his coffee.

"OK, I get most of that. You're fucked. You made your statement. You killed four. You're a serial killer, the IKEA Killer, next year's TV movie, so why the blogger's wife? I get the blogger. I could understand killing Harold Zhang. I'd kill Harold Zhang. But you kill his wife."

Maxwell looked away from the inspector as if searching for something.

"He was uncouth."

"Uncouth?"

"He disrespected the victims."

Low leaned forward.

"So did you. You killed them. You didn't care about the victims, not after the first one, not after Aini, your Aini. That's who he was really disrespecting, right? He can call them *ang mohs* and Chinese gangsters and he can call you anything, but he can't criticise her. She's like family. You can criticise her. You can kill her. But he can't go anywhere near her. But he doesn't leave her alone, does he? No, no, he can't, because his view of women is almost as screwed up as yours. He hates women, loathes them, more than you. Women betray. Women humiliate. Women cheat on their husbands and sleep with white men; disgusting white men like you. So he goes after you. He cheapens you. He cheapens your murders. He wants you to feel like he feels. He wants your woman to become like his woman."

"He called her a whore. Even your media called her a cleaner, but only he called her a whore. She wasn't a whore."

Low was nodding now, empathising with Maxwell.

"So you don't kill him. You don't kill him, do you?"

Maxwell was shaking his head.

"No, you don't kill him," Low continued. "That's a release

from his pain, the uncontrollable pain that he wakes up with
every morning, just like you. Like you said in the note, his show
and your show, his act and your act, the same routine, every day,
different women, but the same pain. But only your woman is
dead. His is still alive. While she's alive, there's a chance that the
pain will go away, that he'll somehow heal and you cannot accept
that. He doesn't *deserve* that, not after what he did to you, not
after what he called her, all those disgusting names. So if you kill
her, you kill him."

Maxwell didn't care now. He looked up towards the light. The
tears glistened.

"Now he's got what I've got."

"And that's how you justify it. You didn't *want* to kill her. No
you didn't. She hadn't done anything to you personally, but it was
the only way he could truly understand real pain, your pain."

"It was quick," Maxwell said, wiping away the tears. "I don't
care if you tell him or not, but I'm telling you. It was quick,
behind that bar. Almost no pain. I was very careful, very quick.
I brushed her hair back as I lowered her to the ground. I told
her. Don't look at me. Look up at the sky. Don't look at me,
I whispered to her. Don't look at my face. Picture his face, on
the beach in Australia, surfing and smiling back at you. And she
smiled. I closed her eyes. I left her there with her dignity. But he
didn't. He took hers away, calling her a whore. She was never like
that, never like *that*."

"You loved Aini?"

Maxwell paused, considering the question carefully.

"Love's a funny thing," he said finally. "I loved what she gave
me. What she represented."

"What was that?"

Maxwell sighed.

"Domination. She allowed me to dominate her. That's what

we really want right, when you get down to it, I got good old-fashioned domination. That's what I got from her. A flashback. How it used to be. When I had them lining up to drop their knickers. When I was king. That's what Asia really gives us you know. That's the lightning in the bottle that every red-blooded expat is trying to capture in Asia. People say it's all about the olive skin, and the skinny legs, but that's the superficial stuff. What it's really about is control. When we come here, we get what we've lost in the west. We get a whiff of that patriarchal society we left behind years ago. We get submissiveness. That's what we pay for. In Asia, the man is still king."

"No, your money is king."

"I always had money. So I always had Aini."

"But it was an illusion."

"It was better than nothing."

"Did she love you?"

"Probably not. In fact, I know she didn't. But it didn't matter. Aini gave me my dignity back. And now, I'm going to do the same for her."

"How?"

"That's up to your Minister."

Chapter 58

THE Kreta Ayer Police Post was a cage filled with trapped, wounded animals. They paced its tiled floor, pawing at each other in feeble displays of patriarchal power. The three investigators surrounded the Minister, crowding his space, closing in. His weary, reddened eyes struggled to focus. At private retreats with Asia's ruling tigers, he had shouted them down, trumpeted Singapore's interests and defied the odds, defeating them all and getting his own way. He was a product of his environment, the embodiment of a country's faith in the inherently superior intellect. Like his nation, he had punched above his weight his entire life. But he couldn't hold his hands up now. He was crumpled, ready to fall, desperate to throw out his arms and grab her, to tell her that everything was going to be OK, tell her how proud he really was, how it wasn't the Asian way to display fatherly love, but he didn't care anymore. He adored her. He loved her more than life. He didn't know that until now, this very minute. His life's work was irrelevant. The study, the knowledge, the experience, the political power, the elitist philosophy all vanished. His mind was a blank space. The proud product of positive eugenics was a cracked, empty shell. Everything had gone except a primeval desire to protect. He just wanted her back.

"I'll do it," he said, dragging a tissue across his blotchy cheeks.

"I'm not sure that's a good idea, sir," Chua said.

"Maybe we should at least recce the site first, check it," Chan suggested.

The Minister pointed at the clock.

"Look at the time, inspector. It's hours now, hours," he shouted, the tears stinging his eyes once more.

"It could already be too late."

The other men faced Low.

"He's playing games," Low continued. "I'm not sure why. He wants to give his dead girlfriend her dignity back. I don't know how. He's using you."

"Of course he's using me," the Minister said. "I know that. I don't care."

"But you must know. There's a chance. After the press conference, he had at least three, maybe four hours."

"Don't say it. Don't you dare. She's fine. She's my daughter. She's fine."

"That's right, sir," Chua said quickly. "So we just need a few minutes to sweep the area, maybe one hour and then we'll consider it. I've got police everywhere, all over the restaurant, checking every shophouse, void deck, back street."

"She is my only daughter, OK and I missed everything, her first day at school, first piano recital, first everything. I sent the maid to watch her first school play. I got my driver to play tennis with her. I made mistakes with my family, my wife, my marriage, everything. And all she did in return was love me. She was proud of me. She was one of the best young doctors in the country and she said she was proud of me. Do you know what that means?"

"Yes, sir," Chua mumbled.

"No, you don't."

The Minister turned to Low. He needed a reckless man who saw a broken father rather than a rank.

"Stanley, what risk is there if we do this now?"

The inspector peered through the window. "Ah, to you, physically, directly, none at all. He's unarmed and handcuffed. We'll have him at all times and there are enough officers. I don't know what other kind of risks. Don't know what he wants."

The Minister wanted to examine the inspector's eyes. He stepped closer.

"You've been talking to him. Is my daughter dead already?"

Low watched the fireworks fall into the dying embers of the fire. He reached out, but they were too far away. He was grasping in the flickering light.

"I don't know, sir."

The Minister instinctively knew that Low was lying. The insufferable inspector had never been deferential before.

"Is it worth trying?"

"I don't know what else we've got to lose."

That answer satisfied the Minister. It sounded truthful.

"OK, we do it now," he said, already reaching for the door. "But this is an order. No matter what he does, you do not shoot him, OK. You do not shoot him."

The Minister left the police post before his breaking voice abandoned him entirely. His emasculating tears would be harder to see outside.

Chapter 59

THE irony was not lost on the Minister of Home Improvement. Hong Lim Park was in lockdown, but few people noticed. Hardly anyone came to Speakers' Corner beyond tourists, dog walkers, gay activists and anti-government crusaders. The first three were benign. The last one lacked the talent pool. Hong Lim Park usually had what the Minister habitually championed.

Calm exteriors.

A dozen or so officers had been discreetly placed around the grass field's perimeter, quietly turning away twilight joggers and sending shoppers the long way round to People's Park Complex. The officers had clear orders from the deputy director. No one comes through. No one leaves. Keep an eye on proceedings in the field, but do not stare. Shoot if he runs, but aim low. Maim, but do not kill. He was already a dead man. They were told nothing else. They didn't ask. This was Singapore.

In the middle of the grassy field stood five men, very near the space when Harold Zhang had recently erected his temporary stage, its muddy imprint barely visible under a dark, cloudy sky.

To the uniformed officers continuously glancing over their shoulders, the IKEA Killer looked like a terrifying monolith. Four Chinese men danced around him, but he was handcuffed and still.

Talek Maxwell was exactly where he wanted to be, where he needed to be.

He had found his spot.

"About here I think," he said.

Low and Chan were flanking Maxwell, their guns drawn, waist high, mindful of the Minister's instructions. They would stay low and wound. At least, that's what they told themselves.

A few steps behind, the deputy director gently held his boss' arm, for support and safety. He wasn't sure what the Minister was capable of. The lost man was no longer a minister. He was a grieving father. He was capable of anything.

Chua had acceded to Maxwell's request, just the five of them, no other officers cluttering the place. Chua was secretly pleased. Maxwell was handcuffed and surrounded. Chaos could be avoided, so could the social media sites, as long as they were quick.

"No more talking cock, Maxwell," Low hissed, wanting nothing more than to put a bullet through the *ang moh's* heart, for the greater good, for Dragon Boy. "We're here, Hong Lim Park, just as you wanted. Where is she?"

Maxwell smiled at the Minister.

"Why do they call it Speakers' Corner?"

"What?" The Minister looked at Low, seeking guidance that wasn't forthcoming.

"This place. Why do they call it Speakers' Corner?"

"Eh, enough already," Low said. "I'll shoot you just to make you stop talking."

Maxwell gazed up at the gloomy sky. "Go ahead, shoot me. But we'll both die tonight won't we, Minister?"

The Minister felt Chua's restraining hand.

"Now you're getting angry, aren't you, Minister? Just like I did. I was raging. It makes you want to kill someone. Just like I did. Do you think I've done it already? Do you think I've stuck a screwdriver through your daughter's heart? Do you think she screamed out 'Daddy' as I shoved my screwdriver through her tits?"

The Minister was pushing the deputy director away and running. He saw the younger inspector lowering his gun, blocking his path, but he wouldn't put his hand on the Minister, wouldn't physically restrain a member of the Cabinet, not while holding a gun in the other hand. The Minister was almost there, his fist clenched, ready to strike, when the blood spray splattered across his cheeks. He recoiled in horror, wiping his eyes in time to see the butt of Low's gun come down again, smashing Maxwell's nasal septum.

The stunned Caucasian fell to his knees, his blood turning black beneath the park's soft lighting.

Maxwell was chuckling.

He was still chuckling when Low pressed the gun into the top of his head.

"What are you doing, Stanley?"

"Fuck off, Charlie. We're not giving him what he wants again. He killed Zhang's wife to kill Zhang. Now he's doing it with the Minister. No more of this living dead shit. I'll save the Minister and shoot him."

Maxwell turned his head slowly, stopping when the gun rested above his bleeding forehead.

"That's even better. Then you are all dead, aren't you?"

"It's borrowed from the British," the Minister exclaimed. "Hyde Park, Speakers' Corner, a place to celebrate free speech, where anyone can speak."

Maxwell nodded slowly, smiling sincerely for the first time.

"Thank you, Minister. Thank you. Now, Ah Lian, if you could move your gun away for a moment. It's making me go cross-eyed."

Low looked over at the Minister and took a half step back. Maxwell spat out the blood in his mouth.

"So, freedom of speech. Freedom of expression and so on. That's what that idiot Harold Zhang said here, playing to the crowd, posing for the cameras. But at least he was honest. He went after me from day one, but you didn't, Minister. Why?"

"I don't understand."

"She's dying, Minister."

"No, really, please, I don't understand."

"You only came after me when I killed my fellow westerners."

"What? Please. I don't know what you want me to say."

"She must have less than an hour now."

"What do you want me to say? Tell me. What do you want from me?"

"I watched your press conferences about me, read all your comments in the media. And you didn't say anything at all. The blogger did. But you didn't, not a word. Why?"

The Minister's imploring eyes sought help from his officers. He couldn't think, couldn't reason; couldn't do anything except see his daughter's dying face.

"I can't remember. I don't know. Please, whatever you want from me. Take it."

"He wants you to dismiss his dead girlfriend," Low shouted. "Wants you to tell him that she wasn't worth bothering with. She was worthless, like Dragon Boy, that he's right and we're all wrong. He wants you to validate his dumb fucking experiment that some lives are worth more than others. He killed the only woman who made him feel good about himself and he wants to pass the guilt onto you."

"You really are good, Ah Lian. I'm going to miss you."

Maxwell savoured the explosive pain as Low's gun tore open

the flesh on his cheek.

"For god's sake, Stanley, he's handcuffed," Chan said, stepping between Low and Maxwell.

"Fuck him."

"Look, that's enough. I'll answer the question," the Minister said. "No, you are incorrect. We do not prioritise people's lives or victims."

"No, that's the politician talking. You're not in parliament now, Minister. You're in Speakers' Corner, where no one ever listens. A dead Indonesian prostitute doesn't matter as much as a dead blonde backpacker, right?"

"Everyone is equal in the law. Everyone."

"But some are more equal than others, not just here, but everywhere. You didn't care about me until I killed the backpackers and your famous blogger's wife. I could've been Singapore's Jack the Ripper forever, killing lowlifes and you would've left me alone."

"No."

"Yes, Minister. There wasn't a press conference from you until I killed the blonde couple, because they were more important than my Aini."

"No, it was because you were a serial killer."

"Bullshit. The numbers don't matter, only the names."

"That's not true."

"She's almost dead now."

"We wouldn't categorise victims like that."

"There's no 'we', only you. I'm talking about you. My Aini didn't matter to you."

"Of course, she did. It's just that we get a lot of . . ."

"A lot of what? Foreigners? Maids? Prostitutes? What?"

"No, a lot of murders."

"No, you don't, not in Singapore. Just give me one answer and she lives."

"I can't say what you want me to say."

"Yes, you can. She didn't count."

"Everybody counts."

"Not my Aini. She scrubbed your floors. She was nothing. She wasn't a doctor. She wasn't a minister's daughter. She was the shit on your shoes."

"Bastard, what do you want from him?" Low shouted.

"Honesty. You've got it from me. I am disgusting. I killed five people to make myself feel better. It'll be six soon. I've answered all your questions. Now answer mine. You didn't give a shit about my Aini, right?"

"That's not true."

"YES, IT FUCKING IS!"

"No, there was a thorough police investigation," the Minister said, wiping the tears from his cheeks.

"Yes, cry for your doctor. Cry your fucking heart out. She means more to you than my Aini, right?"

"How can I answer that?"

"She'll be dead soon. Answer the question. Is a politician's daughter worth more than a foreign cleaner?"

"That's impossible for me . . ."

"ANSWER THE FUCKING QUESTION. Your daughter or my Aini?"

"Well, of course, I'm going to say . . ."

"She dies tonight, alone in the dark, crying for Daddy. Is her life worth more to you?"

"YES! She's my daughter."

"Worth more than my Aini?"

"YES!"

Maxwell closed his eyes, allowing the absolution to wash away his misdeeds. He felt so much better. There was a point to it all now, a *purpose.*

"Call Lock and Store, the storage place in Keppel Road. Tell them to open unit seven, the Porsche inside. Check the boot," he said. "I'd hurry if I were you."

Chapter 60

AZIZ enjoyed his job. Security gave him just that. He didn't understand Asia's relentless pursuit of wealth, wasn't even sure what everyone else was chasing after. He wanted for nothing. His wife made the best *nasi lemak* in Singapore and his three boys had all graduated with diplomas and married well. He looked forward to the grandchildren. He wouldn't retire, but his boss at Lock and Store had agreed to let him go part-time whenever he wanted. Aziz had been with the company since it had opened and saw no reason to look elsewhere. He made his rounds, checked the units, monitored the cameras, answered the overnight calls and ate his wife's homemade meals at his desk. His life was simple because he led a simple life. His boss was a decent man, a fair man, but always fretted over the paperwork, always perspired in the air-conditioned office. He worried over the margins, the foreign competition and even the future itself. He panicked over the long-term plans to redevelop Keppel Harbour and shove the port and storage facilities out to Tuas, the forgotten, industrial corner of Singapore, the end of the world. He worried about things he couldn't control.

Aziz had no interest in that world. He was born breathing the sea air. His father had been a docker at the port and his uncle a sampan operator. His family had all once lived in the old Kampong Silat flats, built by the British and overlooking the burgeoning harbour. Aziz was raised on seawater. He followed his father down to the harbour and ended up managing security at a storage facility. He wore a white shirt to work. He didn't have the sun-crisp skin and coarse hands of a labourer. He left the heavy industry to others. He managed other people's material possessions. He watched strangers work through weekends to buy and store status symbols they didn't need. They hid the fruits of their labour in one of his units. Aziz saw the fruits of his labour every day at the family table, sharing *nasi padang* together. He was a contented man. He left the stress to others.

But now he was running along the corridor, panting loudly, clutching a torch in one hand and a bunch of keys in the other. He never exercised. Singaporean security guards didn't run. There was no one to chase. Aziz heard the raspy rattling in his chest but kept going. He had told the policeman on the phone that he didn't have the authority to open a storage unit without the client's permission.

"*Fuck the authority.*"

Aziz had been appalled by the inspector's belligerence. Aziz rarely swore. He abhorred bad language and wouldn't tolerate it at home. He raised three good boys. He didn't raise *mat rock* clichés.

"*No, cannot wait for the police. No time. Open the fucking unit.*"

The aggression in the voice had been unmistakable. So had the panic. The aggression was less troubling than the panic. This Low character was clearly mad, but he was also scared. And his final words kept Aziz's legs moving.

"*She's probably already dead.*"

Drenched in sweat, Aziz stopped in front of unit seven. There was an electronic keypad for the shutters, but he didn't know the password. He only had a key for emergencies. If the key failed, he had been ordered to smash his way into the unit.

He crouched low, his stomach hanging over his waistline, making it hard to find the lock near his feet. The sweat cascaded. The keys leapt in the palm of his hand. He finally picked out the right one and pulled open the shutters. He almost walked into the back of the Porsche, the car obviously parked in a hurry. The opaque unit was otherwise empty. The Porsche's rear end had been covered in sheets and blankets. Aziz pulled them away and noticed the key taped to the top of the boot. Using his torch, he found the keyhole and flung the boot open.

His torch clattered against the concrete floor.

She looked like a sleeping newborn.

Her hands and feet were tied and her mouth taped. Her knees were tucked into her chest. The foetal position was disconcerting. The peaceful image gave a false impression. The security guard noticed the dried blood on the side of her head.

"Madam," Aziz whispered.

He touched her shoulder, very lightly. She wasn't cold.

"Eh, can hear me or not. It's OK. I'm the security guard here. You're safe now."

He rocked her gently from side to side, pulling the matted hair away from her bloodied face.

"Eh, OK or not?"

There was a sigh. At least Aziz thought there was. There was a distinct echo. He continued to rock her, more forcefully now.

"Eh, come on, police and ambulance on the way already."

He heard a groan, a definite mumble. Aziz leaned closer.

"It's OK. You gonna be OK. My name is Aziz. Uncle Aziz."

Her hands were moving, slowly, sliding across her dress. She fumbled her way along until she found his hand. She squeezed tightly, her eyes still closed.

Aziz swallowed hard. "It's OK now. It's OK."

She mumbled something.

"What's that? It's OK. No need to talk, ambulance coming already."

She mumbled again, desperate to speak, suddenly anxious.

"It's OK. It's OK." Aziz patted her hands.

"Is he gone?"

Aziz tilted his head and leaned closer. "Again?"

"Is he gone?"

Aziz smiled. "He's gone."

Reluctantly, she opened her eyes.

"Thank you, uncle. Thank you."

They ignored each other's tears and continued to hold hands.

Chapter 61

THE police van waited at the traffic lights in North Bridge Road. Inside, Maxwell sat on a bench, handcuffed and manacled, across from Low. Two uniformed officers sat beside them, peering across at the IKEA Killer whenever he and the inspector were looking elsewhere. The van pulled away and changed lanes abruptly, sending Low towards Maxwell.

"You can't stay away from me," Maxwell said. "Shall we attend the next gay rally together?"

"You'll be dead by then."

"Yes, justice is swift in Singapore. How long do you think?"

"I don't care."

"So I'm no Tiger then."

Low rolled his eyes. "He was Premier League. You're non-league."

"I killed more people."

"You killed innocent people."

"Oh dear. You are not seriously going to give me the 'honour among thieves' routine."

"No, but there's got to be a reason at least."

"There was a reason."

"What? Your sociology experiment? Rich people have it better than poor people. Didn't need to kill five people for that. Just read the newspaper."

"I had to know."

"You already knew."

"I wanted to hear it from someone who mattered."

"OK, then what?"

"I got what I wanted."

"You got the Minister to say his daughter was more important than your dead girlfriend. What did you expect him to say?"

"It's all I needed to hear."

"And that's a good enough reason?"

"We kill each other for all sorts of reasons."

"So, you're what then? The first sociology serial killer?"

"No, I was right, Ah Lian. I like being right. I know you'd feel so much better if I just sat in the corner dribbling, telling you that Mummy didn't hug me enough or Daddy didn't turn up for my rugby matches. You can live with that. That fits. But they did. They gave me everything I wanted. And I wanted everything. And out here, in Asia, I had everything. Everything I wanted. Until I messed up with Aini."

"So you had to justify her death, give it some sort of meaning."

Maxwell nodded in agreement.

"Might as well. And I was right. In the end I was right. As soon as I climbed the social ladder, you had to chop me down."

"What if his daughter had died?"

"No chance. I only punched her a couple of times."

"You covered the car with a blanket to muffle the noise. She could've suffocated."

"I had to see if I was right. I knew I would be."

"Why?"

"I made the Minister feel how I felt after Aini died. When you feel that way, you'll do anything to climb out. Anything."

Low was surprised by how much he vehemently disagreed. He

preferred not to climb out.

"What do you think will happen to the Minister now?" Maxwell asked.

"Nothing. Why?"

"Just wondered."

Maxwell looked up at the van's ceiling. "It's quiet, isn't it? Why are there no sirens?"

"You're caught already. No need to make a fuss."

"But you still put me in a van with no windows."

Low smiled at the police officers.

"No choice, *ang moh*. Social media is our biggest killer."

As the policemen laughed, Maxwell leaned back against the van's wall. He was quietly singing to himself.

Tonight, I'm a rock 'n' roll star.

Chapter 62

FOR the first time in days, Harold Zhang was thinking clearly. He had visited the barber for a short back and sides and paid extra for a rare shave with a cutthroat razor. The white shirt was freshly laundered and the black slacks neatly pressed with a sharp line running through the middle. His polished shoes matched his slick hair.

Zhang was going to make a real effort with his physical appearance from now on.

It's what she would've wanted.

He waited for the traffic to clear before making his way across the road. The anticipation was building, but he had to keep a lid on it, stay focused on the job at hand and remain professional.

Everyone had left now, but stealth was still required. The cardboard collectors and the rough sleepers often wandered through Chinatown in the small hours. By morning, the place would be filled with *tai chi* classes, office cleaners on their way to an early shift and maids walking dogs.

Zhang knew that they were reasonably obscured.

But someone would surely find them in the daylight.

He settled on a brisk walk. If anyone recognised him, he was on a recce. That made sense. Running would draw unnecessary attention and make for a trickier explanation. The time of night was odd, but the location wasn't.

He followed the footpath, checking again that he was alone. But no one had loitered. There was no reason to stay. Zhang made his way to the bushes. He knew the spot well. They had sat nearby for many hours, holding hands.

He pushed aside the leaves and soil that he had left earlier and there they were, undisturbed and untouched. Zhang hesitated. The adrenaline that brought him here was now giving way to a nervous tension, leaving him with a sickening sensation in the pit of his stomach. The apprehension made him dizzy.

Zhang checked again, looking over both shoulders this time. He wasn't a fool. She had often said he was, dismissing him as an old Chinaman, a fish-ball noodle man out of touch with his own generation. But Zhang wasn't stupid. He knew it wasn't a trap, not once they had left.

He was less certain when he received the email earlier in the day, telling him what to do and when and where to do it. His first reaction was to throw the keyboard across the room. But he reread the email and considered his options, the potential angles. Somehow, he had to get on with his life.

It's what she would've wanted.

There were three GoPro cameras planted in the soil, hidden between the shrubs, but they still enjoyed an unblocked view of the field. Zhang picked up the one in the middle and connected it to his iPad. His cameras were invaluable. They not only provided terrific clips for YouTube, they also gave Zhang a snapshot of the crowd. After the first few rallies, he had learned how to pick out the zealots from the rubberneckers, the foreigners from the tourists. Most of all, he could identify the plants from the Internal Security Department. They were the ones who always pretended to pay attention, even during the really tedious speeches.

It took him a while to find what he was looking for, lots of rewinding and mistimed pauses, until he found them.

There they were, five men in a field, four Chinese guys and a foreigner on his knees. Zhang enjoyed the symbolism, but was hesitant to press play. His conscience complicated things. He had to weigh up the pros and cons. He would make a decision after seeing it.

He pressed play and watched the scene unfold.

"*Is a politician's daughter worth more than a foreign cleaner?*"

"*That's impossible for me . . .*"

"*ANSWER THE FUCKING QUESTION. Your daughter or my Aini?*"

"*Well, of course, I'm going to say . . .*"

Zhang hit the fast forward button.

"*Is her life worth more to you?*"

"*YES! She's my daughter.*"

"*Worth more than my Aini?*"

"*YES!*"

Zhang watched it again.

"*Is a politician's daughter worth more than a foreign cleaner?*"

Zhang hit the fast forward bottom.

"*YES! She's my daughter.*"

Zhang played it back.

"*Is a politician's daughter worth more than a foreign cleaner?*"

Zhang hit the fast forward bottom.

"*YES! She's my daughter.*"

He would re-edit, obviously. He would cut out the word "foreign" of course. He had his target audience to think about. He would incorporate the footage of all three cameras if the content was usable and zoom in on the Minister's face. He would repeat those two lines on a loop. He would amplify the most important message that the neglected, downtrodden victims of globalisation needed to hear. He would kick-start the campaign to take his country back. He would ensure that his wife did not die in vain. He would finish what they had started together.

He would manipulate the footage to create the most politically inaccurate video in Singapore's history. He would master the masses. And he would win.

Finally, he would win.

It's what his dead wife would've wanted.

Chapter 63

DR Tracy Lai had spent the previous hour cleaning her own office. She had cancelled another patient's appointment to accommodate him. Her secretary had been told to block all calls except suicide risks.

Lai was rather ashamed of herself. The curiosity had nagged away at her for days. Professionally, he was unusual, but certainly not unique. Personally, she felt like a nosy auntie, a supermarket magazine junkie.

She was desperate to see him.

"I read the newspapers," she said brightly.

"Yeah, well, you did go to university."

His appearance was even scruffier than usual. His shorts and T-shirt hadn't been washed for days.

"You must be pleased."

"OK."

"You caught the serial killer."

"He caught himself."

Low picked at a mosquito bite on his leg.

"That'll bleed," Lai said.

"Hope so."

"It'll make it worse, it won't heal."

"Sounds familiar."

Lai scribbled a note in her pad. His health was clearly deteriorating. The highs needed to be more frequent, more intense to ward off the increasing lows. He was at risk of being engulfed.

"Catching him wasn't enough, was it?"

"I did my job."

"That must make your bosses happy."

"I did my job. So they cannot fire me this week."

"Is there a part of you that wishes he was still out there?"

Low glared at his psychiatrist.

"He killed five people. He beat a young woman and left her in a car boot to die. He did all this to make himself feel better, just so there was a *point* to it all, so he didn't have to feel guilty about killing the one person who treated him kindly. So, no, I don't wish he was still out there."

"He killed your friend."

"He did."

"Does that bother you?"

"Would it bother you?"

"Of course. How do you feel about it?"

"How do I feel about it? I want to pick up this chair and smash it through that wall, but what for? It's over."

"I've heard you speak about your friend fondly in the past. I'm concerned that it may trigger further episodes."

"I'm fine."

"Really?"

"No, I'm fucked, but what difference does it make?"

Lai put down the notepad.

"Maybe we need to consider taking certain steps to work towards achieving a degree of closure."

"What closure? He's as good as dead. I'm closed."

"But did you get the outcome you wanted?"

"You read the newspaper. He'll be hanged."

"Is that the kind of justice you want?"

Low smiled for the first time.

"Justice is beyond my pay grade."

COMPUTER access was Maxwell's highlight of the week. For one hour, once a week, he was allowed to use one of the Changi Prison laptops in his cell, under strict supervision. He couldn't participate in the communal computer classes. His daily movements had initially proved to be a logistical nightmare and he now spent most of his days in solitary confinement.

"How much longer have I got?"

Standing by the cell door, the prison officer checked his watch.

"About 10 minutes. Hurry up *ah*, must sign for me after."

The officers often wanted signed photos for eBay auctions. The sales topped up their mediocre salaries. Maxwell didn't mind. They usually gave him something in return. A young and impressionable prison officer had informed him that an IKEA Killer Facebook page had picked up almost 50,000 followers before it was shut down. He was denied access to social media sites and couldn't see the Facebook pages that had been established under his name. There were rumours that they ran into the hundreds. The government struggled to close them all down, particularly when they were registered overseas. His mail was also vetted. He'd heard about all the marriage proposals, but they rarely reached him.

Maxwell glanced at the clock on the screen. He had five minutes left to complete his search. He was only interested in one subject.

Himself.

"Eh, you're that *ang moh*, right?"

Maxwell exhaled loudly.

"I'm not allowed to sign prison property of any kind," he said, not looking up, engrossed in his special subject. "We will both get into trouble."

"No, no, no, you're that one *ah*, right? The IKEA Killer."

"Look, could you please . . ."

Maxwell turned towards the cell door. The prison officer had gone.

"Who are you?"

"You don't know?"

"No, I don't know."

"Strange *ah*? You knew my boy last time."

For an old man, the portly, tattooed prisoner moved quickly and gracefully across the cell. Maxwell had just enough time to close his laptop.

And then Tiger went to work.

About the Author

Neil Humphreys grew up in Dagenham, England, before travelling to Singapore when he was 21 for a short holiday. He stayed a bit longer and became one of the country's best-selling authors. His works on Singapore – *Notes from an Even Smaller Island* (2001), *Scribbles from the Same Island* (2003), and *Final Notes from a Great Island* (2006), the omnibus *Complete Notes from Singapore* (2007) and *Return to a Sexy Island: Notes from a New Singapore* (2012) – are among the most popular titles in the past decade. His book *Be My Baby* (2008) chronicled his journey to parenthood and was his first international best-seller. His two novels – *Match Fixer* (2010) and *Premier Leech* (2011) – were also released to critical acclaim. He believes *Marina Bay Sins* is *Match Fixer's* evil twin. When he's not researching a fresh murder case, he writes further adventures for his popular children's book series *Abbie Rose and the Magic Suitcase*. He still lives in Singapore and explains himself in further, excruciating detail here: *www.neilhumphreys.net*

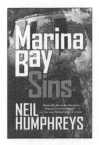

Marina Bay Sins
In this first book of the Inspector Low series, Detective Inspector Stanley Low is having a really bad day. His bipolar condition is already ruining another therapy session when a sadistic sex murder-suicide at Singapore's most prestigious hotel plunges him back into a sordid underworld he was desperate to leave behind.

He has no choice. Dead bodies at Marina Bay Sands are bad for business. They ask questions of a sanitized society no one is keen to answer. As the case spirals out of control, Inspector Low encounters a self-help celebrity couple, an expat CEO addicted to Asian women and an elusive foreign businessman playing pimp for exiled military generals ... all thriving in Asia's cleanest city. None of them can get their story straight.

As Inspector Low gets closer to the unpalatable truth, the search for the murderer races to a gripping, horrifying finish.

Other Books by Neil Humphreys

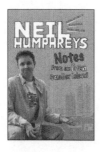

Notes from an Even Smaller Island
Knowing nothing of Singapore, a young Englishman arrives in the land of "air-conned" shopping centres and Lee Kuan Yew. He explores all aspects of Singaporean life, taking in the sights, dissecting the culture and illuminating each place and person with his perceptive and witty observations.

Scribbles from the Same Island
Humphreys is back with yet more observations and ruminations about the oddball aspects of Singapore and its people. *Scribbles* also contains a selection of his work as a humour columnist.

Final Notes from a Great Island
All good things must come to an end, and before Humphreys makes his move Down Under, he revisits all the people and places he loves in his final, comprehensive tour of Singapore.

Complete Notes from Singapore (The Omnibus Edition)
All three of Humphreys' best-selling works, *Notes from an Even Smaller Island*, *Scribbles from the Same Island* and *Final Notes from a Great Island*, in one classic, updated book.

Be My Baby: On the Road to Fatherhood
Follow Humphreys on his most terrifying and hilarious journey yet – travelling the unfamiliar road to fatherhood.

Return to a Sexy Island

Singapore got sexy and the country's best-selling author got jealous. After five years chasing echidnas and platypuses in Australia, Neil Humphreys returns to Singapore to see if the rumours are true. Like an old girlfriend getting a lusty makeover, the island transformed while Humphreys was away. Singapore is not just a sexier island, it's a different world.

Match Fixer

Once a promising graduate of West Ham United's Academy and tipped to play for England, Chris Osborne arrives on the Singapore football scene in a bid to right his faltering football career. But nothing has prepared him for the underground party drugs scene, the bent bookies, dubious teammates and a seductively beautiful journalist who welcome him to life in paradise.

Premier Leech

English Football Clubs are dying but club captain, Scott, couldn't give a toss. As long as he delivers on the pitch, he can do whatever he likes off it. That's the right and privilege of an English Premier League footballer – until he sleeps with his best mate's wife. The tabloids go wild and a team of investigative reporters are hot on the trails of both Scott and his manager, Charlie, who's been lining up a secret takeover with a Saudi businessman more interested in property and blonde hookers than football. In a world where the only currency is fame, how much are they willing to sacrifice to stay in the game?